Fay Cunningham was born in north London but now lives in Essex with her husband and a very old cat. She has been short-listed for the CWA Debut Dagger prize three times and has had a number of short stories published in women's magazines.

CRY BABY

Gina Cross has a talent: she puts the flesh back on the bones of the dead, working for the police as a forensic artist. Gina is convinced there's a connection between the body of a teenage mother and a friend's missing sister. She enlists the help of investigative journalist Adam Shaw to help her find the missing girl. Their search eventually takes them to the mysterious Willow Bank hospital — which hides a deadly secret. But if Gina and Adam learn the truth about Willow Bank they may have to be eliminated . . .

Books by Fay Cunningham
Published by The House of Ulverscroft:

SNOWBOUND
DECEPTION
LOVE OR MARRIAGE

FAY CUNNINGHAM

CRY BABY

Complete and Unabridged

ULVERSCROFT
Leicester

First published in Great Britain in 2010 by
Robert Hale Limited
London

First Large Print Edition
published 2012
by arrangement with
Robert Hale Limited
London

British Library CIP Data

Cunningham, Fay.
   Cry baby.
   1. Police artists- -Great Britain- -Fiction.
   2. Journalists- -Great Britain- -Fiction.
   3. Missing persons- -Investigation- -Great Britain- -
   Fiction.
   4. Detective and mystery stories.
   5. Large type books.
   I. Title
   823.9'2–dc23

   ISBN 978–1–4448–0957–2

Published by
F. A. Thorpe (Publishing)
Anstey, Leicestershire

Set by Words & Graphics Ltd.
Anstey, Leicestershire
Printed and bound in Great Britain by
T. J. International Ltd., Padstow, Cornwall

This book is printed on acid-free paper

*To my family for their encouragement
and to the RNA
for my new friends.*

Before

The body lay at her feet, naked and crusted with blood, and when she looked at it she felt her stomach lurch.

It wasn't supposed to be like this.

The room was dim, a single window the only source of light. Filtered through the dusty glass, a square of diluted sunlight lay on the floor. A sad little square, far too small to frighten away the black shadows that crouched in every corner. Fear had brought her here, fear of the unknown, and a tiny glimmer of hope.

But now that hope was gone.

Tears ran down her face as she looked at the body. It was far too late for remorse. She knew it was already dead, long dead, before it fell and smashed its head on the wooden floor. Once there had been life. She had felt it. A flutter of anticipation that made her smile. But now the waiting was over, a life had ended, and she was on her own.

Her stomach heaved again as she pushed herself away from the wall on unsteady legs. She was weak from loss of blood, but she had to find the strength to leave this place before

1

he came and found her. Once she had been an asset: now she was just a liability.

She moved away from the body and stumbled across the dimly lit room, and when the rock he was carrying descended on her head she hardly made a sound.

And in that lonely, tragic place, where the floor was still wet with her blood, he put the body of her newborn baby in a Tesco carrier bag and tied the handles nice and tight.

1

The flat Essex countryside basked in the late afternoon sunshine, the heat trembling above the dry grass, bending the light and turning the metal bridge over the river into a shimmering mirage. Earlier, the river had rushed eagerly towards the town, swept along by the tide, but now the thick brown water nudged the bank listlessly on its way back down to the sea. Soon it would be no more than a thin trickle between the mud banks.

In the background, the university blocks thrust their ugly towers towards a cloudless blue sky, and bees buzzed beside the cycle path looking for late summer flowers. But it wasn't the drone of the bees that kept Gina Cross silent and still beside the ditch. It was the sound of the flies.

The body lay a few feet from a well-frequented cycle path. The ditch was overgrown with nettles and it was only the stink of rotting flesh that had eventually prompted a couple of students to investigate. A breeding ground for the young of the blowfly, the body moved restlessly in its shallow grave, brought to life by a seething mass of larvae.

Standing just outside the small tent that had been erected to shield the body, Gina Cross clutched her sketchpad in front of her like a shield. Her shoulders were burning and sweat beaded her upper lip. It was too damned hot for late September. A fly landed on her face and she slapped at it in disgust. She knew where it had been. Moving nearer, she watched Sheila Avery, the pathologist, kneel beside the body and pluck a single larva from the decomposing corpse with a pair of tweezers, holding the convulsing maggot a few inches from her eyes.

'Second instar,' Avery told Inspector Reagan. 'The body's not been here long. The ditch is like a compost heap and there are lots of flies around in September. They'd have found the body in minutes.'

Gina saw Reagan frown. 'What's not long? Hours? Days? Weeks?'

'Not much more than a couple of days, most likely. The blowfly eggs take eighteen hours to hatch and twenty hours to first instar. They would've moulted to this stage sometime within the last twelve hours. Work it out for yourself.' Avery dropped the maggot into a plastic tub and screwed on the lid.

'What else?' Reagan asked.

'Female, but you could've worked that out from the clothes, and quite young — late teens or early twenties. Severe head trauma, but I'll be able to tell you more about that when we get the body moved.'

'Definitely murder then?'

Avery managed a sour smile. 'Unless hitting yourself on the head with a blunt instrument is a new form of suicide.' She pushed herself painfully to her feet, arthritis making her knees crack. 'I don't make guesses, Detective. It looks like the blow to the head killed her, but not here, not in this ditch. Somebody moved the body. Whether it was murder or not is your problem, not mine.' The pathologist turned to Gina Cross. 'You got a picture?'

Gina inched further inside the tent and handed the woman her sketch. Reagan moved up close to Avery, looking over her shoulder. Gina had drawn the face of a young girl with long straight hair and a turned-up nose, her mouth a second short of laughter.

'Quite pretty when she was alive.'

Avery frowned at the drawing. 'Yeah. Most of them are when they're alive.'

Gina knew her artwork didn't impress the pathologist. The faces she drew were too lifelike — the faces of the living, rather than the dead.

Reagan took the sketch and rolled it up. 'I'll see if we've got a missing persons that matches. At the very least we've got a case of concealment. Someone knew this poor kid had died, but didn't report it.'

'If the girl's a student the staff may not know she's missing,' Gina suggested. 'The new term's only just started.' She ducked out through the flap of the tent and looked at the muddy sweep of the river. 'And this is a cycle path. Have you found a bike?'

Reagan followed her out and called to a young officer who was standing well back behind the tape cordoning off the area. 'Look for a bike, Robbins.' He stared at the slow-moving water morosely. 'I don't want to have to search the mud for a bleedin' bike.'

As a forensic artist, Gina's work was done, but there was something about the body she hadn't told the policeman.

It wasn't a bike they should be looking for.

As Gina started to walk away the big policeman called after her. 'Don't get involved with this one, Gina. Leave it to us.'

Fine. They'd discover what she'd seen when they did the post-mortem. If anything was out there, they'd find it.

She pulled off the blue gloves and booties, handing them to one of the young policemen. Give him something to do and he might not throw up again. Her hands and feet were hot and sticky and she probably smelt almost as bad as the corpse.

She had parked her car outside a block of student accommodation and, as she walked to her car, her mobile phone burbled quietly, reminding her yet again that she hadn't listened to the call. She pulled the phone from the pocket of her jeans and tossed it on the passenger seat of her ancient Metro. Adam Shaw had kept her waiting almost four months. Now it was his turn to wait.

She was halfway home when the phone on the seat beside her set up a persistent ringing. She ignored the sound, knowing her messaging service would pick up. A few minutes later the phone rang again. Damn the man! Couldn't he take a hint? She carried on driving. All she wanted to do was get home and stand under a hot shower.

She pulled up outside her studio and saw the windows were dark. It was gone six, and Megan would have locked up by now and gone home. Gina parked her car around the corner and climbed the metal stairs to the flat above the studio. Once inside, she stripped off and let the water from the shower pummel her into oblivion. She was always afraid a maggot might have strayed, or a blowfly tangled itself in her hair.

Ten minutes later she felt reasonably clean. Dressed in tracksuit bottoms and a blue shirt, her shoulder-length hair a mess of still-wet curls, she took a bottle of Stella out of the fridge and popped the top. Her mobile phone rang again, dancing around on the glass-topped coffee table in front of the sofa. Gina glanced at the dial and turned it off. After a full day in the studio and then a call-out for Reagan, she was far too tired to cope with her wayward lover.

She had just taken half a pizza out of the freezer when the doorbell rang.

Adam Shaw looked much the same as he had four months ago. A tall, rangy man with short dark hair and intense blue eyes dimmed now with jetlag, the stubble on his chin at least two days old. The sight of him still made her stomach flip and she cursed herself for it.

He leant against the doorframe waiting for her to ask him in. When she didn't, he walked past her into her living room. She smiled as he cracked his shin on her new glass coffee table. Her own legs were already black and blue.

'That's new.'

'Yep.' She grinned at him. 'And it gets you every time.' She watched him flop down on her sofa. He looked tired, but she couldn't dredge up any sympathy.

'Make yourself at home.'

'God, Gina, what have I done this time? My plane only landed a couple of hours ago and I came straight here. What more do you want?'

'You didn't phone while you were away. Not once. It's been four months, Adam, and not even a postcard.'

'I'm a journalist, not a tourist. And Thailand is still a mess. They've cleaned up the resort areas, but the rest is a shambles, and most of the time we weren't anywhere near a working phone, let alone a post office. What did you expect? A 'wish you were here' card?'

She sighed. Nothing had changed. Five minutes together and they were already snapping at one another. She'd missed him, but she wasn't about to tell him that. She pulled another bottle of beer from the fridge and handed it to him. He had the top off before she could give him the bottle opener.

'I tried to phone you but you weren't answering.' He took a long swallow of his beer straight from the bottle. 'Jack won't be back until tomorrow; he's gone up to Norfolk to see his family. His sister's missing.'

Jack Lowry was a young freelance photographer who often worked with Adam. The two had known one another for several years and were good friends, in spite of an eleven-year age gap.

Gina poured her own beer into a glass. 'I didn't know Jack had a sister.'

'She was supposed to start her first year at university, but instead of turning up for the new term, she disappeared. No one knows where she is.'

Gina felt a tiny brush of fear. 'She was a student? What university?'

'Norwich.'

Norwich University was miles away from Castlebury. So why the scary feeling? She picked up Adam's empty bottle and stood up. 'There was a body today. In a ditch beside the university cycle path. A young girl.'

He looked at her curiously. 'So?'

She fetched another beer from the fridge and handed it to him. 'I don't know. Connections, I suppose. Jack lives in Castlebury; his sister lives in Norwich. University towns. Missing girls.'

'But nowhere near one another. What are you trying to say, Gina? You think the dead girl might be Jack's sister?'

'No, of course not.' She shook her head. She didn't know what she was trying to say. No good mentioning bad vibes. Adam dealt in absolutes.

Flipping the top on the new bottle, he said,

10

'Probably nothing to worry about, anyway. Sophie told her friends she was taking a gap year before she started university. She informed all her tutors, all her friends. She just didn't bother to tell her family.'

'Have her parents told the police she's missing?'

He raised an eyebrow. 'They reported her disappearance and the police made some enquiries at the university, but Sophie's over eighteen. As far as the law is concerned she can go where she pleases.'

Gina refused to acknowledge she had any psychic talent. She was a good forensic artist and that was all, but she wished her gut feeling of impending disaster was a little less ambiguous. Something was wrong and specifics would be nice.

'I only met Sophie once,' Adam said, 'about five years ago. Kids change a lot in five years. Did you do a sketch of the body you saw today?'

'Yes, but Reagan kept it to do copies.'

'If you're still spooked when Jack gets back, show him a copy of your sketch.' He yawned and pushed himself upright. 'I take it you're not going to invite me to stay the night, so I'm going home to sleep.' In the doorway he bent down and kissed her lightly on the lips. 'See you tomorrow.'

Gina shut the door behind him with more force than necessary. The annoying thing was he had absolutely no idea why he had upset her. Even if he couldn't find a phone in Thailand, he could have texted her.

She put the half-thawed pizza back in the freezer, her appetite gone. Hearing that Jack's sister was missing had unsettled her. Earlier that day she had looked at the face of a pretty young girl. Now all she could remember were the maggots. That was the downside to her gift. While she was looking at a body, however badly decomposed, the face came alive in front of her, but afterwards she had no idea what she had seen. Her sketch was her only reminder and Reagan had taken that away from her.

She picked up the phone and punched in the number of Castlebury Police Station.

'I need a copy of my sketch. I don't want the original back, just a copy for my files.'

She realized after the first five minutes of being shunted from one person to another she wasn't going to get a copy of her sketch from anybody at the police station. None of them wanted to talk to her. She was a freak. She drew lifelike pictures of dead people, and there was no knowing what she might do next. Put a hex on the whole of Castlebury Police Force, no doubt. The forensic team had always disliked her, but now it seemed to have spread to the rest of the force, and even Sheila Avery looked at her suspiciously every time they met. Gina knew any good computer programme could do exactly what she did, visually resurrect the dead, but people still looked at her as if she was about to grow horns. However much she tried to tone down her talent, she was an anomaly. And there is nothing science hates more than an anomaly.

The only way she was going to get hold of a picture to show Jack was to drive to the mortuary and do another sketch of the body. Hoping one beer wouldn't put her over the limit; she grabbed her car keys and headed back down the stairs. Michael Morgan, the mortuary attendant, or anatomical pathology technician as he preferred to be called, was always willing to help, and he was weirder than she was. Besides, she consoled herself, as she drove towards the hospital, there was one big difference between the girl in the ditch and the missing Sophie.

The dead girl had recently given birth.

2

Why is a mortuary always in a basement, Gina wondered, as she parked around the back of the hospital? A post-mortem could just as easily be performed in a light, air-conditioned room on the top floor of the building. This was the NHS equivalent of the London Dungeon. She pushed open the squeaky double doors, trying not to catch her fingers.

When Michael Morgan saw her come in he put down the newspaper he had been reading. 'Good evening, Gina my love. What brings you here? I thought you already looked at our latest occupant.'

'I did, Mick, but Reagan kept my drawing. I need another look at the body.'

The mortuary attendant was on the wrong side of 40, a little tubby, with the pale skin of a redhead and a shock of curls that looked pink in the overhead lights. The more white hairs that got mixed in with the original red, the pinker his curls became. Everyone knew Michael was gay, but sometimes he was so camp it bordered on the ridiculous. When Gina told him what she wanted, he consulted

14

a list on his computer screen before rising reluctantly from behind his desk and pulling out a drawer.

'Goodness, Gina dear, you do like to punish yourself, don't you? This one's not pretty.'

Gina sighed. Taking a pad and pencil out of her bag, she said, 'I know.'

She pulled on the thin latex gloves Mick handed her — 'just in case you touch anything nasty' — and waited while he unzipped the body bag. The maggots had gone, supposedly chilled to death, unless Sheila Avery had taken the entire batch for some strange reason of her own. In spite of the ravages to her face, the dead girl looked quietly calm. Peaceful at last.

Gina finished drawing and closed her pad. 'Has anyone examined her yet?'

Mick gave Gina a sly smile. 'Are you asking if I know she recently popped out a baby? Sheila Avery came in for a quick poke around a while ago. Picked up on the baby thing while she was doing the swabs and temperature readings. Can't cut our little mother up yet, though, not until someone identifies her, or they confirm she died from a bang on the head. Avery needs parental permission, or at least good cause, before she can do a full PM.'

15

'Isn't a missing baby good cause?'

'The baby was born several days ago. They won't find the baby until they identify the mother.'

'Avery doesn't think she died in the ditch.'

'Hardly any blood at the scene, according to our favourite pathologist, and the lividity is wrong, see?' He pointed to the blue bruising where blood had pooled on one side of the body. 'She was lying on her side somewhere before she was dumped in the ditch.'

'So someone probably drove to the car-park beside the river and then carried the body to the ditch. About fifty yards if you park at the far end of the car-park. Could one person have carried her on their own, do you think?'

'Possibly. Like you, she's only a little thing.'

Gina put up her hand to stop him before he closed the bag. The girl was tiny, with a small, heart-shaped face and long blonde hair, matted now with blood. Jack also had fair hair, but he was tall, and from what Gina could remember he had a square jaw like Brad Pitt. There was no obvious family resemblance that she could see.

'Did she have any identification on her?' Gina remembered the girl had been wearing a short denim skirt and a crop-top, not many places to put anything, but teens usually had a purse and a mobile phone at the very least, and probably a front-door key.

'Strange you should ask that. She had nothing with her and an initial search found nothing nearby. No purse, no keys, no nothing.' Mick held up a plastic evidence bag. 'Apart from this.'

In the corner of the evidence bag, visible through the clear plastic, was something orange.

Gina held out her hand, but Mick snatched the bag away. 'You are joking, dear? If I let you handle this I'll get a boot up my pretty backside. This is a folded piece of paper, found with the body, and sealed in a police evidence bag. That's all I can tell you. It's stuck together with the victim's sweat and God knows what else, and no one, but no one, is allowed to touch it until forensics have carefully peeled it apart.'

She held out her hand again. 'Can I just look, please?'

Reluctantly, Mick handed her the bag. 'Don't try and open it. It's sealed.'

She held the bag up to the light. The paper was flattened and creased, folded to about the size of a credit card. 'Where was it found? You said it was with the body, but where on the body?'

'Believe it or not,' Mick said, 'it was in her shoe.'

She handed the bag back. Trainers. She remembered trainers. Probably a very good hiding place, no one in their right mind would go rooting about in somebody else's sweaty trainers, but what was so important about the little square of paper that it needed hiding? She stepped to one side so Mick could zip the bag shut over the girl's face and close the drawer. 'Any idea when Avery is likely to get permission to do the post-mortem?'

'No idea, darling.' He gave her an artful smile. 'I can't see into the future like some people.'

Gina knew Mick was teasing, but it still annoyed her. She had absolutely no idea what was going to happen in the future. All her ghosts lived in the past.

She thanked Mick for his help and drove back to her flat, the sketch rolled up on the passenger seat. What was she supposed to say to Jack when she saw him? This is a sketch of a dead girl. If it's your sister, she's lying in a drawer at the mortuary waiting to be carved up like next Sunday's roast.

But Sophie hadn't been pregnant. Some-one would have noticed — wouldn't they?

Gina parked her car outside the studio and hurried up the stairs to her flat. After her grandmother died, she sold the old house with its mixed memories and used the money from the sale to buy an art studio, a small Victorian house near the centre of town. The space on the floor above had originally been used for storage, and it had taken a lot of work, and not a little imagination, to rearrange it to her liking. Now she had two bedrooms — one used as an office — a living room, kitchen, and a bathroom. The bathroom was her favourite, and where she had spent a good percentage of the money. A proper wet room would have been a problem because the property was so old, but she had a walk-in shower cubicle, complete with power shower, and a bath big enough for the occasional soak. The rest of the flat was furnished with a mix of antiques from her grandmother's house and new pieces she had chosen herself. She liked the mix of old and new, the glass coffee table being her latest acquisition.

Still not really in the mood for food, she made do with the remaining bottle of Stella, which had enough calories to keep her going, and wondered about Jack's sister. From what she could remember, Jack's father was something to do with the church. A vicar or something. Had a religious upbringing been too much for Sophie? Or had she been pressured into going to university and then decided she didn't really like the idea? In that case, perhaps a year out wasn't such a bad thing, but you'd think the girl would have told someone what she was doing — unless, of course, she couldn't.

Gina slept badly and got out of bed just after seven. She needed to run. She felt uptight and edgy, and Castlebury was a much nicer place early in the morning. The usual rush-hour traffic hadn't yet built up and her run through the park was a pleasure. The trees still had most of their leaves and, although the summer bedding plants were beginning to fade, the ornamental bushes were full of flower. A couple of squirrels stopped what they were doing to stare at her, wondering if she had brought them food, and a blackbird sang prettily in the branches of a tree.

Here in the park, on a perfect sunny morning, there was no smell of death in the air.

At the bottom gate, where she could have turned for home, she glanced at her watch and headed along the cycle path to the spot where the body had been discovered. Just around a bend in the river blue and white tape still straddled the path, and a large policeman blocked the way.

'Path's closed, luv.' He looked her up and

down, taking in her shorts and running shoes. 'Do you run along here every day?'

'Most days,' she told him. 'Why?'

'Little bit of an accident yesterday, so we're asking a few questions. See if anyone saw anything suspicious.'

'Like what?' Gina asked, amused. There were obviously different interpretations of accident. 'Like what do I know about a dead body in a ditch?'

Startled, the man fumbled with his phone. 'Stay right there, miss, while I get someone to come and talk to you.'

She shook her head. 'I'm sorry. I was here yesterday because I work for Inspector Reagan. My name's Gina Cross. I'm a forensic artist.' She smiled, feeling sorry for teasing the poor man. 'Just get someone to verify me. I came to see if the path was still cordoned off.'

The policeman finished talking on his phone and it was his turn to smile. 'Detective Inspector Reagan says if you're a pretty little thing with dark curly hair, I'm to let you go.'

Gina's eyes widened in surprise. 'He didn't say that.'

The big man laughed. 'No, he didn't. Just getting my own back. Take care now.'

Gina turned and ran back the way she had come until she was out of sight of the policeman, then she slowed her pace. The tide was out again and gulls were walking tippy-toe across the mud, looking for breakfast. The river smelt of sewage and old dead things, and Gina knew the mud, which supported the gull's three-toed feet so easily, would suck her in like a hungry leech if she ventured too far. But she liked the continuity of the river, the inevitability of its tides, and its overriding sense of purpose.

As she headed for home, she wondered again why the dead girl had hidden the piece of orange paper so carefully.

3

Once she got back to her flat she had a quick shower, changed into jeans and a comfortable top, and headed downstairs. When she walked into the studio, her nineteen-year-old assistant was already at the computer. Megan looked up as Gina came through the door and waved her hand at the new coffee machine.

'I can fill a kettle, but I don't know what to do with that thing. The coffee runs straight through.'

'Did you put a filter paper in?'

'Ah,' Megan said. 'I wondered what they were for.'

Gina took the machine to bits and rinsed it out in the little sink. She'd bought the new coffee machine because Adam hated her instant coffee. It had been sitting in her flat, unused, for weeks, but she'd taken it down to the studio on her way out last night. Why? So she could earn his approval if he bothered to call in? God, she hoped not.

'Adam's back,' she told Megan.

'I know.' Megan stopped typing. 'Jack phoned from Norwich. He's going to try and get here today. Did you know his sister's gone missing?'

Gina nodded while she reassembled the coffee machine and put in a filter. 'Adam came round last night. He didn't stay,' she added quickly, before Megan had time to ask. She spooned coffee into the filter, filled the reservoir with water from the glass jug, and turned on the machine. 'That body I looked at yesterday evening, it was a girl about your age, probably from the university, left in a ditch by the cycle path.'

'Killed by someone?'

'She'd been hit on the head with something, and then her body was moved to the ditch.' Gina paused, frowning. 'She had something hidden in her trainer, a piece of orange paper folded up really small, but I've no idea what it was because Mick wouldn't let me look.'

'Good place to hide something. No one would want to go poking around in *my* trainers.'

'Exactly.'

The coffee machine made a noise like a prolonged death rattle and they both jumped. 'Shit,' Megan said, 'what if it does that when you've got a shopful of people?'

Gina cautiously removed the jug and poured steaming coffee into mugs. 'When do we ever have a shopful of people?'

'Good point.' Megan reached for the milk. 'But the kettle is a lot quieter and not nearly so scary.'

'I know. I'll take the machine back upstairs. That girl, the dead one, she'd just had a baby.'

Megan was quiet for too long. 'Did you find it?'

Gina shook her head. 'No, it was born a day or two ago. The girl probably left it with friends or family. The police will be looking for it.'

'But they don't know who the girl is or where she lived. How do you know she'd had a baby?'

'She was a mess when I first saw her, maggots and things had got to her, so I had to regress her a bit to sketch her face. She was pregnant before she was killed. Michael Morgan confirmed that last night. The police are looking for the baby, Megan. If it's still alive, they'll find it.'

'You go back in time, don't you? When you look at someone who's had their face bashed in, or when you only have bones to work with, you go back in time to see what they used to look like. Can't you see the place where they died? That would help the police find the baby.'

25

Gina wished she hadn't told Megan about the baby. It was stupid and insensitive. 'I'm not a time traveller, Megan. I just regenerate people in my head and then draw them. A computer can do that. It's not magic.'

Megan looked unconvinced. She had discarded her Goth look some weeks ago and was dressed in indigo jeans topped with an acid yellow T-shirt, her multi-coloured hair tied back in a ponytail. 'I still think you should try. You might be able to do more than you think, and it's important they find the baby.'

'And they will find it, but right now we have to help Jack find his sister. That's the priority. Any ideas where to start?'

'You're changing the subject, but you could start with Sophie's friends, I suppose. Pretty well all of them live in Castlebury. She lived here all her life, went to school here and everything, until her parents up and moved to Norwich. Jack said she hated leaving Castlebury. Hated Norwich. Hated her parents for a while. She could have gone to uni here, but they made her go to UEA.'

'Could that be a reason for her to take off without telling anyone?'

Megan shrugged. 'No idea. I don't know her, only what Jack told me.'

'Do you know any of Sophie's friends?'

'You having a laugh? Sophie went to the Girls' High School. I went to the worst school in town. Drugs and knives instead of books. Yeah, of course we shared the same friends.'

Gina raised an eyebrow. 'I thought there wasn't any such thing as class distinction these days.'

Megan just snorted.

Leaving Megan to her accounts, Gina moved to the other end of the open space that was both shop and studio. The building was ancient, with massive beams supporting the flat above. A large bay window at the front, and French doors at the back, helped fill the area with light. Gina had partitioned the space with open shelving filled with the artists' materials she sold to the general public. Her workspace was behind the shelving, which gave her a degree of privacy. In front was the shop, laid out with pictures for sale, Megan's desk, and a leather chair for prospective clients. Gina was about to start on a portrait she was copying from an old photograph when the door opened and Jack Lowry walked in. He looked tired, she thought, and older than his twenty-six years.

'Is Adam here? I need to talk to him.'

She shook her head. 'I haven't seen him since yesterday evening.'

'Shit! He's not answering the phone in his

27

flat and his mobile's turned off.'

'You know Adam turns his mobile off if he's working,' she said carefully. 'Why don't you sit down, Jack?'

He ran a hand through his hair and dropped into the armchair she kept for her clients. 'Sorry. I thought Adam might be here.'

She took a mug from the cupboard over the sink and poured in scalding coffee. As he reached for the mug she moved it out of range. 'Wait, it's hot, I'll get some milk.' She put in just enough to cool the coffee and added sugar. He looked as if he needed it sweet and dark. He took a sip of his coffee and she saw his hands were shaking.

'I'm sorry,' he said again. 'I haven't seen either of you for ages and I didn't even say hi.' He shifted in the chair. 'I just found out she's here in town. All the time we've been looking for her she's been living in my house.'

Gina felt a little icy trickle down her spine. She presumed Jack was talking about his sister. The sister everyone thought was somewhere in Norwich, or gone abroad on a gap year. Nowhere near a ditch in Castlebury.

'Are you sure?'

He took something out of his pocket and held it out. 'It's her ear-ring. Mum and Dad gave her ear-rings for her eighteenth birthday.

Sapphires. Her birthstone.' He shook his head in bewilderment. 'Why didn't she tell us where she was? She could've phoned. Saved Mum and Dad worrying so much.' He held the ear-ring flat on his palm, a small blue stone glinting at the centre of an intricate twist of gold. 'It was in my bed.'

No arguing with that, Gina thought, but was Sophie alone in her brother's bed when she lost the ear-ring? A little bit of extracurricular activity that her parents didn't know about would explain a lot. 'I take it she's not still at your house?'

He shook his head. 'No. She hasn't left anything. No clothes, no nothing, apart from the ear-ring. She cleaned up after herself pretty well, but the place smelt different, you know? Perfume and make-up and stuff. And some things had been moved around, mugs in the kitchen, towels in the bathroom. I know if things are out of place.'

'He's anal,' Megan butted in. 'All the mugs with the handles the same way round. Saucepans in a line. No crooked pictures on the wall.'

He smiled for the first time. 'Just because you lived with me for a while.'

Megan's face went pink. 'I rented a room from you while I was waiting for my new council flat. It wasn't like we were living

29

together.' She looked at Gina, suddenly serious. 'If Sophie is back in Castlebury . . . you don't think . . . '

'I don't know,' Gina said. There was only one way to find out. She took the rolled-up sketch out of her bag and passed it to Jack. If Megan hadn't spoken she would probably have handled it differently but, one way or another, it had to be done.

He unrolled the drawing and studied it for a long moment. 'She's dead, isn't she?' He looked up at Gina. 'No, it's not my sister, but it could be, couldn't it? We still don't know where she is. She could be lying dead somewhere like this girl.' He looked at the picture again, took a wallet out of his pocket and pulled out a small photo, handing it to Gina. 'She looks like Sophie, a little bit.'

Girl students always look alike, Gina thought, and the girl in the photo was no exception. Clones, all of them. Tall and skinny, with long straight hair and bare middles, even in winter. She envied them. At school she had always craved to be one of the crowd, but the dark Italian looks inherited from her father, and her small build, had set her apart. The foreign runt. She had been a prime target for bullying until she learnt to use her gift, drawing pictures of the offenders as they would look in their eighties, and threatening to put a curse on them. After that, they called her a witch, and no one spoke to her, but the bullying stopped.

'We'll find her, Jack,' she said, with more confidence than she was feeling. 'Now we know she's not far away.' She poured more coffee into his empty mug and added milk and sugar. 'Tell us exactly what happened. How did your parents find out Sophie hadn't turned up for the new term?'

'She's been away for most of the summer. Staying in Spain with a friend whose parents have a villa there. She came back home to pick up her stuff and we all thought she'd gone straight to the university, but she left a folder behind with a load of work in it and my mother thought it might be important. She phoned the student accommodation department and they said Sophie wouldn't be back until after Christmas. Neither of my parents believed Sophie would lie to them, but when my father talked to Sophie's tutor and some of the other staff, they all said the same thing. She'd told them she needed some time out.'

'Did Sophie tell anyone where she was going?'

'No one at the university knew where she was going. The police made some enquiries, but she'd gone of her own accord, hadn't been abducted or anything, so what could they do?' He shook his head. 'It's not like her. She usually does everything by the book.'

But she's a vicar's daughter, Gina thought, brought up to be a good little girl, and good little girls were often the first to go off the rails. Maybe Sophie got fed up with doing everything by the book.

'If she's here in Castlebury, she has to be staying somewhere. I can check with her friends if you want me to. You need some sleep.'

He knuckled his eyes like a child. 'I can't remember when I last slept. On the plane, I think. I came back to Castlebury today intending to go straight to bed,' he looked down at the ear-ring in his hand. 'But then I found this.'

'Have you got an address for the girl Sophie went to Spain with?'

'Amber Beaumont; they've been friends since junior school, but I can go and see her tomorrow. It's not fair to dump this on you.'

'Go home, Jack. Get some sleep. You found the ear-ring, so you know Sophie's OK. She's not hurt, hasn't been kidnapped, and is probably close by. Besides, the friend is more likely to talk to another female, rather than an angry, stressed-out brother. I'll close up here, get something to eat, and see if I can talk to Amber. Girls tell their best friend everything.'

'I don't,' Megan said, after he had gone. 'I don't have a best friend, but even if I did, I wouldn't tell her everything.'

'Neither would I,' Gina agreed, 'but Jack doesn't know that.'

Megan tidied her desk and turned off the computer. 'I'll come with you in case you need some help. It's a long time since you were nineteen.'

Only ten years, Gina thought, as she turned out the lights and locked the door. But, yes, ten years is a long time.

4

Megan's new council flat was near the river but well away from the expensive private apartments. Her window overlooked the supermarket car-park. As Gina got out of her car she noticed the glass in the door to the entrance lobby had been broken and someone had nailed a strip of plywood over the hole.

Megan was waiting outside. 'Someone threw up in there last night so the place stinks.' She was wearing a bright pink top and a very short denim skirt over black leggings. Her bare arms showed off the bracelet tattoo just above her elbow and the baby dragon on her forearm. Gina felt decidedly under-dressed in jeans and a black sweater with not a tattoo in sight — but at least she was warm.

Amber Beaumont lived with her parents in a village just outside the town. The house was in a cul-de-sac of individually designed properties, the front lawns cropped close and very green. The house they were looking for was set back from the road with a double garage in a faux hayloft and parking for several more cars on the drive. Gina drove through the open gates and parked between a black BMW and a red Mini. With two cars in the drive, somebody was probably at home. The house looked even bigger up close. Mostly mock Tudor, with lattice windows and stone pillars either side of the front door. She wished developers wouldn't mix their periods, but the house was still quite impressive, even in semi-darkness.

As they were getting out of the car, Megan's mobile phone started playing a pop tune. She glanced down at the screen and pushed a button. 'I'll turn it off while we're in the house.'

Gina turned off her own phone. 'Should we have phoned first, do you think?'

Megan shook her head. 'Better to take them by surprise.'

The woman who answered the door was dressed almost identically to Gina, except the jeans were probably designer and the pale-cream sweater definitely cashmere. She was tall and slim, with flawless skin and white-blonde hair brushed back off her face in a style that was deceptively casual. Well into her forties, Gina decided, but wearing well.

'Sorry to bother you, Mrs Beaumont.' Gina thought she must sound like a double-glazing salesman and wished she had rehearsed what she was going to say. 'I believe your daughter knew Sophie Lowry. She's missing and her brother's worried about her. Could we talk to Amber for a few minutes?'

The woman held the door wide. 'Please come in. Grace Lowry phoned me last week. Have they still not found Sophie?'

Before Gina could answer, a girl appeared beside Mrs Beaumont, scowling at them. 'Why are these people asking questions about Sophie?'

Gina blinked. Amber Beaumont was a total surprise. Tall and very dark, with skin the colour of espresso coffee and dead straight, jet-black hair, she looked like a younger edition of Naomi Campbell. Dark eyes brushed indifferently over Gina and settled on Megan. 'I've seen you before.'

'We go to the same bar sometimes.'

Amber nodded, her eyes suddenly hooded. 'That must be it.'

Mrs Beaumont looked puzzled, as if she couldn't imagine why Amber would frequent the same bar as Megan, but she smiled politely and ushered them into a large sitting room with double French doors. The room was furnished in a style Gina hated; leather, chrome and glass, with nothing to soften the minimalist look except a white fur rug. She looked around for the obligatory gas-flame fire and found it, complete with a hearth full of shiny pebbles.

Mrs Beaumont waited until they were seated on a white leather sofa and then sank gracefully on to a matching pouffe, folding her long legs to one side. Amber remained standing.

'The girls have spent most of the summer at our villa in Spain,' the woman said. 'A treat for them both before Sophie started her new term in Norwich. I can't think where she could have gone; she always seemed such a nice, sensible girl. She didn't tell you where she was going, did she, Amber?'

Amber studied her silver nails. 'No.'

'We know she's back in Castlebury,' Gina said. 'If she's your friend, Amber, surely she told you something about her plans?'

'Well, she didn't. I don't know where she is.' Amber looked at her mother. 'I'm going out, remember?'

Gina tried a last ditch plea. 'Please, Amber. We need to find her.'

Amber got as far as the door without saying a word, then she turned round and stared straight at Gina. 'No, you don't need to find her. You need to leave her alone.'

Gina got to her feet as Amber disappeared out of the door, but Mrs Beaumont put a hand on her arm. 'She won't tell you anything. Not if she doesn't want to. She's very like her father.'

In more ways than one, Gina thought. The girl certainly didn't take after her mother. 'I have a studio in town. If Amber tells you anything at all, perhaps you could let me know.' She fished in her bag and handed Mrs Beaumont a business card. 'Sophie's brother is really worried about her.'

'I'm sorry I can't be more help. Amber is my stepdaughter, I've only been married to her father for just over a year, and things between Amber and myself are still a little difficult, but I'll do what I can. I know how Amber's father would feel if his daughter went missing.'

But not you, Gina thought. You'd be glad to get rid of her.

They thanked Mrs Beaumont and went back to the car. As she was driving out through the gates, Gina said, 'I wanted to shake that damned girl.' It was now quite dark and she had to concentrate on finding her way through the country lanes, but she risked a quick glance at Megan. 'How come you know her?'

Megan made sure her seat belt was fastened securely. Gina was driving awfully close to the ditch. 'I don't. Not really. We hang out in the same places, that's all. She's not my type. So up herself it's not real. The last time I saw her, she was tanked up on ket.'

'Ket?'

'Ketamine. Vets give it to horses. It's supposed to be safer than coke, but it makes you see things that aren't there, and your legs go wobbly. Amber was staggering around like she was drunk before she fell on the floor. I wouldn't take something they give to horses.'

Gina missed the last part because she was trying to get her head around the image of a hallucinating horse with wobbly legs. 'Why do they give it to horses?'

'No idea. I'm not a vet.' Megan ducked as the branch of a tree hit the car window. 'After they took Gary away, I gave up going to the regular places. I've been back a few times since, but mostly I leave the stuff alone now. I haven't seen Amber for ages.'

'Because she was in Spain with Sophie — if that's really where they went. It shouldn't be too hard to check.'

'Get Adam to find out,' Megan suggested. 'He'll be able to do that.'

Gina swerved to avoid something dead in the road. She hated driving on unlit roads. 'If I ever see him again. I reckon he's disappeared as well.'

But he hadn't. When Gina got home and walked round the corner to the stairs leading up to her flat, he was sitting on the bottom step.

'Where the hell have you been? You had your bloody phone turned off.'

Gina pushed past him and started up the stairs, glad she had never given him a key. It would be like coming home to a houseful of angry bear. She almost slammed the door on him, but he was too quick for her. He caught the door as it was about to close and just missed losing his fingers.

'I went round to see Jack but he wasn't answering, then I came round here and you were out. You never go out in the evening.' He said it accusingly, as if she had no right to go out without telling him. Perhaps he'd like an itinerary, she thought, or he could have her tagged so he could find her with a sat-nav or something.

He walked into the kitchen and took a bottle and glasses out of the cabinet, handing her a full glass of red wine as she kicked off her shoes and flopped down on the sofa.

'Jack came to the studio looking for you. He hadn't slept, so I sent him home to bed. He's probably still sleeping.'

Adam filled a glass for himself and sat down on the other side of the coffee table. 'What did he want? Has he found out any more about his sister?'

40

'Yes, but he couldn't find you to tell you.'

'The *Castlebury Times* asked me to do a follow up on the murdered girl. They've got a statement from the police, but they want a story, which means I've got to try and find someone to interview. Difficult if no one knows who she is. I've been at the hospital most of the day with Sheila Avery. The dead girl wasn't a student — not at this university, anyway.' He looked at Gina over the top of his glass. 'So you were wrong, there's no connection between her and Jack's sister. Not with the town and not with the university. She could have come from anywhere.' When Gina didn't answer, he said, 'You don't look convinced.'

She shook her head. 'It's not that. It's just that you seem more interested in getting a story than finding Jack's sister. He's your friend, Adam, and you promised to help him.'

'For Christ's sake, Gina, Sophie's a teen. She's lived in a church environment all her life: I'm not surprised she's rebelled. She went abroad with a friend, didn't she? Got a taste of freedom, probably met a Spanish waiter. Maybe she's eloped. Jack's getting himself worked up over nothing.'

'Sophie's been staying in his house. That's what he wanted to tell you. He found her ear-ring in his bed. All the time his parents

41

were looking for her in Norwich she was here in Castlebury, and he can't understand why she'd do something like that, worry them to death when there was no need. Now she's gone missing again.'

'Perhaps she brought the Spanish waiter back with her and stashed him in Jack's house.' He saw Gina wasn't amused and raised his hands in surrender. 'What do you want me to do?'

'You're a bloody investigative journalist. So investigate. I went round to the friend's house this evening, a girl called Amber Beaumont. I think she knows where Sophie is, but she's not telling.'

How could she explain the feeling of dread she felt every time she thought of Sophie? There was no rational explanation, and Adam was probably right, a secret boyfriend would explain her disappearance and Amber's silence, but there was more, Gina was sure of that. Sophie was in danger.

'How do you find a nineteen year old who went missing of her own accord in a town full of nineteen year olds?' he asked reasonably. 'That's like looking for a bit of hay in a haystack. This is a university town; we have a sixth form college, a couple of art centres, a drama school, and every other person on the street is a student of some sort. But' — and he actually had the temerity to point a finger at her — 'somebody killed a young girl, dumped her body in a ditch, and left her to the maggots. That is something that needs investigating.'

Why did he come round, she wondered, when he was in such a filthy mood? 'She was pregnant, the dead girl. Had a baby just before she died. Did Avery tell you that?'

He emptied his glass. 'Yes, she told me that, and they've found it, or at least they think they have.'

Something in his face told her she shouldn't get excited. 'Alive?'

He shook his head. 'A baby's body was discovered at an infill site early this morning. Hidden in a black bag and collected with the rubbish. The men just pick up the bags and throw them in the back of the refuse truck. They have this crushing thing — '

'Don't. I don't want to think about it.'

'Christ, Gina, neither do I. Trouble is, once you've seen something like that, you keep thinking about it, whether you want to or not.'

She reached for the wine bottle. 'Was the baby already dead? Before the crusher thing?'

'Avery says so. It never took its first breath. She's doing the post-mortem on Monday morning. If there's a DNA match, she'll most

43

likely get permission to do a PM on the mother, even if she hasn't been officially identified.' He held out his glass for a refill. 'If you thought the girl was a mess, you should have been there when they brought the baby in. The guy who found it is going to need counselling.'

Gina filled Adam's glass and poured the last of the wine into her own glass. No wonder he was in a bad mood.

'Fine,' she said. 'You carry on with your story on the dead girl, and I'll help Jack find his sister. Someone's got to. He's going nuts, not knowing where she is. Amber Beaumont was high on something called ketamine last time Megan saw her, scrabbling around on the floor of some bar.'

'That wouldn't please her father. He's got some high-powered hospital job. Consultant, something like that.'

'Well paid, too, from the look of their house.' She had a sudden thought. 'Drugs, hospitals? Is that where Amber gets the ketamine?'

Adam shook his head. 'Not likely. You have to sign for everything in a hospital, and ketamine is readily available on the Internet. The kids can buy anything they want on line. Ecstasy pills are a couple of quid, which is less than a pint of beer. Not pure, though.

44

There won't be much MDMA in it. The stuff you get for that price has been cut with god knows what. They call it mud, and that's what it looks like.'

'MDMA?'

'Don't ask me to spell it. Started out as a slimming aid, but it gave everyone such a nice feeling it became popular in the eighties as a recreational drug.'

'Lot's of happy, thin people. Where can I buy some?'

He laughed. 'You're skinny enough already.' He stood up and held out his hands to pull her to her feet. 'We got off on the wrong foot again, didn't we?'

She pulled her hands free and picked up the empty wine glasses, moving into her tiny kitchen. 'We always do, Adam.'

He was right behind her. 'Why is that, do you think?' He waited until she turned round. 'I quite like the sparks, don't you, when we rub one another up the wrong way?'

Before she could stop him, he lifted her up and sat her on the work surface. Sometimes she hated her humiliating lack of height, but his face was now on a level with hers, which meant they were eye to eye, and his eyes were so incredibly blue . . . but he was a manipulative bastard, and she wasn't about to be manipulated.

'Put me down, Adam.'

'Because I don't know where you've been?' He grinned at her. 'I don't think you've been far, have you, Gina? You've got that hungry look, like someone who's been starved for quite a while.'

She raised her knee. Suddenly, unexpectedly, and with a great deal of force. As he backed away, his breath whooshing out and his hands going to his crotch, she slid down off the counter and marched out of the kitchen. 'Fuck off, Adam,' she told him over her shoulder.

'Bloody hell,' he whimpered, still holding himself. 'If that knee had connected properly, I'd be a eunuch.'

She smiled at him sweetly. 'I'll pour some cold water down the front of your trousers, if you like. Take the pain away.'

He leered at her. 'How about kissing it all better?'

She laughed. What else could she do? She was pretty sure she'd hurt him, but he was taking it like a man. 'It's late. How about we start again tomorrow, when we've both had some sleep? I promise not to rub you up the wrong way.'

He groaned. 'That's not fair, talking dirty to me when I'm injured.'

She walked with him to the front door.

'Can you let me know when the results of the DNA come in for the baby match? Or if anyone identifies the girl.'

He didn't answer, just bent down and kissed her long and hard, and he was right, she had been starved, but just as she was about to give in to her melting bones and beg him to stay the night, he gave her one of his wickedly sexy grins. 'God, I missed that, Gina. Those Thai girls aren't a patch on you.'

5

The next day was completely manic. In the morning a group of students from the Arts College decided to buy all their materials from Gina's studio. They consulted lists, yelled back and forth to one another, and picked up everything in sight, usually moving it to another part of the shop where Gina knew she would never find it again. In the end, Megan took over.

'Shut up, the lot of you,' she shouted over the general bedlam. 'If you give Gina your lists, she'll find the stuff for you.'

Now why didn't I think of that, Gina wondered, as the students formed an orderly line, each holding a list? She found them what they wanted and they moved to Megan, who rang the purchases up on the till and handed out change. Within twenty minutes, order had been restored, and the students had left.

The rest of the day passed quickly. Two people came in to order portraits, both of which had to be completed before Christmas, and Gina sold several small drawings of views she had sketched from the balcony of Adam's riverside apartment before he went away. All in all, a good day. After Megan had gone, she finished a long overdue picture of a fat Persian cat, and then locked up the studio, tired, but content.

Her personal mail was always delivered straight to the studio, mainly to save the poor overworked postman having to climb the stairs to her flat, but also because she didn't have a letterbox. The plain white envelope sitting on her doormat had obviously been pushed under her door. She picked it up, thinking she would have to do something about a draught excluder before the winter gales started whistling in off the river. There was nothing on the front of the envelope except her name, written in large upper-case letters and underlined with a heavy diagonal slash. She ran her thumb under the flap and ripped open the envelope.

For a moment she just stared, not touching the bright orange paper, almost afraid to remove it from the envelope. But then curiosity got the better of her. It wasn't exactly the same, of course. The small square of paper in the evidence bag had been folded a number of times, stuck together, Mick had told her, with God knows what. This paper was pristine, folded just once to fit inside the envelope, the wording fresh and black.

ABORTION IS NOT THE ONLY OPTION.

The single line of print was followed by a local telephone number, and she actually had her hand on the phone before she reined herself in and stopped to think. If someone answered, what was she going to say? She had no idea who had posted the leaflet through her door; a normal flyer wouldn't be in an envelope.

And why had it been sent to her?

She smoothed the paper out on top of her coffee table. What is another option to abortion? The only alternative she could think of was to keep the baby, and you didn't need to phone somebody to be told that.

Her feet were hurting and she didn't want to go out again, but she needed to make sure the leaflet was the same as the one tucked in the girl's shoe. If she got something to eat before she left, she might miss Mick, so she grabbed her car keys, put the leaflet back in the envelope it had come in, and ran down the stairs to her car. As she slid behind the wheel she decided she was making far too many trips to the mortuary.

She had expected to find Mick alone, but Sheila Avery and Reagan were standing at one of the metal tables, looking down at something. Gina hesitated in the doorway wondering if she could make a quick getaway, but it was too late. Avery spotted her and straightened up slowly.

'Why, if it isn't the little psychic artist.' She moved away from the table. 'Come to draw the baby?'

Gina shook her head, staying where she was. 'I need to speak to Inspector Reagan.' It was as good a reason as any to be at the mortuary, but Avery wasn't done yet.

'What's the matter? I thought you liked drawing dead bodies. The girl in the ditch didn't seem to bother you. You drew a really pretty picture in spite of the maggots.'

The pathologist was baiting her and Gina wasn't sure why. 'A baby is different,' she said quietly.

Avery was silent for a moment, staring at Gina thoughtfully, then she nodded. 'Yes, it is.'

Reagan moved away from the table, frowning. 'What did you want to see me about?' His irritation was tangible. He had told her to stay away, not to interfere, and now here she was, like the proverbial bad penny. Besides, Reagan had kids, and now he had two dead ones to deal with. A baby and a teenage mum.

She took the envelope out of her bag and handed it to him. 'This was pushed under my door.' Reagan pulled the orange leaflet out of the envelope and unfolded it. She caught a glimpse of Mick out of the corner of her eye. He looked as if he was about to have a heart attack. 'I have no idea why someone would send this to me,' she said. 'It probably has nothing to do with your investigation, but I thought I'd better let you see it before I throw it away.'

'Why?' Reagan held the leaflet by one corner as if it might bite him. 'Why would you think a flyer through your door had anything to do with my investigation?'

'Because a flyer doesn't usually come in an envelope with my name written on the front.' She paused, not looking at Mick. 'And I saw the evidence bag when I was here last.'

Reagan's bushy eyebrows came together in an angry V above his nose. He looked across at the technician. 'I thought evidence was supposed to be locked up.'

'It is,' Mick said with a nervous little wave of his hand. 'When it's been catalogued I lock it away safely, but your little dears leave stuff lying around all over the place. It's a wonder more of it doesn't get lost.'

Nicely done, Mick, Gina thought. She didn't want to get the technician into trouble. 'I came straight over as soon as I opened the envelope. My sketch of the girl was in the paper this morning and people know I work

52

for you. I think someone is using me as a messenger.'

Reagan held the paper up to the light. 'No doubt you've had your sticky little fingers all over this. Not much help if we want to look for prints.'

'I didn't think to take the paper out of the envelope with kitchen tongs,' Gina said tartly. 'I'll remember next time. Besides, we both know it's almost impossible to lift prints from ordinary paper.'

'Has the bit of paper from the girl's shoe been processed yet?' Reagan asked no one in particular.

Mick trotted to the back of the room and unlocked a cupboard. He took out a plastic box and carried it back to his desk. 'If the evidence had been processed it wouldn't still be here, but there's a backlog at the lab, same as always.' He opened the box and handed Reagan the plastic bag with the small square of orange paper. 'See? Still here. So are her trainers, if you want them as well.'

Reagan didn't attempt to open the sealed bag. He put it on Mick's desk and spread the leaflet out beside it. 'Slightly different colour, but this one is fresh. Looks newly printed.' He folded the paper into an approximation of the piece in the evidence bag and laid one on top of the other. The fit was perfect. He looked at Gina, pursing his mouth, and then took a mobile phone out of his pocket and tapped in a number, pushing the dial button. He looked surprised when someone answered almost at once. Clamping the phone tight against his ear he walked to the other side of the room, frowning when he saw all three of them straining to hear.

'I'm Detective Inspector Reagan, Castlebury Police. I'm following up a lead that might be related to the death of a young girl . . . Yes, that's right, the picture in the paper. What is it you do exactly?' He listened for a moment in silence. 'Thank you for your help, Miss Valentine. I can't give you any more information over the phone, but I'll send someone round in the morning to speak to you.' He put his phone away and walked back to Avery. 'Some sort of counselling service for pregnant women. I'll get it checked out.'

Avery looked at her watch. 'They work late, same as us. I've got the DNA samples, so I'll push off home.' She turned to Mick. 'Get the remains ready for transporting in the morning. We won't be doing the post-mortem here. This one will need specialist treatment.'

Gina wondered if Avery was trying to distance herself from the dead baby, or if she was really as callous as she pretended to be. That was the body of a tiny baby on the table, not remains. The big difference between their respective jobs was that Avery took a body apart, while Gina put it back together again.

Trying not to look at the table, she asked, 'How was the baby found? The infill site is enormous.'

'Seagulls,' Reagan said, 'and some poor bloke in a truck sent to scare them off. The bag had been torn open by the birds and he saw a little foot. Thought it was a doll — until he got out of his truck for a closer look. Now I've got men I can't really spare crawling about on a dump looking through other people's rubbish. Bloody waste of time. Whoever stuck that baby in a carrier bag won't have left their wallet behind, will they?'

'Was it a boy or girl?' She needed to give the baby an identity, the chance to be a person.

'Girl.'

Gina thought of Megan and her baby, Rosie. Another baby girl who didn't live to see the light of day.

'Stay out of it, Gina,' Reagan said. 'Don't make this personal.'

'I'm not.' She shook her head. 'Jack Lowry's sister has gone missing. I'm just trying to help him find her. As far as I know, her disappearance has nothing to do with your dead mother and baby.'

Reagan waved to Sheila Avery as she closed her bag and hurried out. 'Then why did the flyer get pushed under your door?'

Gina shook her head again, this time in exasperation. 'I don't know. Maybe because I drew a picture of the dead girl. Maybe because I work for you. Maybe because I know Adam Shaw and he's doing an article for the local paper. I really don't know. I promise I'm not trying to muck up your investigation.'

'I spoke to Shaw about his photographer friend and the missing sister. The parents are driving down from Norwich this weekend. I'll try and find time to have a word with them, but if the girl buggered off because she wanted to, there's not a lot the police can do.'

Gina wanted to go home. She wanted to leave this cold, miserable place, with its metal tables and stark white tiles, and go home to her nice warm flat. But she didn't often get the chance to question Reagan.

'You must have dealt with missing girls before. Why do they do it? Sophie Lowry had a nice home, a family who obviously loved her, and she was just about to start her first term at Norwich University. Why would she take off without telling her family?'

'Depends.' Reagan hitched his bottom up

on Mick's desk. 'Depends whether the problem started at home or outside. Abuse at home, physical, mental, sexual, will make a kid run. Bullying, or an inability to cope with the school workload, can cause them to take off as well — or hang themselves. Then there's drug addiction, or an unwanted pregnancy. Both unlikely, I would think, in this case. The kid's parents would have noticed that much of a change.'

'How about a secret boyfriend? I know that sounds extreme, but Sophie's dad is a vicar. Could it be that she hitched up with someone really unsuitable and knew dad wouldn't approve?'

'Mmm. Doesn't really fit, does it? First off, if she'd run away with some kid who plays the drums and smokes pot she'd leave a note. Rub her parents' noses in the fact that she had to leave home because they wouldn't accept him. And if it was a married man, she'd have nowhere to run to, would she? She could hardly move in with him.'

Reagan got to his feet and waved a hand at Mick. 'I'm off, Mick, but I'll be back for the girl's post-mortem. Let's hope someone recognizes the drawing in the paper. The poor kid must belong to someone.' He turned back to Gina. 'Speak to the parents of the missing sister when they get here. They'll tell you

57

things they won't tell the police. There's a reason the girl's gone missing, probably a good one, and if you can find out what it is, you'll probably find the girl.'

6

'Let me phone the clinic,' Megan said.

Gina shook her head violently. 'God, no! Reagan's already spoken to them. Can you imagine what he'd do to me if he found out?' She had just finished telling Megan about the orange flyer and her visit to the hospital mortuary.

'He won't know. I'll just be another pregnant teenager, sick with worry and looking for this amazing 'other option'. I could have done with another option when I needed it.' Megan was silent for a moment. 'Do you think Sophie is pregnant?'

'I don't know,' Gina answered honestly. 'The thought crossed my mind. If she is, I think Amber would know. Maybe that's why she's so protective. But where would Sophie go? She has to live somewhere.' It was Gina's turn to pause. 'Unless she's gone back to Spain. Back to the villa. Something else for Adam to check out.'

Having sidetracked Gina, Megan picked up the phone. 'Good job you made a note of the number before Reagan took the flyer from you.' She punched in the number Gina had

59

written on a scrap of paper, holding up her hand for quiet. 'Hello,' she said, in a soft, hesitant little voice. 'I've got, like, a leaflet someone gave me, with this number on it.' She winked at Gina. 'Yes, I would like to talk to someone . . . Oh, only a few weeks. I've only just found out for sure.' Her voice broke convincingly. 'I don't know what to do.' She listened for a few moments longer, and then put the phone back in its rest. 'Someone will be at the clinic on Monday,' she said. 'I've got an appointment at ten in the morning, so you'll have to manage here by yourself.'

'The police are sending someone to the clinic as well. You'll lose me my job, Megan.'

'No, I won't. Reagan's sending someone today, you said. I'm not going until Monday. And I want to know what they're telling these girls, because one of them stuffed her baby in a bin and ended up murdered. Reagan won't tell you anything. You know he won't.'

Someone came in to buy a picture frame, which started a small rush that lasted until lunchtime. As soon as the studio was empty, Gina grabbed the closed sign and put it on the door. 'Tea,' she said, making a dive for the kettle. 'If we don't shut shop for an hour, we won't get a break.'

There was a bang on the window and Gina looked up to see Adam grinning at her.

'Timed that right, didn't I?' he said, as she closed the door quickly behind him. He produced three packs of sandwiches and a bag of doughnuts and put them on Megan's desk. 'As you can see, I didn't come empty handed, all you have to do is make the tea.'

'I'll do it,' Megan said, 'but I get first pick of the sarnies.'

Adam looked round the studio. 'You've changed things a bit. New shelves. It looks good.'

'If I do a sketch for a portrait, it gives the clients a bit of privacy.'

Adam wandered round the studio studying Gina's sketches. 'This one was done from my balcony. I remember you sitting in the sun with very little on, a sketch pad on your lap and a glass of wine beside you.'

'I work better that way, but it's a little impractical here at the studio.' She changed the subject. 'Have you spoken to Reagan recently? They found something hidden in the dead girl's shoe.'

'Yeah, Sheila Avery told me. That was all the girl had on her, she said, a bit of orange paper.'

'Someone put an orange leaflet through my door last night. It was a flyer about help with unwanted pregnancies.' She held up her hands as he went to speak. 'I don't know why, so don't ask.'

'How do you know it's the same?'

'Because I took it to Inspector Reagan and he confirmed it. It's some sort of counselling service operating from the clinic in town. It seems legit.'

'And I've got an appointment with them on Monday,' Megan said. 'I told them I was pregnant.'

Adam looked at her in surprise. 'Why?'

'Because they're telling people there's some miracle cure for getting knocked up, and there isn't. Whatever happens, you still get stuck with what comes after.' Embarrassed by their silence, Megan started fussing with the packs of sandwiches. 'Who wants chicken?'

'This is some sort of abortion clinic?' Adam asked.

'No,' Gina said. 'It seems to be the opposite. The message on the flyer said there is an alternative to abortion, and there was a telephone number. Reagan rang it while I was there. He's sending someone to check it out today.'

'The dead girl didn't have an abortion, did she? She gave birth full term.' He frowned. 'But in that case why would she hide the leaflet in her shoe?'

'Exactly,' Megan said. 'That's what I'm going to find out. I'll say a friend sent me and see if I can discover whether the girl went to

62

the clinic before she died.'

'I wish you wouldn't.' Gina chose a pack of sandwiches without looking at them and handed the other pack to Adam. 'I have a nasty feeling about all this. Reagan told me not to get involved with his murder case.'

'You're not,' Megan said. 'I am.'

'Do we know any more about the dead girl?' Adam asked. 'Has anyone identified her?'

Gina took a bite out of her sandwich. Ham and pickle. Not her favourite. 'Do you want to swap?' she asked Adam. 'I don't like brown pickle.'

He handed her his unopened packet with a sigh. 'Read the label next time before you take a bite.'

She grinned at him. 'You don't like tuna, otherwise you wouldn't have swapped. No, in answer to your question, no one has identified the dead girl or the baby. The blood type matches, but that doesn't mean a lot. Sheila Avery took a DNA sample to send off, and they're sending the baby's body some- where else for the post-mortem. Probably Addenbrooks. I think whoever put the flyer through my door knew I'd show it to Reagan. It was like an anonymous phone call. Someone trying to help. But you can't put it in your story because Reagan would kill me.'

'Was the leaflet supposed to help us find the identity of the girl, or help us find the person who murdered her? If someone bashed her on the head and killed her, why not leave her where she was, why go to all the trouble of moving the body?'

'Perhaps she was somewhere she shouldn't be,' Megan said. 'Like a drug dealer's house, or a squat. Somewhere you wouldn't want the police to come calling, not with blood all over the place and a dead body. When you think about it, no one would want that.'

They finished their sandwiches in silence. Megan poured the tea.

'Getting back to Sophie,' Gina said, taking the mug Megan handed her. 'I was thinking about Spain. She was there most of the summer. Do you think she could have gone back there?'

Adam shook his head. 'Not in the last few days, and not from Stansted. You told me I wasn't helping enough, so I checked. Besides, I think Jack told me the Beaumont's Spanish villa is rented out during the winter months. Some Spanish agency handles the rental and keeps an eye on the place.'

'So Sophie isn't likely to be in Spain? If she was, the Beaumonts would know.'

'Yes, and she isn't at the YWCA or any of the hostels in Castlebury, because I checked them as well. But she could be dossing down with a friend somewhere.'

'Reagan said if we can find out what made her run in the first place, we'll find her.'

'Jack's picking up his parents from the station today and taking them back to his house. I suggest we meet them somewhere for Sunday lunch, fill them in on what we know, and try and put their minds at rest. As far as we know Sophie is alive and well and living somewhere in Castlebury.'

'What are they like, Jack's parents?' Megan asked.

'Grace and Brian Lowry? I've only met them a couple of times. Brian's a typical vicar, if there is such a thing. Tall, like Jack, and rake thin. Grace had Jack in her early thirties, thought that was going to be it, and then got pregnant again seven years later with Sophie. They must both be in their sixties now. Grace was teaching in Castlebury until they moved to Norwich, and she's always had a lot to do with the running of the church, the social side and all that, so I think Jack spent a lot of time with Sophie. He thinks the world of his little sister.'

'She could have sent him a message to stop him worrying.'

'She hasn't contacted anyone as far as we know.' He sighed. 'In a way, I hope she has run off with some local boy. A teenage girl on her own, however well she knows the area, could be in danger.'

'She is,' Gina said.

'Wow, you said that with conviction. Was that another of those psychic moments you say you don't have?'

'Just a feeling.' She looked at him coldly. 'Most normal people have them.'

He looked as if he was about to say something, changed his mind and looked at his watch. 'Time to go. I have to get down to the police station. A little bird told me they might have a lead on the dead girl's mother.' He waved goodbye from the door. 'See you both on Sunday.'

'Avery,' Gina said crossly, as she shut the door behind him and turned the sign round. 'That woman tells him everything, even though he's a bloody reporter. She hardly speaks to me.'

'Because she doesn't understand you,' Megan said. 'She's afraid of you. She thinks you really are a witch.'

Sometimes Gina thought it might be a good idea to walk around in a pointy hat. Something to give her a bit of status. The broomstick might be a bit of a nuisance, though. Why did a wizard have a nice wand that did magical things and a witch have a bloody broom? Definitely a case of sexual discrimination.

She started a rough sketch of a bloodhound she was copying from a photo, wondering if the owner really wanted her to include the skeins of drool hanging from the animal's jaws, but her heart wasn't in it. Sophie was running out of time and Gina didn't know what to do about it.

The question was still haunting her when she said goodnight to Megan, locked the door, and climbed the stairs to her flat. She had just started to sort her post when the phone rang.

'They've found the girl's mother,' Adam said. 'I'm going to try and arrange an interview with her.'

He hung up before Gina could ask any questions. Her drawing of the dead girl had been good, a near perfect likeness that had appeared on TV and in most of the daily tabloids, not counting the local papers, so why had it taken the mother this long to come forward? And why hadn't she reported her missing daughter to the police?

7

Sunday started out sunny, a shaft of light catching Gina right between the eyes just as she was thinking of having another ten minutes in bed. Rather than risk being blinded, she got up and shuffled into the bathroom. She ran the shower longer than usual, turning the hot water to cold at the last moment to wake her up. Strong coffee made in her new coffee machine finished the recuperation job, and she scrapped her usual run around the park in favour of scrambled eggs on toast. A girl needed a treat now and again.

Saturday had been frustrating. The studio had been exceptionally busy, which was a good thing, but she needed to get out there and find Sophie. The feeling of impending danger was like a toothache, niggling away in the background. She had arranged to pick Megan up at one o'clock for Sunday lunch with the parents. Maybe they would have some idea where Sophie might have gone.

She changed into her best jeans and a lightweight sweater, piling her hair on top of her head and securing the unruly curls with a black scrunchy. The early morning sun had given way to heavy clouds, and if it rained her hair would turn to frizz. Leaving it loose was not an option.

The housing association flat where Megan lived had French doors and a safety railing instead of a balcony. As Gina got out of the car, a sound that couldn't possibly be called a miaow made Gina look up. Megan had left one of the French doors open and Gina watched the Siamese push her head through the railings, a disapproving scowl on her pointed face. She gave another shriek as Megan came out of the lobby downstairs.

'Won't she jump?' Gina asked worriedly.

Megan looked up at the third floor window. 'It's a bloody long way down. She's not that stupid.'

The restaurant by the river was crowded, a blanket of noise and warmth enveloping them as they walked inside. Adam was already seated at a table by the window with Jack and his parents. Brian Lowry looked tall, even sitting down, his dog collar just visible over his black polo-neck sweater. He had the same colour eyes as his son, but his hair had once been darker, turned cappuccino now as white mixed with the brown. He was frowning into his glass of ale. His wife sat opposite him, a little dumpling of a woman, still pretty, with soft curls and a dimple in her cheek. Her hair was pale gold with barely a hint of white; it was easy to see where Jack got his looks.

Gina asked for two Stellas at the bar and slipped into a seat next to Grace Lowry. She handed a beer to Megan and took off her jacket, glad Adam had booked a table inside. The weather had changed, and beneath the window the estuary water moved like black treacle under a heavy sky, fat little boats bobbing in the cool breeze coming off the sea.

'Thank you for helping,' Grace said, covering Gina's hand with her own. 'We need all the help we can get.'

'I haven't done much.' Gina wondered if she could remove her hand without appearing rude. 'I spoke to Amber and her mother, but Amber wasn't very forthcoming.'

'She wouldn't be,' Grace said. 'She dislikes her stepmother and makes no bones about it, but her father dotes on her. I worried about Sophie going around with Amber, she's not a good influence, but you can't pick your children's friends.'

Gina thought Grace flicked a glance at Megan, but she could have been mistaken. 'They went on holiday together, didn't they? Before Sophie went missing.' Gina took the menu Adam handed her, glad of an excuse to take back her hand.

Grace Lowry nodded. 'To the villa in Spain. She came home in time for the new term. Everything was fine then.'

But it wasn't, Gina thought. And Grace should have known that. Adam had mentioned the woman was a retired teacher, so poor Sophie had been raised by a teacher and a vicar, not Gina's idea of ideal parents, but if Sophie had grown up in that environment it wouldn't have been enough to make her run, not on its own. There had to be something else.

'So when Sophie went to Spain with Amber, everything was fine? Then she came home, back to your house in Norwich, and packed ready for the new term at university. How did she seem?'

'She was home for such a short while, only a few days, just enough time to pack a bag, really, and we were both busy with the new parish.' Grace Lowry shrugged apologetically. 'I certainly didn't notice anything wrong. Sophie seemed her usual self. Excited about going to university.'

'Did you take her? Drop her off at the student accommodation? Or did she go on her own?'

'I took her.' Grace Lowry stared down at her plate. 'That was the last time I saw her.'

Gina suddenly thought of something. 'When she went missing, did Sophie have her passport with her?'

Grace shook her head. 'No. She took her chequebook and credit card, and some personal things, but her passport is still in her bedroom.'

'Well, that's something. At least we know she's still in this country.'

The waiter arrived and they all ordered. Gina was glad of the respite. She glanced across the table at Adam for support, but he was chatting to Brian Lowry, with Jack intervening now and again. She drank half her beer in silence, trying to hear what the men were saying above the hubbub of the crowded restaurant, and wondering what else she could ask Grace Lowry without upsetting the woman. She looked at Megan, wondering why the girl was so quiet. In the end she settled for the question that had been uppermost in all their minds.

'Did Sophie have a boyfriend?' she asked Grace. 'Someone who lives here in Castlebury?'

Brian Lowry didn't give his wife a chance to answer. 'No,' he said forcefully, leaning across the table. 'The police asked the same thing. She wasn't interested in boys. If she'd had a boyfriend, we would have known about it. She tells us everything.'

No, she doesn't, Gina thought, and what teenage girl isn't interested in boys? She turned to look directly at the vicar. 'Do you have any idea why Sophie might have gone missing? Was there anything different about her behaviour before she went to Spain? Or after she got back? Anything worrying her?'

'She's been abducted. Kidnapped, or something. I kept telling the police she wouldn't have left of her own accord, but they wouldn't listen. Treated me as if I was a suspect myself.'

The waiter brought the food on a trolley and carefully put a plate in front of each of them, reminding them the plates were hot.

'She was staying at my house, Dad,' Jack said, after the waiter had gone. 'I told you, I found her ear-ring.'

'Planted,' Brian Lowry said. 'Whoever took her wanted us to think she was staying there. You read about that sort of thing all the time. A false trail, to lead the police astray.'

'She hasn't been abducted,' Jack said quietly. 'That's ridiculous.'

'How would you know?' his father shot back. 'You weren't there. You were too busy taking your pictures to care about your baby sister.'

After a couple of seconds of embarrassed

73

silence, Grace put her hand on her husband's arm. He shook it off. 'Best eat your lunch, Grace. It's getting cold.'

Any attempt at normal conversation after that was a lost cause. When the meal was finished, Brian Lowry went outside to stand on the wooden deck and watch the boats. A moment or two later Grace followed.

'I'll take them home,' Jack said, pushing his chair back. 'This is stressing them both out.'

When no one came back in to say goodbye, Adam ordered coffee. 'They're not the only ones stressed out,' he said. 'Bloody hell, no wonder the girl did a runner.'

Megan took a long breath and let it out with a whoosh. 'I think I stopped breathing for a bit. I hate watching people winding one another up.'

'You were very quiet,' Gina said. 'Not like you.'

'It was Jack's mum. Did you see the look she gave me? The thought of her son shacked up with someone like me was worse than her daughter running off with a Spanish waiter.'

Gina didn't disagree.

'Although they've found the dead girl's mother,' Adam said, changing the subject, 'the identification isn't official yet. Avery didn't want the mother to see her daughter's body, so ID was based on a tattoo. The girl hasn't been to a dentist since she lost her baby teeth, as far as the mother knows, so it's no good chasing up dental records. The woman recognized your sketch, Gina, and at the moment it looks as if the dead girl's name was Madonna Price. Known to her friends as Donna. When Donna told her mother she was pregnant, she was kicked out. Mum has enough to cope with already, evidently. Like a petty crimes list as long as your arm, a drug habit, and several visits to a clinic that specializes in sexually transmitted diseases.'

Megan laughed. 'And I thought I had problems.'

'It's sad, though, isn't it?' Gina said. 'Sophie's parents are desperate to find her, and that poor kid was slung out on her ear.'

Adam looked thoughtful. 'How would the vicar and his wife react, do you think, if they found out their daughter was pregnant?'

'Her dad wouldn't believe it,' Megan said. 'He'd swear she had a pillow stuffed up her jumper, or it was another virgin birth.'

'Total denial,' Adam agreed. 'If they'd only admit Sophie might have a few problems they don't know about, it would be easier to discover why she went missing.'

Gina took a sip of her coffee and added more cream. 'If she is pregnant, all the more reason to find her quickly.'

'It makes sense,' Adam said. 'It's the one thing that would make her take off without telling anyone, but if she was several months' pregnant surely her mother would have noticed.'

'Not necessarily,' Gina said. 'Baggy clothes can hide a bump for ages. I didn't know Megan was pregnant for nearly six months.'

Megan grinned. 'Because you thought I was just getting fatter. A girl I knew still thought it was something she'd eaten when she was giving birth. How's that for denial?'

'So what do we do?' Adam said. 'Put forward our idea to the good vicar and his wife?'

Gina made a face. 'Rather you than me. And what would be the point? As Megan said, they wouldn't believe you, and we might be completely wrong. How about putting the idea to Amber? If she thinks we know already, she might talk.'

'I'll do that,' Megan said. 'I know most of the places she hangs out.'

'If we're wrong,' Adam said, 'we're wasting time following a dud trail.'

'Maybe,' Gina answered. 'But at least it's a trail, which is more than we had before.'

As they were about to leave, Megan said, 'I've got an appointment at that 'other option' clinic tomorrow. It would be interesting to find out if Sophie went there, wouldn't it?'

8

Megan stood outside the clinic for a few moments, plucking up the courage to go in. She had walked from her flat, and felt hot and sticky in spite of a thin rain that misted on her face and denim jacket. She wiped her face with the back of her hand and brushed ineffectually at her jacket, stalling for time. This was harder than she had thought it would be.

She wore no make-up, apart from a slash of lipstick, and her hair was pulled back into an untidy ponytail. Finding clothes in her wardrobe slightly on the shabby side had not been a problem. She was aiming at a desperate look, one she knew only too well, brought on by a pregnancy as terrifying as it was unexpected. She had to keep reminding herself she was only play-acting.

Housed in a small Victorian building well away from the bustle of the main shopping area, the clinic was made up of separate advisory services where you could get the morning-after pill, have a smear test, or talk to someone about the dose of clap you'd picked up seemingly by magic. Megan had been here before, several times.

She took a breath and pushed through the doors, her heart rate escalating as soon as she got inside. She didn't have to pretend to be nervous, she was. She had forgotten how much she hated this place.

'I have an appointment,' she told the woman at the desk. 'With a Miss Valentine.'

The woman checked a computer screen and pointed to a row of chairs. 'Have a seat. She should see you in a minute or two.'

The building was old, the chairs too low and too small to be comfortable, but the people coming in through the doors didn't care. The staff might be a bit abrupt on occasions, but nothing shocked them. They had seen and heard it all before. By the time Megan was called she had spoken to several people she knew by sight, both staff and patients. A girl she had met at the clinic months before came over to talk to her, and a boy she had seen at one of the clubs gave her a nod before scuttling into a room that dealt with sexually transmitted diseases. Megan knew for a fact he was only just fifteen.

When her name was called she was shown into a room with a desk, two plastic chairs, and a table strewn with leaflets and magazines. A picture hanging on the wall moved uneasily as she shut the door, as if its location was only a temporary arrangement.

The woman sitting on a plain wooden chair behind the table looked to be in her late thirties. She was wearing the obligatory white coat over what looked like a trouser suit. She had very fair skin, chocolate brown eyes, and shoulder-length hair too dark to be natural. A large mole on her chin looked as if it was waiting to sprout hairs. Apart from the mole, she was quite attractive.

The woman looked up as Megan approached. 'I'm Lucinda Valentine.' She opened a pink folder and took out a sheet of paper. 'And you're Megan Pritchard.' She looked down at the paper. 'You've been here before, haven't you, Megan? Is this the same problem?'

What problem was that? Megan stared at the woman, her brain no longer capable of coherent thought. Was it a problem she had when she was expecting Rosie? Or was this some other problem she couldn't even remember having? She had been here on several occasions wondering what new and undiscovered venereal disease Gary had given her. She associated this place with fear, and it took her a moment to remember there was nothing wrong with her.

'A friend of mine came to see you, but I don't think I've spoken to you before,' she said.

'No, I usually work over at the hospital.' Lucinda Valentine flipped through the pages from the file. 'Your boyfriend beat you up, didn't he? I have a note here to say you were warned not to stay with him.'

Gary had taken her in when her mother changed the lock on the front door. Where else was she supposed to go? 'He's in prison. I think I'm pregnant and I don't want another baby.'

'No, of course you don't,' Lucinda said soothingly. She had an accent Megan couldn't quite place, like an American trying to sound English. 'But abortion is such a difficult option, isn't it? Particularly in your situation. We can help you, Megan. But first, you have to answer a few questions for me, and we need to make sure you really are pregnant.' She smiled, showing perfectly even teeth. 'You might have nothing to worry about. Can you let me have a urine sample in the next couple of days? Mid-stream. Once that's sorted we can talk about the other options we can offer you. What was your friend's name, by the way?'

Megan took a chance. 'Donna. Donna Price.' She would have missed the slight flicker in Lucinda's eyes unless she'd been looking for it. The woman was good, the smile only a fraction tighter.

'Even if she had been to see us, Megan, I couldn't tell you. We keep all our consultations private.' Then, almost casually. 'Have you seen your friend recently?'

Megan shook her head. 'No. Not for a long time. I think she must have gone away somewhere.' As she had once told Gina, she was very good at lying.

Lucinda stared at Megan for a moment, the brown eyes flat. 'Right. Let's get the questions out of the way then.' Lucinda opened a drawer in the desk and took out a form. 'Your name is Megan Pritchard and you live at number 11 Tower Court. You live alone, is that right?' When Megan nodded she made a note on the form. 'You are nineteen years old and you have no major medical problems, apart from a history of drug abuse.'

As that didn't seem to be a question, Megan didn't answer.

'Are you still taking drugs?'

That was a question. 'No.'

The woman looked up. 'Are you being honest with me, Megan?'

Why was it, Megan wondered, that if you said you were using, everybody believed you, but if you said you weren't, no one did. 'I haven't taken anything since . . . ' She took a breath. 'Not for a long time.'

'Very well.' Lucinda turned the form over.

'What is your natural hair colour?'

'What?' Megan had never been asked that before.

'We need to update your record for the files. Height, weight, hair and eye colour. Things like that. We have your height and weight already.'

'Oh.' Still Megan hesitated. 'My hair is sort of straw-coloured, I think,' she said at last. 'That's what my mum called it. Like dirty straw, she said it was. That's why I colour it. I lost some weight, I'm about eleven stone now, and my eyes are a sort of bluey-grey colour.'

'Natural blonde, blue eyed.' She made a note on her form and looked up. 'And the father's nationality?'

Megan's mind went blank again. Gary? No, not Gary the father of this fictitious baby she was supposed to be carrying. Perhaps lying wasn't as easy as she thought.

'He wasn't foreign, was he?' Lucinda said impatiently. 'He was a local boy, yes?'

Megan got her wits back together and nodded her head. 'Yes. Local. You don't need to know his name, do you?'

'Not right now.' The woman stared at the form on the desk in front of her. 'So, what was his colouring? Fair? Dark?' She looked up. 'If you know, of course.'

What was that supposed to mean? Megan

felt her skin go hot, sweat beading her upper lip. Of course she knew who the father was. Only she didn't, did she? She had no idea. Make it up, she thought frantically, the way you made up everything else. Not dark. Lucinda didn't want dark. 'He was fair,' she said. 'Fair hair, blue eyes. Like me.'

'Good. That's excellent.' Lucinda beamed at her. 'Watch your diet, though, Megan. It's not good for the baby if you put on too much weight.' She tucked the form back in the folder, reached into the drawer again, and handed Megan a brown envelope. 'That's all, then. Bring the urine sample to the hospital within the next two days, we'll check everything out and I'll talk to you again.' As Megan headed for the door, the woman stood up and put her hand on Megan's arm. 'Remember, Megan, everyone makes mistakes, but not all mistakes turn out to be a disaster.'

Which was a load of bollocks, Megan thought. She got as far as the door and then turned back as if she had just remembered something. 'There was someone else who came to see you,' she said. 'Sophie Lowry.'

'Is she another friend?' Lucinda was shuffling brochures on her desk, seemingly uninterested.

'Not really. Amber Beaumont knows her

and I know Amber, that's all.'

'You know Dr Beaumont's daughter?' Now there was surprise in the voice, and a hint of something else. Probably disbelief.

Megan stuffed the envelope into her bag, slinging the bag over her shoulder. 'We go to the same clubs.'

'Do you?' The scepticism was obvious. 'Just take the sample to the hospital. They'll be expecting you. The quicker the better for obvious reasons.'

'Right. Thanks.' Megan left as quickly as she could without running. Had she learned anything? Probably not. Except never to go back to that place again.

She walked down the steps on shaky legs, glad to be outside, and then stopped and looked back. This place was part of her old life, the life she had left behind when she watched Gary being bundled into a police car.

9

By the time Megan got back to the studio Gina was trying to deal with a customer who didn't really know what she wanted, and a telephone that wouldn't stop ringing. Megan slid her arms out of her jacket and picked up the phone, watching Gina hang on to her cool by a thread. She held out the phone. 'It's for you.'

Once she had sorted out the customer, Gina took the phone and left Megan to ring up the sale.

Adam didn't bother to introduce himself. 'Got a definite ID on Madonna Price,' he said. 'The mother recognized a birthmark. They're rushing through the DNA samples, as much as you *can* rush a bloody technician. I thought I might have a word with Ms Price as soon as Reagan lets her go. She'll talk to me if I make it worth her while.'

'Let me come as well,' Gina said. 'She'll talk more to another woman.'

'She'll talk to whoever has the cash,' Adam said.

Gina handed the phone back to Megan when the line went dead, then she picked up the kettle and filled it at the sink. 'I need a cup of coffee.'

'What did Adam want?' Megan asked.

'The dead girl is definitely Madonna Price. They got a positive ID from the mother.' She got two mugs out of the cupboard and spooned in instant coffee. 'What happened at the clinic?'

'The woman I saw, Lucinda Valentine, she's not like the women who usually work there. She had this very white skin and black hair and a big brown mole on her chin. She looked really smart, like she worked in an office, not a hospital. She knows something about Donna Price, but she's not talking. Says it's confidential.' Megan took the kettle from Gina and plugged it in. 'She definitely recognized Donna's name, I could tell, but nothing happened when I mentioned Sophie Lowry. Not that I noticed, anyway. I told the Valentine woman I knew Amber Beaumont and her family, and she seemed really surprised.'

'I wonder why,' Gina said with a smile.

'All I said was, me and Amber go to the same clubs sometimes, which is true.' Megan took the envelope out of her bag and shook the contents on to the desk. She held up the plastic bottle. 'How am I supposed to pee into this little thing? Usually they give you a plastic beaker at the clinic and check it while you wait. That woman asked some funny questions, since I'm just supposed to be pregnant.'

'Like what?'

'Like what colour my hair is, and if the father of my baby is foreign. She meant black, but she wasn't going to say it.'

'Why would they want to know that? A white girl having a black baby isn't going to be much of a shock these days, is it? And I would have thought the question was politically incorrect, apart from the fact that it's none of their business.' Gina shrugged. 'Anyway, it doesn't matter because you're not really pregnant.' She looked up at Megan. 'You're not, are you?'

Megan rolled her eyes. 'No, I'm not.' She patted her stomach. 'I think I look more like a belly dancer than a Sumo wrestler since I lost weight, but the stomach is all mine. No one in there but me.'

Gina finished making the coffee and handed Megan a mug. 'So we're never going to find out what the mysterious other option is.'

'We might. I've got an idea how I can make the wee sample work. But it was scary going there, and that woman is not nice. Most of the people at the clinic really care about you.

She didn't. She's got an accent, like American or something, not Essex.'

'And not one of the regular counsellors at the clinic?'

'No. Not since I was there last. When I was with Gary I was there all the time.'

'I still can't work out who would put a leaflet about abortion under my door.'

'You said the orange flyer was meant for Inspector Reagan, not you. You were just a messenger. That's what you said.'

'I know.' Gina finished her coffee and rinsed the mug in the sink. 'But I'm worried for Sophie. No one has seen or heard of her for nearly a week, and I keep connecting that second leaflet to her, for some reason.'

'You think she's going to finish up murdered like Donna Price?'

Gina shook her head. 'I don't know, Megan. I just don't know.'

The shop became busy again and Gina didn't have time to think about anything except work for the next few hours. 'Don't do anything without running it by me first,' she told Megan as they were packing up for the day. 'I know you. Once you get a bone to gnaw on you won't let it go. We don't know where Lucinda what's-her-name fits in, so just take it easy for the time being, OK?' She knew it was no use telling Megan not to do anything once she set her mind to it. 'Just be careful until we know what's going on. I've got a funny feeling about Lucinda and her anti-abortion clinic.'

A funny feeling was putting it mildly, Gina thought, as she locked up and climbed the stairs to her flat. The nervous flutter in her stomach and the feeling that something was hovering just out of reach was really irritating. If she did have psychic tendencies, they were pretty damned cryptic. She hated the sense of unease that was following her around like an itch she couldn't scratch.

Lucinda Valentine. Could that possibly be her real name? If she was American, probably yes. If Lucinda worked at the hospital she ought to be legit, but it depended on what she was employed to do. From the way Megan described her, she wasn't part of the medical staff. More likely some admin assistant. Gina thought for a moment, chewing her bottom lip. Who would have a list of all the hospital employees? She picked up the phone, hoping Mick was still speaking to her.

'Don't worry about it,' he said, when she apologized again. 'I didn't do anything wrong, and Detective Inspector Reagan loves me. He just likes to slap me around a little.'

'Can you get a staff list for the hospital up

on your computer, Mick? I'm looking for somebody called Lucinda Valentine. Probably works in admin.'

'Lucinda Valentine? Known as Lucy?'

'You know her?'

'No, but if my name was Lucinda I'd want to be called Lucy. Much prettier, don't you think?'

'It wouldn't suit you. You may feel like a Lucy, but you still look like a Mick.'

'I know, I keep forgetting. But I'll keep that name in mind in case I decide to have the operation one day. Hang on, I've got a list of staff up on the screen, all sorted into different departments. Lucinda Valentine? Spelt just as it sounds?'

Gina nodded, and then realized he couldn't see her. 'Yes.'

After a few moments Mick said, 'No one working here by that name. I had a look at the part-time staff as well. Absolutely nothing, darling. Sorry.'

Gina thanked him and put down the phone. So Lucinda was lying about where she worked. But Megan had been told to take her urine sample to the hospital. Strange. Gina grabbed the phone again and dialled Megan's home number.

'Sorry to bother you, Megan, but I got Mick to look at the hospital staff list and the

Valentine woman isn't on there. She did tell you she worked at the hospital?'

'Yes.' Megan was quiet for a moment. 'She said she *usually* works at the hospital. Perhaps she isn't listed as staff.'

'She'd have to be, in case of a fire or some other disaster. They need to know exactly who is in the hospital at any one time for security purposes.' It was her turn to pause for thought. 'Get the envelope, Megan. Check where you have to take the sample. See if it gives a department.'

Gina heard Megan put the phone down. 'Wrong hospital,' she said, a few moments later. 'The sample has to go to Willow Bank.'

'The private hospital?'

'Yeah.' The silence lasted longer this time. 'Wow! How did I get on their register? That's like, you know, the Hilton of hospitals.'

'I've no idea,' Gina said slowly. 'Willow Bank being a private hospital, I don't know what they deal with. Maybe they do abortions.'

'You know what? I bet when I go to the hospital I'll get a lecture on how lucky I am, and how I should keep the baby even if I don't want it. There aren't any magic choices, Gina. You either have it, or you get rid.'

'Megan, listen to me. You are not pregnant. You are not going to the hospital. And you are not going to have an abortion.' Gina took a breath. 'I'm sorry, love, I should never have got you mixed up in all this.'

'You didn't,' Megan said quietly. 'I got mixed up in it because I wanted to. I just forget sometimes it isn't real.'

Gina hung up, made herself something to eat, and sat at her small dining table staring at the blank television screen. Megan shouldn't be going anywhere near a hospital, it was too soon after Rosie, and if the orange leaflet had nothing to do with Sophie's disappearance, Gina knew she shouldn't get involved either. But Lucinda Valentine had responded to the name Donna Price, Megan had seemed sure about that, and Donna had finished up dead in a ditch.

Gina suddenly had another thought. She finished her dinner quickly and tossed the container in the bin. Mick sounded surprised to hear from her again so soon.

'This is nice, Gina. I've been alone all day and none of these dead people will talk to me. Now you ring me twice in half an hour.'

'Dr Beaumont,' she said. 'Where does he work?'

'I can tell you that without looking on the computer. Willow Bank, the posh hospital on the Greenacres estate. He's listed as chief consultant.'

Gina gave herself a high five. Yes! That's how Lucinda Valentine knew Dr Beaumont and his family so well. They both worked at the same hospital. 'Thanks Mick. It's a private hospital, isn't it?'

'Yes, and it's got a good reputation. We don't get much business from there.'

'What sort of hospital is it?'

'Hang on, I'll look them up on the computer.' He came back to her a few moments later. 'They deal mainly with IVF, but they've also got a fertility clinic to help you get pregnant naturally, an antenatal department and a small maternity unit. One of the few places, evidently, that sees the whole thing through from beginning to end.'

Gina thanked Mick, although she wasn't sure what she had really achieved. It looked as if Dr Beaumont and the Valentine woman both worked at Willow Bank, which was presumably where the orange leaflet had originated. Donna Price had a leaflet hidden in her shoe, and someone had pushed an identical leaflet under Gina's door. But there was nothing to connect any of that to the missing Sophie, and Gina knew she had to forget about Donna Price and concentrate on Sophie Lowry. She could still hear the unmistakable sound of time ticking away in the background. The girl had to be found quickly, or it would be too late.

Adam phoned her just as she was about to slide into bed. It wasn't chilly enough yet for a hot-water bottle, but bed socks, definitely. Sleeping alone had its drawbacks.

'I shall be seeing Donna's mother tomorrow. She wants a photographer along and I can't ask Jack, he's still ferrying his parents around, so do you fancy being a photographer for an hour or two?'

Gina hesitated, and then realized if she didn't answer he would probably hang up on her. 'I'm not a photographer.'

'Don't have to be. State of the art, digital SLR, borrowed from Jack. All you have to do is press the button. Besides, I'm not going to give the woman a free photo shoot. All I want is a black and white to put in the paper.'

'OK. What time?'

'Ms Price suggested lunchtime.' Gina could almost see his smile. 'Wants a free lunch. Can't blame her, I suppose.'

'Her daughter just got murdered.'

'So? The woman's still got to eat. I'll pick you up about twelve-thirty and we'll go to the Bear. Never too crowded at that time.'

It was Gina's turn to smile. 'And I expect it's cheap.'

He laughed. A deep throaty sound that had her wishing he was right there beside her instead of on the other end of a phone. 'I only do cheap when it's my money, and this will go on expenses. The Bear does good food, so shut up and be grateful.'

She put the phone back on the bedside table and went to sleep hugging her pillow.

10

The Bear Inn advertised itself as rustic, which meant old beams and rickety tables ringed with beer stains. Call it rustic and there's no need for a makeover. A family of mum, dad, and two kids, sat at a table studying the menu; a foreign gentleman stared gloomily at his laptop; and a group of businessmen talked loudly in a corner.

Adam pointed to a table for four. 'Sit down,' he said. 'I'll get the drinks.'

Gina did as she was told. 'No sign of the grieving mother?'

'No. She'll be late so she doesn't have to pay for her drink.'

'You don't have a very high opinion of Ms Price.'

'She kicked her daughter out because she was pregnant.'

'Megan's mum did the same. Sophie's parents don't know where she is and, if she is pregnant, they don't know that either. She could die all alone and no one would know.' A lot of people die alone, Gina thought. That's why it would be nice to have a family. Someone to miss you when you're gone.

Adam handed her a small but impressive looking camera. 'It's set on automatic focus. All you have to do is point and click.'

Gina turned the camera round. 'Where's the screen?'

'Use the viewfinder, it looks more professional.'

Gina peered through the viewfinder and swung the camera round the room. The children stared at her and she moved the camera away quickly. Not a good idea to take pictures of other people's children when you can get locked up for taking pictures of your own. The face of a woman came sharply into focus and Gina nearly dropped the camera. Angela Price, close up and personal.

The woman sat down and crossed her legs. The black leather skirt rode up high as she sat, leaving a lot of leg showing between the bottom of her skirt and the top of her high-heeled boots. The lipstick was red and shiny, the black eyelashes straight out of a TV ad. This wasn't a woman mourning her dead daughter.

'Ms Price,' Adam said. 'What can I get you?'

'Call me Angie. One of them cocktail things would be nice. The one that tastes of coconut.'

Adam cocked an eyebrow. 'A pina colada?

If they've got it, you shall have it.' He looked at Gina. 'Stella?'

She nodded. She was beginning to understand why he didn't like Angela Price.

The woman took a mirror out of her handbag and inspected her face. 'How long have you been taking pictures? You don't see many women photographers.'

And you're not seeing one now, Gina thought. She slipped the camera strap round her neck. 'The camera does all the work these days. Don't worry, I'll take some good pictures of you.' Fingers crossed behind the back probably didn't work, but it was worth a try.

Angela looked over at the bar and lowered her voice. 'I've got a few lines here and there, and I wondered if you could, you know, touch them up a bit.'

'Oh, it would be a shame to do that. Your daughter's just been murdered. If you look too glamorous in the pictures it might make people think you don't care.'

Adam smiled as he put a tall glass, complete with paper umbrella, in front of Angela. 'My photographer is very good,' he said. 'She'll make it look as if you've been crying for days.'

He let Angela finish her scampi and chips before he started asking her questions. She avoided answering anything directly, but he was good at his job. 'You said you kept in touch with your daughter after she left home. Do you know who got her pregnant?'

'Oh, yeah. Pretty much for sure. No-good son of a bitch has probably knocked up half of Castlebury. Name's Gilmore, Steve Gilmore. Just wanted to add Donna to his list. I told her that, but she wouldn't listen.'

'Teenagers never do,' Gina said, with mock sympathy. 'He's local, then?'

Angie nodded. 'Look, can we go outside so I can have a smoke? It's a fucking laugh when you can't have a smoke in a pub.'

While Angela Price finished her cigarette, Adam managed to get a list of Donna's friends, both male and female, and the names of the clubs and bars she'd visited. He didn't mention the orange leaflet.

Gina took half a dozen photos with the woman posing in front of the camera like Britain's Next Top Model, pulling faces that were supposed to represent grief.

'Don't worry about it,' Adam said, after Angela had taken her money, complained about the amount, and driven off in a shower of gravel. 'You got just the look I wanted. My article will be just about as sincere as your photographs.'

'She mentioned a boyfriend. Steve Gilmore.

Do you think he had anything to do with Donna's death?'

'If she went round to his house when she was in labour he might have panicked, but I doubt he'd kill her, and he wouldn't be able to move her to that ditch on his own. Carrying a dead body isn't as easy as it looks.'

And Adam would know, Gina thought. He had been in Iraq during the worst of the fighting. Plenty of dead bodies there. 'So it would've taken two people to move her? Wouldn't two people carrying a body look even more suspicious?'

'Not necessarily. Two people supporting a girl, late at night, her arms across their shoulders, her legs dragging. If anyone sees them, they call out she's had a bit too much to drink and they're taking her home. No one is going to question it.'

'But why that ditch? It's right beside the cycle path, so someone was bound to see Donna's body eventually. Why not drive somewhere out into the country and roll her into a ditch miles from anywhere?'

Adam got up from the table and pulled on his leather jacket. 'Whoever it was wanted her found quickly.'

Gina pulled her own jacket off the back of the chair. 'I have to get back to the studio. I don't like leaving Megan on her own.'

100

He paid the tab at the bar and they walked to his car. 'I'll see if I can find out where the Gilmore boy lives and have a word. No doubt the police have already questioned him, but he might tell me something he wouldn't tell the police.'

'And someone has to find Sophie. It's over a week since you told me she was missing. Jack and his parents must be worried sick about her.'

'Mrs Lowry doesn't seem that bothered,' Adam said. 'She told Jack not to worry, says she's sure Sophie is safe somewhere. He reckons all the stress has sent her round the twist.'

'I just hope Sophie is still alive. If she is, you'd think she'd pick up a phone and let one of them know she's OK.'

'Teenagers don't think, that's the problem. I'm sure she's fine. She'll turn up eventually wondering what all the fuss is about.'

Adam dropped Gina outside the studio. 'I won't come in. I'll see if I can trace Steve Gilmore. He might know more about her than her mother does.' He caught Gina's arm as she was about to open the door. 'Are you doing anything special tonight?'

She looked at him warily. 'Why? What do you want me to do this time?'

He grinned. 'Come out to dinner with me.'

It was impossible to refuse when he looked at her like that. 'OK,' she said, trying to sound nonchalant. 'What time?'

He promised to pick her up about seven o'clock and she walked into the studio feeling better than she had all week.

She didn't stop work until nearly six o'clock and still had to shower and change before meeting Adam. 'What are you doing tonight?' she asked Megan, as they were closing up the studio.

'Clubbing.' Megan gave a sly little grin. 'You never know who you might meet.'

'You're going to look for Amber, aren't you? Please don't, Megan. I've got a really bad feeling about Amber.'

'Amber may be taller than me, but I beat her hands down on weight. Look, stop worrying Gina. You said we need to find Sophie quickly, and Amber knows where she is.'

'We don't know that. Go tomorrow night instead and I'll come with you.'

Megan shook her head. 'Amber fancies the DJ. She'll be there tonight.'

Gina thought wistfully of the dinner she was going to miss. 'I'll come with you tonight then.' She frowned when Megan looked at her in disbelief. 'Come on, Meg, I don't look that old when I'm dressed up, and it's so dark in those places I could take my granny along and no one would notice.'

'They probably would,' Megan said. 'She's been dead for three years.'

Adam wasn't answering his phone so Gina sent a text to him. Her phone rang while she was trying to decide what she had in her wardrobe that looked remotely club-like.

'What the hell do you mean, you can't make it?'

'I have to go out.'

'Yes you do. With me.' There was no disappointment in his voice, only outrage.

'And I cancelled,' she said crisply. 'Perhaps we can make it another time.'

'Sure. Just let me know when you can fit me in.' His voice dripped with sarcasm. 'Have a look in your diary and see if you have a free evening sometime.'

'Oh, for goodness sake, Adam! Stop behaving like a spoiled child. Megan is going after Amber tonight and I need to go with her.'

'Megan is more than capable of looking after herself.'

'Well, I'm sorry . . . ' she began, but he'd hung up on her.

Hunting in her wardrobe she found a top that had shrunk so much it left a gap above the top of her best skinny jeans. She added black ankle boots and a studded belt, hoping she didn't look too much like a geriatric biker. Her hair was loose, tumbling round her shoulders in a mass of dark-chocolate curls. She hated it like that, but if she scraped it back off her face people might think she was Megan's mum.

She was still seething about Adam. He was so caught up in his newspaper story he refused to believe Sophie was in any sort of trouble, while Gina could feel the danger like a physical thing. It was a wonder Grace Lowry couldn't feel it as well. She was the girl's mother. Was she trying to comfort Jack when she told him Sophie was fine, or was she, like her husband, in total denial?

Gina sat quite still on her dressing-table stool and closed her eyes. If she really was psychic like everyone seemed to think she was, she ought to be able to see something. But the only picture in her head was of a girl in a ditch with maggots crawling out of her eyes.

11

Gina caught her foot on the leg of a chair and cursed. 'Why is it so dark? Or have I gone completely blind?'

Megan might have laughed, but any normal sound would have been lost in the general cacophony, so Gina gave up, following Megan to the bar by some sense other than sight. The air was smoke free, she noticed. Since cigarettes had been banned, pills had taken over completely, a knock on effect that should have been predicted and was probably far more dangerous than the odd spliff.

Gina took the bottle of beer Megan shoved in her hand and looked at the DJ. In the spotlight aimed at the decks, she could see he was tall and not bad looking. His hair had been styled with a razor and his clothes were jumble-sale casual, but most of the girls in the room had their eyes on him. Amber was standing as close as she could get without actually sitting in his lap.

Megan pointed and Gina nodded. They were too close to the speakers to hear one another. Then Gina spotted a table in a corner that looked far enough away to make conversation possible, and pulled Megan in that direction.

'What's his name?' she asked, when they were seated.

Megan looked over at the DJ. 'Roddy McBride. Calls himself the Nighthawk. He's quite good, went to Australia last year for a three-month gig, but he was born in Castlebury so he DJs here when he's in town. I went to school with him. He was just about to leave when I started. He must be about twenty-five, I reckon.'

Gina watched Amber, clad in a thin gold vest that clearly showed her dark nipples, lean over to whisper something in Roddy's ear, her hand on his arm. Gina watched with interest as he drew back. The movement was slight, almost a reflex action. He spotted Megan and waved, and when Amber turned her head to follow his line of sight her expression changed.

'Uh oh,' Megan said. 'She's spotted me.'

Amber slid away from the DJ like some exotic snake, leaving her hand on his arm until the last moment, heading straight for Megan. From his slightly elevated position on the DJ stand, Roddy McBride watched.

'Can you fight your way to the bar and get us another couple of beers?' Megan said. 'She won't talk to me if you're here.'

Gina hesitated, but Megan looked relaxed and Amber had stopped to speak to someone a couple of tables away. Neither girl looked as if they were about to do battle. 'OK,' she said, 'but promise to tell me what she said when I get back.' Megan nodded, and Gina fought her way to the bar as instructed. Fifteen minutes later, when she got back to the table, Amber had gone back to Roddy. 'Ten quid for two halves. How do you manage to afford this place?' she asked Megan.

'I don't usually drink beer. The shots are cheaper.' Megan opened her hand. 'Or these.'

Gina stared at the two little pills. 'You got those from Amber?'

'Yep. Two quid each. Want to try one?'

'No, thank you.'

'Me neither. I bought them for research — and to make Amber think I was still in the market.' She picked up her bottle. 'Can I claim the money back from expenses?'

'If I can claim for the beer, but then we won't have any money left in the petty-cash box.'

Megan twisted her bottle on the table, making wet patterns. 'She told me to lay off Roddy, and she says Sophie is fine. She just needs some time out, Amber reckons, so no one is to go looking for her.'

'You and Roddy? You never mentioned him before.'

'Because there's nothing to mention. He's OK, but I've never fancied him.'

Gina was dying to ask more questions but then she shrugged, it was none of her business. 'We need to find Sophie, Megan. We'll have to tell the police if you think Amber really knows where she is. We'll get Reagan to talk to her.'

'And you think she'll talk to Reagan? She'll just deny everything. We can't make her tell us if she doesn't want to, and she's Sophie's best friend. I don't think she'd say everything was all right if it wasn't.'

Gina pushed back her chair and stood up. 'I'll talk to her. Tell her I think Sophie's in danger.' She got halfway to the DJ stand when she felt a hand on her arm.

'You best go back to your table, Miss Cross. Miss Beaumont doesn't want to talk to you.'

He was tall, and built like the proverbial toilet block, his head shaved to black shadow on pale skin, an old scar bisecting his bottom lip. He slid a hand down her arm and twisted slightly, his thumb pressing into the soft skin just above her wrist. She whooshed out air, the pain so intense there was no breath left in her lungs to cry out. She must have made some sound, or perhaps it was the shocked expression on her face, but a man standing a few feet away started towards them. Her captor turned and looked, and the man backed off, muttering some apology.

'Take my advice and keep your nose out of other people's business.' He gave her a little shove. 'Now turn around and walk back to your table.'

She really didn't have any choice. He had released the pressure, but he still had hold of her wrist. Her arm was numb right up to her shoulder and she wondered if she would ever be able to move her fingers again. He didn't let go until she sat down on her chair.

'Have a nice evening, ladies.'

'Who was that?' Megan asked curiously as the man disappeared into the crowd around the bar. 'I haven't seen him here before. Was he holding your hand?' She bent forward to peer at Gina's face. 'Whoa, are you crying?'

Gina brushed a hand angrily across her face. 'No. I'm just cross I let him get away with it. He really hurt me.'

'What did he do? Should we tell someone?'

Gina shook her head, rubbing her arm where a little knot of pain throbbed like a bad tooth. 'He didn't want me to talk to Amber. Did you see where he went?'

Megan looked around. 'No. The place is

really crowded now. He could be anywhere.'

'Let's get out of here, then.'

'Finish your beer,' Megan said, not moving. 'You paid enough for it. Besides, you need to tell me what happened. I watched you get halfway to Amber, then you stopped.'

'Because that man grabbed my arm and dug his thumb in my wrist where it hurt like hell. He walked me back here like a dog on a lead and I let him. I should have shouted, or screamed, or at least done something.'

'If you'd shouted or screamed you'd have been thrown out. He's probably a new bouncer. They think they're God, sometimes.'

'He didn't act like a bouncer, and he knew my name. Whoever he is, he's a really nasty piece of work.'

Gina didn't believe for one moment the man was a bouncer. Besides, there was no reason to stop her talking to Amber. She hadn't been looking for trouble. And how did he know where she was heading? She could have been going to the loo.

She looked around, breathing through her nose, still angry enough to snort fire. The man was nowhere to be seen and now Amber had disappeared as well. Roddy caught her eye and looked away quickly, picking up the microphone to deliver his next round of patter.

If Amber had gone walkabout, it might be worth talking to Roddy, but she wasn't prepared to walk across the room without a bodyguard. Adam would have come in handy, but he was no doubt out somewhere having a hissy fit because she hadn't dropped everything to meet him for dinner.

Sighing, she pulled her jacket off the back of the chair and slipped it on. 'Adam is wrong,' she told Megan. 'This isn't just about a girl who took off without telling her parents. There's a lot more going on than that. One good thing, though, if someone is going to that much trouble to stop us finding Sophie, I think she must still be alive.'

'Did you really think she was dead?'

Gina pushed back her chair and got to her feet. 'Maybe not yet, but something bad is going to happen.'

Megan shivered. 'OK, let's get home. I've gone right off this place.'

Before either of them could move, Roddy appeared in front of them. 'Sit down for a minute. I need to talk to you.' He glanced over his shoulder and then slid into a vacant chair. 'I've only got a ten minute break, so I need to talk quick and you need to listen. Stop looking for Sophie. Like Amber told you, she just needs to be left alone for a bit.'

'She needs to get in touch with someone

then, and tell them where she is, or I'll go to the police.' Gina refused to sit down, she'd been pushed around enough for one evening.

Roddy shook his head in disbelief. 'Don't be fucking stupid, lady. You saw Crawford, you saw what he can do, and that's nothing.'

'What do you mean, nothing?' Gina sat down again, not wanting to draw attention to herself. It hadn't felt like nothing.

'He can do a lot worse than that.' Roddy turned to look at Megan, something like pleading in his eyes. 'Keep out of it, Meg. You'll get hurt if you don't.'

'Keep out of what?' Gina leant across the table. 'Roddy, what's going on? Do you know where Sophie is? People are worried about her. Is she all right?'

The questions were too much for the DJ. 'I've got to go.' He got to his feet and looked at Megan again. 'Keep away from Amber, Meg. And her dad.'

Megan watched Roddy weave his way back to the DJ stand. 'What has Amber's dad got to do with anything? I've never even met him.'

Gina shook her head. 'I have no idea. Unless Roddy knows you're supposed to be going to Willow Bank. Doctor Beaumont works there.'

'Does he? How'd you find that out?'

'I checked. Look, aren't we supposed to be going home. Do we get a taxi, or walk?'

Megan looked at her watch. 'It's only just gone midnight. Early yet. Let's walk and save money.'

The walk took them twenty minutes and the roads were well lit, but after saying goodbye to Megan outside her block of flats, Gina had to fight a sudden urge to run the rest of the way.

As she got ready for bed she noticed the red light flashing on her phone telling her she had missed a call. She pushed the button absently.

'Just to let you know I have an interesting snippet of information I had intended sharing over dinner. That was before you stood me up. As you're obviously not home yet, I'll speak to you tomorrow. Hope you had a good time.'

Gina really didn't care what interesting snippet of information Adam had discovered. It was well past her usual bedtime and she was tired of fighting with him, but he always managed to have the last word, and now she was going to have to go to sleep one more time thinking about him.

How did he manage that, she wondered?

12

Whatever information Adam had couldn't have been that important, because he didn't come into the studio the next morning, or bother to phone. The message on her answer phone was probably just a way of getting back at her for reneging on their date. He was small minded and petty, she decided, and whatever snippet he had come across he could stuff wherever he liked, preferably somewhere painful.

The day passed quickly. The sun was shining outside the big bay window of the studio and Gina felt restless. She promised herself she'd find some time over the next weekend to get out into the countryside and do some sketching. Landscape art wasn't her first love, but her little watercolours sold well, helping to pay the seemingly exorbitant electricity bills. She always left the light on in the studio overnight as a deterrent to anyone who thought it would be a good idea to rob the shop. Her flat had been burgled earlier in the year, and it was not an experience she wanted to go through again.

When she went upstairs she turned the key

that set the dead bolt. Usually, she didn't bother, but the experience with the man at the club had made her edgy. She jumped when her doorbell rang. She didn't have a chain on her door, and it wasn't the first time she had wished she had a spy hole. Not wanting to sound stupid shouting through the door, and fed up with being scared, she eased open the door, ready to slam it shut again if necessary.

Adam peered at her through the four inches of space she had left him. 'Who were you expecting?' he asked. 'The bailiffs?'

Controlling her instinct to shut the door in his face, she grudgingly eased the door open another few inches. Bailiffs she could cope with.

He produced two bottles of wine from behind his back. 'I come bearing gifts.'

At least he knew how to get on her good side. Flowers wouldn't have done it. She pulled the door all the way open. 'The wine can come in,' she said. 'I'm not sure about the bearer of the gift, though.'

'Can't have one without the other.' He pushed past her and walked straight into her kitchen. 'Are all your wine glasses still in the dishwasher?'

'All two of them, yes. That's all I have left since the burglary and, as there are never more than two people drinking here at any one time, it didn't seem worth buying more.'

'Sensible,' he said. 'Until you have a party and have to share the glassware. That's no fun.' He found the wine glasses in the dishwasher and rinsed them out. 'See? I'm quite domesticated when I have to be.' He opened one of the screw cap bottles and filled both glasses to the brim, handing her one. 'From the way you're behaving, I must owe you an apology. I thought it was the other way round.'

She followed him back into the living room. 'I couldn't help missing our date, but you could certainly help your attitude.'

'You didn't say sorry for standing me up.'

'I was about to, as it happens, but you hung up on me.'

He laughed. 'Oh, Gina, why do we do this?' He took the glass out of her hand and pulled her against him, tilting her chin with one finger so he could kiss her. 'You see?' he said a few seconds later, when her world had tilted, spun, and teetered on the brink of oblivion. 'This is so much better than fighting.'

'You can't do that whenever — '

'I feel like it? I thought I just did.'

He really was insufferable sometimes. She wasn't going to bed with him. That was what he was working up to, and she wouldn't do it. But he had brought wine, and she was having real trouble with his smile. Defences crumbling, she grabbed her glass back. 'What was it you wanted to tell me? The little snippet you mentioned on the phone.'

He sprawled on her sofa, smiling when she sat on one of the hard chairs on the other side of the table. 'You know we were talking about Sophie staying at the Beaumonts' place in Spain, and then discounted it because the villa was already rented out to someone else?' When she nodded, he said, 'Well, that's not the only property they own. They have two houses they rent out here in Castlebury. One unoccupied as far as I could tell when I drove past.'

'You think Sophie might be holed up in the empty one?'

'I don't — but I knew you would. They're a pair of farm cottages on the edge of a field. On their own, but not isolated. There are one or two bungalows up the same lane. One of the cottages has a neat front garden and a car parked outside. The next-door one looks deserted. Blinds down on the windows, weeds in the garden. A bit tatty and uncared for.'

'But she could be there, couldn't she? She must be somewhere.' Gina got up to pace. 'I had a funny experience last night at the club I went to with Megan. I got warned off by this really nasty guy. A big hulk with a shaved head and a scar on his lip. He stopped me when I was on my way to speak to Amber and tried to make a hole in my wrist with his thumb. It hurt like hell. Then the DJ, some bloke named Roddy McBride, told Megan to keep away from Amber and — this is the funny bit — to keep away from Amber's dad as well.'

'Doctor Beaumont?' Adam said slowly. 'Now that is strange, isn't it?'

'Considering he owns the houses you were talking about, and Megan is supposed to take her sample to the hospital where he works, yes, it does begin to get a bit strange.'

'Hang on,' Adam said. 'You've lost me.'

'Willow Bank is the private hospital where Dr Beaumont works, and Megan has to take a urine sample there to prove she's pregnant. The woman at the clinic, Lucinda what's her name, works at the hospital as well, so it's all tied in with that abortion leaflet somehow.'

Adam still looked confused, so Gina went through the whole thing again. How she found out where Lucinda Valentine worked, Megan's visit to the clinic, and the strange happenings at the club.

'Megan had to answer some very peculiar questions at the clinic, as well. Like, if she's a natural blonde, and whether the father of the baby is Caucasian. Why would it matter?'

'Perhaps they're doing some sort of study in genetics at the hospital. They are a fertility hospital, after all. They'd want a core sample to judge everything else against. Perhaps they think Megan is what they're looking for. Pale skin, blue eyes, fair hair; a perfect example of the English rose.'

'Only she can't be a sample,' Gina said, 'because she's not really pregnant.'

'Damn.' Adam slapped his forehead with the palm of his hand. 'I'd forgotten that. If she'd really been pregnant, we could have sent her in undercover to report back on the strange experiments going on at Willow Bank.' He grinned at Gina's shocked expression. 'Only joking. What exactly did this man at the club do to you? You said he pushed his thumb into your wrist. Did your arm go numb?'

Gina rubbed her arm. 'After a somewhat excruciating pain, yes. Like pins and needles, only not the prickling sensation. Just a sort of dead feeling, like my arm didn't belong to me.'

'It's caused by nerve compression. If his hand had been on your neck, you'd be dead.'

Gina's hand moved to her neck. 'Gee, thanks.'

'How did you get mixed up in this, Gina? Why do the bad guys always home in on you? You promised Reagan it wouldn't happen again.'

'I was trying to find Sophie, but the leaflet someone pushed under my front door has to do with the dead girl, not Sophie.'

'Castlebury is a small town. Everybody knows everybody else, so paths are bound to cross. If you're asking if I think Sophie's disappearance has anything to do with Donna Price, no, I don't.'

'And you don't think Sophie might have got a key from Amber and be hiding out in the empty house Dr Beaumont owns?'

'No, I don't.' He looked at her with interest. 'Are we arguing again? Or is this a discussion? Sometimes I find it hard to tell the difference.'

She bit back an angry retort. 'I'm discussing. I don't know what you're doing. So where does the man at the club come in?'

'Just a heavy, working for the club. The clubs don't want trouble or they get shut down. If you were storming towards Amber and the DJ, he'd have to try and stop you.'

'I wasn't storming,' she protested, knowing she was fighting a battle already lost. She was never going to make Adam believe there was anything sinister going on. Perhaps the man really had just been a bouncer. It would be nice to believe that.

Adam suggested pizza and she agreed, suddenly hungry. He phoned for a takeaway and they kept off the subject of Sophie and the dead girl while they ate pizza and coleslaw, demolished a tub of ice cream, and finished off the wine. She asked him about Thailand, and listened to his tales about the rebuilding of the islands and the gradual return of tourism, which was the main source of income. Adam could be really good company, she thought, when he wasn't being argumentative and bigoted.

'Something else I was going to tell you,' he said, as she carried the empty plates into the kitchen. 'Angela Price got herself a slot on Look East last night. The epitome of the grieving mother. She looked pretty convincing, I'll give her that. She took your advice — hardly any make-up and red eyes — but she spoilt it with lashings of mascara. No tears on screen in case it all smudged. The interviewer commented on how brave she was.'

'God, that woman is something else.'

'Don't be too quick to put her down. She said she would never have identified her daughter if it wasn't for your sketch. How lifelike it was, and all that.'

Gina made a growling noise. 'As long as no reporters come knocking on my door.'

She made coffee in her new coffee machine and they watched a silly game show on TV. When she looked at her watch again it was almost eleven o'clock. 'I need to sleep,' she told him. 'I have to go to work tomorrow.'

'So do I.' He took his jacket off the chair and started towards the door with her following, but then he stopped suddenly and turned round so she almost ran into him.

'I can't do this, Gina. I can't just go home.' He looked at her hungrily. 'Christ, I shall be awake all night.'

She backed off a few steps, watching him warily. 'I'm not going to bed with you.'

He dropped his jacket on the floor and pulled her towards him. 'No problem, the sofa will do fine.' Before she had time to catch her breath, he picked her up as easily as a kitten, kissing her while he held her in his arms, and then deposited her gently on the sofa.

'There's not room for both of us,' she said lamely, trying to get her heart rate back to normal.

'Just shut up and relax. There's plenty of room.'

'Adam, we'll fall — '

'Shut up,' he said again. And this time, she did.

At some point he must have carried her into the bedroom, because when she woke up the next morning she was in bed. Alone.

13

By the time she got out of bed the next morning she was beginning to regret being such a pushover. He only had to snap his fingers and there she was, flat on her back. That annoyed her. It was probably a good job he had left early. Breakfast together could have been difficult.

She had only just walked into the studio when Megan's mobile phone rang. Megan looked at Gina apologetically as she answered it.

'Yes, I'm Megan Pritchard.' Her eyes went wide. 'Today? I don't know if I . . . yes, I know it's urgent.' She listened for a few moments, panic written all over her face. 'No, I understand. Yes, I promise. I'll bring it to you in my lunch break.'

Megan put the phone back in its holder very slowly, as if it might bite her. 'That was Lucinda Valentine. I have to take my wee sample to the hospital today. She says she'll be waiting for it.'

'But you can't. You're not pregnant and they'll know straight away.' Gina thought for a moment. 'I suppose you could say you thought you were, and be relieved when you find out you aren't. But why go at all? You could have told her you'd made a mistake over the phone.'

'Because I want to see the inside of Willow Bank, and I have an idea that might work. I just have to pop out and see one of my friends.'

'Megan, no. Whatever it is you're thinking of, you're not to do it.'

Megan turned round as the doorbell pinged and a woman walked into the studio. 'We have a customer,' she said. 'I'll tell you all about my clever plan when we get a break.'

'I don't like it,' Gina said, as they discussed Megan's idea over coffee. 'If they find out you've tricked them, you don't know what they might do.'

'Oh, for goodness sake, Gina. I'm going to a proper hospital with doctors and nurses and things. This has nothing to do with what happened at the club last night, or your evil bouncer. This is about a murdered girl and a dead baby. I have to find out what really happened or I shall just keep thinking about it. I wouldn't have wanted Rosie to finish up on a rubbish tip.'

Gina gave her friend a worried smile. 'I can't stop you going, but if you're not back in an hour, I'll send out a search party.'

She watched Megan leave and spent the next fifty minutes watching the clock, but Megan was back within the hour, a smug smile on her face.

'I'm now officially pregnant. I'll have to text Marcie and thank her for the loan of her wee.'

'I doubt if she'll want it back,' Gina said drily. 'How was Willow Bank?'

Seeing the studio was empty, Megan pulled off her jacket and flopped down in the visitors' chair. 'That place is something else. Not a bit like a hospital, more like one of those posh spa places. People wander around in white dressing gowns with little white slippers on their feet and everything is real quiet. They made me wait while they checked Marcie's wee and told me I was pregnant, and then I had a consultation with a doctor. He told me they don't do terminations. They just help women decide what's best for them.'

'We knew that already, didn't we? The leaflet is anti-abortion. But what's this other option?'

Megan shook her head. 'I'm not sure yet, but listen to this. The doctor told me they're doing a special study and they'll pay me for answering some questions.'

It looked as if Adam was right, Gina thought. Everything was beginning to point towards some sort of drug test. 'I don't want you to go back to the hospital, Meg. It's just plain stupid — and possibly dangerous. What if they're involved in some genetic experiment, or want you to try out some new drug?'

'I shall be in a posh private hospital. They're not going to chop me up and put me in a test tube, are they? And if they want me to take any drugs, I'll just refuse. They can't make me do something I don't want to.'

Gina grudgingly agreed, but she spent most of the afternoon worrying about Megan and the rest of the time worrying about Sophie. Jack's parents were going home at the weekend and it was almost as if they'd given up on their daughter. Reagan had been as good as his word and listened sympathetically to their story, but there was little he could do. Sophie appeared to have left of her own free will.

Late in the afternoon, Jack called in at the studio. He looked weary, but found a smile for Megan.

'Just to let you know Sophie sent a text to my mother to say she's well and not to worry.' He sat on the edge of Megan's desk. 'Of course we *are* still worried about her, but at least we know she's safe.'

Megan looked at Gina and then got up

from her desk to fill the kettle. 'What did Sophie say, Jack?'

'Just what I told you, that's she OK and not to worry. Mum always said Sophie was fine, but Dad was practically psychotic. This has helped a bit, I suppose.' He took a deep breath in and then let it out in a sigh. 'I can only think she's run off with some boy, in spite of Dad being so sure she wouldn't. I just want to know where she is. She must've known she could phone me and I wouldn't tell anyone.'

'Yes, you would.' Megan handed him a mug of coffee. 'You know you would.'

He looked into his mug as if he might find a solution in there somewhere. 'The trouble is, even though Mum's quite happy — no need to worry any more and all that — I'm still worrying. So is Dad.'

Megan sat beside him on the desk and for a moment Gina thought she was going to take his hand. 'You shouldn't feel responsible for Sophie. I know she's your sister, but she's grown up now, and you don't have to look after her any more. Your dad's behaving as if she's still a little girl.'

'To him, she still is. He didn't want her to grow up. He wanted her to stay a little girl. He kept reminding her she was a vicar's daughter, as if she didn't know that already.

128

Sometimes I wonder if he's really worried about Sophie, or just his reputation if she goes off the rails again.'

'Again?' Gina asked. 'What was it before? Boys, drugs, partying? I need to know who she is, Jack, what she's like as a person, or I can't find her.'

He sipped his coffee and pulled a face. 'Christ, I know what Adam means about your coffee. I thought you bought a new machine?' He didn't give her time to answer. 'Sophie is completely different from what Dad thinks she is, what he wants her to be. Mum knows how much Sophie wanted to get away from the restrictions that came with being a vicar's daughter. I knew as well, but she promised me if she ever left home she'd let me know where she was going.' He ran a hand through his hair. 'I still don't know why she didn't. When we were kids, every time Sophie was naughty I took the blame. I was her big brother and it was up to me to look after her. But I couldn't make her the little angel Dad wanted her to be.' He gave a half-hearted grin. 'So I suppose I failed them both.'

This time Megan did squeeze his hand and he looked at her gratefully.

'While she was still at sixth-form college, Sophie had an affair with one of her tutors. Something I couldn't take the blame for.

When my father found out, he wanted to get as far away from Castlebury as possible, but Mum wouldn't move any further than Norwich. She wanted to keep in touch with her friends, and she thought Norwich was far enough. The guy had gone, for God's sake.'

'Who knew about the affair?' Gina asked. She was having to revise everything she knew about Sophie and her parents. Reinventing them in her head as Jack spoke.

'Amber knew, that's why they're so close, and my parents. I don't think anyone else did, but I couldn't be sure.'

'And the affair? Is it over?'

He shrugged. 'We all thought so. He's married. He took his wife and kids and moved up North somewhere. Now, I don't know.'

It was Gina's turn to take a deep breath. No wonder the Reverend Brian Lowry was having a hard time. A vicar's teenage daughter having an affair with a school-teacher was enough to make the London tabloids. If she was pregnant, goodness knows how far it would go. There would probably be a film out in under a year. The vicar must have thought the nightmare had gone away for good — until Sophie went missing. Adam had been right about girls and their secrets.

'Another worrying thing is we don't know

what Sophie's doing for money. She had a couple of hundred in her personal account but that's still in there.'

'Did your mother tell all this to the police?'

'I very much doubt it.' Jack laughed bitterly. 'Family secrets don't get bandied about in our house. I looked out for Sophie right from the time she was born. My mother and father did their best, we all did. But Sophie wanted more than any of us could give her, and somewhere along the way we all let her down.' He got to his feet. 'I must go. The parents are staying a few more days and then going home. They've given up looking for her.'

'Well, we haven't,' Megan said with some force. 'Me and Gina are following up leads, and if Sophie is still in Castlebury, we'll find her.'

'Thanks, Meg.' He put his arm round Megan's shoulders and gave her a squeeze. 'But if Sophie doesn't want to be found perhaps we should leave her alone. I'll be glad to get Mum and Dad on a train home and get back to normal. No doubt my sister will come home when she's good and ready.'

'I'm sure she will,' Gina told him, hoping he believed her. She didn't believe it for a minute.

Jack's departure was followed by the arrival

of a customer wanting to book an appointment for a portrait of her three children. She was quite argumentative when Gina suggested a home visit, and couldn't understand why Gina didn't want them all in the studio, complete with nanny.

'Put the closed sign on the door,' she said, when the woman had gone. 'It's nearly time to shut up shop, anyway.'

Megan opened the fridge and pulled out two bottles of Stella. 'Wow! I'm still trying to imagine Sophie shagging a married teacher. We were mega wrong about her, weren't we? Do you reckon he got her pregnant and that's why she's run away from her family? You can't blame her, can you?'

'We've got to find her, Megan. I know she's in danger. I can feel it.'

'Amber won't talk, not unless you can get Adam to torture her. He's been in the army so I bet he knows how.'

'Probably.' Gina finished her beer and tossed the bottle in the bin they kept for recycled glass. It landed with a resounding crash and she wondered if anybody else recycled as many bottles as they did each week. They were keeping the planet green practically single-handed. Yes, she thought, Adam knew all about torture. The methods he used in bed were positively inspired. She shook her head to clear it and get back to the matter in hand. 'I can't believe Amber is the only person who knows about any of this. Someone else must know.'

'If she's pregnant, she must have been to a doctor or a hospital. Perhaps she went to Willow Bank.'

Gina felt her stomach lurch. Even the name of that place gave her the heebie-jeebies. 'Let's hope she's not pregnant, because if she is she needs her family, and I'm not sure how her parents would take the news.'

'I bet Sophie's got a pretty good idea. That's why she ran. If those two were my parents, I'd run as well. My mum was a bitch, but she didn't frighten me as much as Mr Lowry. He's a scary man. You can imagine him waving a pitchfork and calling down the wrath of God.'

'I don't think it's normally a pitchfork,' Gina said with a smile.

'Whatever. You know what I mean, though.'

Gina did. She sent Megan home and closed the shop. All she could think of was a pregnant Sophie roaming the streets of Castlebury with nowhere to stay and no money. The real scenario was probably completely different but the image stayed in her head. The girl needed her mother and father. Parents, however difficult they might be at times, were better than no parents at all.

She had been four years old when she was told her mother and father were both dead, killed in a plane crash. She remembered her grandmother telling her they were gone, and suggesting she go to her room until supper was ready.

'If you need to cry, it is something best done alone.'

She couldn't remember if those had been her grandmother's exact words, but she remembered being in her room alone, trying to understand why she would never see her mummy or daddy again. It was years before she realized it was her grandmother who needed to cry alone.

And then, after her grandmother died, she found out her father might still be alive.

She walked up the stairs and let herself into a flat that seemed as cold and grey as the evening outside. She needed to eat, but first she had something to do.

Grabbing her car keys, she ran down the stairs and slid into the driving seat of her red Metro. Sometime soon the car would have to be replaced. She had a feeling the noises emanating from the engine might turn into a death rattle at any moment. The little car didn't get used much as she lived over the studio, but the poor thing was beginning to wheeze like an asthmatic whenever it came to a hill.

She got to the outskirts of the town just as the first spot of rain landed heavily on the windscreen. This was followed by several more. She turned on the windscreen wipers and notched up the heater, trying to remember exactly what Adam had said about Dr Beaumont's rental houses. The villages surrounding the town were right on top of one another, one running into the next, and finding a small lane in the dark was proving to be almost impossible. The rain had turned the evening into dusk sooner than she had anticipated, and if she didn't find the houses quickly she would have to turn around and go home.

A dead-end lane off the main road through the village was what she was looking for, but she didn't want to get stuck up some rutted farm track unable to turn round. Most of the narrow turnings led to a house up a long drive, or to a farm building. There were no road names, just an occasional house half hidden in the trees, the house names impossible to read. The rain beat against the windscreen and the heater was misting up the windows rather than clearing them. She

135

turned off the heater and opened the driver's window a crack, hoping that would solve the problem. She was beginning to think this had been a really silly idea.

A leaning pub sign suddenly appeared through the driving rain. Thankful for signs of life and hoping to get help, she parked in the miniscule car-park and ran for the door, bursting into a dimly lit room with a wood-panelled bar and a cheerful gas fire. Pausing to get her bearings, she looked around and realized she was the only customer.

''Get you, dear?' the woman behind the bar asked.

'Oh,' Gina hesitated. She hadn't eaten yet and was one beer down already. 'I just popped in to ask directions. I hope you don't mind.'

'Been here twenty-five. Know most places.'

'Two semi-detached cottages up a lane with bungalows. Rented.' She found she was copying the woman's shorthand style of speech. At least it saved time.

'Owned by a doctor. One rented out. Other's empty. You looking?'

Gina shook her head. 'No. Just visiting.'

'Left out of here, first right, lane on your left, dead end. Plenty room to turn.'

It was a bit like texting, she thought, as she climbed back into her car. Perhaps it would catch on.

She found the lane without any trouble. A little road flanked by new-looking bungalows with small front gardens. The two semi-detached houses were right at the end of the lane and much older, probably farm cottages originally. One had lights in a downstairs window behind net curtains and a car parked on the gravel beside the front door. Adam had been right about the other cottage. The windows were dark, the front garden untidy, and the place had a general feeling of neglect.

Gina could hear music coming from the occupied cottage, but as she got out and slammed her car door, the music stopped abruptly. Someone was listening — and probably watching. She had intended having a quick look at the empty cottage, then turning the car around and heading for home, but now she was here there seemed no harm in asking a few questions.

She pulled the hood of her jacket up over her head and headed for the front door, making up excuses for calling as she went. The door was answered almost before she had time to ring the bell — and then all thoughts of an excuse went right out of her head. Standing just inside the open door, a puzzled frown on her pale face, was Lucinda Valentine.

14

Gina had never met the woman, but Megan's description had been near perfect.

'Er,' she said, pulling the hood of her jacket further over her face and completely forgetting the story she had rehearsed. The mole on the woman's chin drew her eyes like a magnet.

'You gonna tell me what you want, or are you planning on standing there all night?' Lucinda asked. 'You're getting kinda wet.'

The accent was stronger than Gina had expected. 'Danny Pearson,' she said, the lie now sounding pathetic. 'I was told he was renting one of Dr Beaumont's cottages.'

Lucinda shook her head, her black hair swinging. 'I've only been here a few months. I know nothing about the last rental. I only just got in and I really have to get on.'

'How about next door?' Lucinda was right. She was getting wet.

'Empty. Has been for a while. Now, like I said . . . '

The door was shut firmly in Gina's face before she had time to ask any more questions, so she beat a hasty retreat back to her car. It was too dark and too wet to explore the empty house tonight. Better to come back in daylight when Lucinda was at work. Putting the car into gear, Gina managed a relatively tidy three-point turn without ending up in a ditch, and took pointers so she could find the place more easily next time. She supposed it was logical the Valentine woman would rent one of the doctor's houses as she worked at the hospital, but coming face to face with Megan's nemesis had been quite a shock. Lucinda was everything Megan had described and more. She reminded Gina of a female contestant in The Apprentice. All power-suit and attitude. The accent was definitely North American, and the hair too dark for the skin tone, but that wasn't all.

Lucinda Valentine's face wasn't really her own.

There had been a lot of work done to make it different from the one she had been born with. The nose job and overbite correction were legitimate cosmetic surgery, but why the eyebrow realignment? And why plant a mole on someone's face when it hadn't been there in the first place?

Gina parked round the corner from her flat and hurried upstairs. It was still raining so hard she wondered if she should start work on an ark. The houses near the river would be flooded again if the rain kept up much longer.

Stripping off her clothes she made for the shower, the quickest way of getting warm. Clean and dry, dressed in a sweatshirt and jog bottoms, she microwaved food and poured herself a glass of Tesco's Cabernet Sauvignon. Well deserved, she thought. She needed someone to talk to, someone to bounce ideas off, but Megan would probably be out, and she wouldn't phone Adam on principle. She hadn't heard a word from him since last night. He could have phoned and said thanks for the great sex, that would have been better than nothing.

Only it wouldn't, of course. Not really.

Her grandmother told her she picked the wrong men and the old lady had probably been right. Simon had been a disaster, a control freak who wanted a Stepford wife. She'd done her best, but obviously not well enough, because Simon had left her for someone else, someone nearer to his idea of a perfect wife. Even at school she had chosen badly. A boy she fancied had offered to carry her school bag and then tipped the contents into a rain-filled ditch, laughing gleefully as she squelched around trying to salvage her homework.

She was obviously doomed to become a

spinster. An old crone living alone with her cat, frightening small children with her toothless smile and shunned as a witch by the locals. The thought was so horrifying, she drank a second glass of wine and felt much better.

Besides, she didn't actually have a cat.

Her mobile phone trilled to tell her she had a message just as she was about to go to bed. The phone was still plugged into the charger where she had left it before she went out, and Adam had left a text message. *Thanks for last night*.

She was surprised he hadn't left twenty quid under her pillow.

When she went down to the studio the next morning she was still in a grumpy mood after a restless night, but the studio was always busy on a Friday and the day passed quickly. By evening the rain had stopped and Gina was looking forward to a weekend that promised to be warm and sunny, summer still not quite gone. She closed the shop at midday on Saturday so they could make the most of the sunshine, then grabbed a sketchpad and headed for the river.

On the way she popped into the sandwich bar for a tuna and cucumber bagel with extra grated cheese. Megan could never understand how anyone could eat fish and cheese together, but Gina thought they tasted just fine. By the time she reached the river-bank she was drooling with anticipation. She sat down on her favourite bench and started to unwrap her lunch, ignoring a couple of ducks that waddled up to her expectantly. 'No way,' she told them. 'This is all mine.'

She was vaguely annoyed when a young girl sat down on the seat next to her. There were several empty benches. Why choose hers? She took a bite of bagel and opened her sketchpad.

'Miss Cross?' the girl asked hesitantly. 'My name's Shelly. Donna's mum was on TV. She said you drew that picture.' Shelly was late teens, early twenties, wearing jeans and a lightweight sweater, a black belt sitting on narrow hips. 'I didn't know Donna was dead.'

'I'm sorry,' Gina said. The sentiment would have sounded more convincing if her mouth hadn't been full of bagel. She chewed and swallowed quickly. 'You're one of Donna's friends?'

The girl nodded. 'They showed your drawing of Donna on TV. Said no one would have known who she was if it weren't for your drawing.' Shelly stared at the ducks as they plodded disconsolately back to the river. 'They said she was murdered.'

Gina took another bite of her bagel. 'Yes.'

'I can't think why anyone would want to murder Donna. Do the police know who did it?'

Gina shook her head. She had given up on the bagel. 'Did you know she was pregnant?'

'Donna went to the clinic to get a pregnancy test and some pills. You know, the ones you take after? I don't know what they said to her, but she must have changed her mind about getting rid of the baby. She reckoned she could live on the handouts from Social and not have to work any more. Someone explained it all to her.'

'Is that the reason she changed her mind? So she wouldn't have to work anymore?' Gina couldn't believe anyone could be that stupid. Why did these young girls think a baby didn't involve any work?

'A woman at the clinic told Donna she would get a new flat and new furniture, like a cooker and fridge and things, and stuff for the baby, as well as lots of allowances. Donna said she was very helpful.'

The ducks had crept back and Gina shooed them away. It looked as if Lucinda Valentine really was advising unfortunate teenagers on the merits of keeping their babies. The alternative to abortion was evidently having a baby and living off benefit. Did that mean the leaflets were pro life and nothing more? A gut feeling told her there was more to it than that.

'Did the police find out where Donna was killed?' When Gina shook her head, the girl said, 'So the police don't know where she was staying, or anything, do they?'

'They don't tell me everything they know. I'm sure they'll find Donna's killer quite soon.'

'But you work for the police, don't you?'

'Only as an artist.' Gina finished her bagel in silence, tipping the crumbs out of the bag for the ducks. Their squabbling antics round her feet put paid to conversation for a few minutes. 'A baby wouldn't have been easy to look after, Shelly. You're quite sure Donna intended keeping it?'

Shelly shrugged. 'I suppose she thought it was worth it. Get a flat and not have to kip down with friends.' She stood up. 'Thanks for talking to me, Miss Cross.'

Gina watched the girl walk away, thinking if cosmetic surgery could give her longer legs she might just start saving up.

She found it difficult getting back into the right sort of mood to draw. The good weather had brought out a nurseryload of kids who were throwing endless rounds of bread to ducks stuffed so full they were eating for the sake of it. Just like people, Gina thought. She sketched a couple of fat white ducks with round bodies and small heads, their tummies practically dragging on the ground, and wondered if a duck had ever been diagnosed as clinically obese.

She found a bin for her empty bag and headed for home, the mood to sketch fields and trees long gone.

* * *

Gina got up late on Sunday morning. She woke early, but she had promised herself a lie-in so that was what she had, even though lying in bed bored the hell out of her. A quick glance through the window told her the day was dull and grey, hardly worth getting out of bed, but after half an hour she couldn't stand the inactivity any longer.

Breakfast consisted of toast and marmalade and orange juice. All very healthy. A cold beer would have been much nicer, but the sun wasn't yet over the mainbrace or yardarm, or wherever it was supposed to be. Bacon and eggs and things were probably sitting in the refrigerator but she couldn't be bothered to cook. Even getting dressed was an effort. She sighed and glanced again at the phone. Adam hadn't rung — or left a message. She had checked her mobile phone twice already and cursed herself for doing it.

Deciding that moping around was getting her nowhere, she dumped her plate and glass in the sink and picked up her phone. It hadn't occurred to her that he might be out, and when she got his messaging service she almost disconnected, but in the end she left a message asking him to call her back. Most of the time she enjoyed being alone, but now she needed someone to talk to, and Adam was very good at listening. Which made her wonder why he was never around when she needed him.

She grabbed her jacket and car keys and let herself out into the grey mist that hung in the air like wet cotton wool. Hospitals didn't close on a Sunday, but she had no idea what Lucinda Valentine really did. Whether she was medical staff or admin. Only one way to find out. If Lucinda was at home, her car would be in the driveway of her house.

Finding the little dead-end lane was easier the second time around. The change in the weather had kept people indoors. No one was washing a car or mowing a lawn, which suited Gina just fine. She parked outside one of the bungalows and walked casually down the road to the cottages. There was no sign of Lucinda's car and the house looked dark and deserted. So did the one next door.

She strolled past the cottages and slipped under a single strand of wire between the end of the road and a field. That way she could get to the back of both houses.

The occupied cottage had a neat little back garden with a rotary clothesline, a small shed, and a patch of lawn, but no sign of Lucinda. The empty house had a path that led from a low wooden gate to a half glazed back door. Bushes overhung the path and weeds had sprung up between the paving slabs. She didn't want to try opening the gate in case it fell off its hinges, and it was low enough to swing a leg over — if you were fairly tall. To someone not much over five feet, it represented quite a hazard, but she made it without mortally injuring herself, and then realized she needn't have bothered. The weeds were already squashed flat.

Someone had opened the gate quite recently.

Paint was peeling from the back door, but the old wood looked solid and the locks were new. The frosted glazing in the top half of the door threw her reflection back at her, distorting her image and making her jump. She took a step back and looked at the upstairs windows. The windows were dark, the blinds pulled down, but then she thought she saw a tiny sliver of light. She turned her head for a better look and it was gone. Probably another reflection, she told herself.

She inched sideways along the back wall of the house, trying to avoid a nasty looking bramble and hoping to get a look in the downstairs window, but that was going to be difficult. The window was hidden behind a dark green bush with thorns. She found out about the thorns when she squeezed behind the bush and got snagged by the sleeve of her jacket. Trying to go back the way she had come made matters worse, so she pushed on, and found she could see into the room on the other side of the window. No blind this time, most likely because the bush completely shielded the window.

The window was dusty, but she could see a table and chairs, pictures on the wall, and a door that probably led to a hall. All very clean and tidy and completely at odds with the outside of the house. As she wriggled sideways to get a better view, her foot caught on a root and she pitched forward, grabbing the window ledge for support. A thorn raked her face and she stayed on her knees, willing herself not to cry out. When she put her hand to her face there was blood on her fingers, but she doubted she'd be scarred for life. All she had to do now was get back on her feet, which was easier said than done with a thorn

148

bush wrapped around her like a roll of barbed wire.

As she pulled herself upright by hanging on to the window ledge, a large chunk of rotting wood broke away, almost sending her back down to the ground. Completely forgetting the damage to her face, she stared at the gap under the sash window where the beading had broken off. If the window wasn't locked . . .

Climbing over the sill was no problem, keeping completely quiet was, but if anyone was at home they would have heard her crashing around in the undergrowth. The window jammed halfway up but she managed to squeeze through the opening. She stood still for a moment in the room, waiting for her eyes to adjust to the dim light from the window. A few seconds later she crept across the bare boards of the stripped oak floor as quietly as she could, no sense in making more noise than she had to, and eased open the door. The blinds were down on all the windows and the hallway was dark.

Raising the blinds was not a good idea. That would announce her presence to anyone walking past. So would turning on the lights. Then she remembered her car keys were in her pocket and the key fob had a light on it. A light big enough to find a lock on a car door, or make a small hole in the dark.

She stepped out into a rectangular hallway, the front door on her right, a kitchen on her left, and the banister of a stairway straight ahead. She moved to the bottom of the stairs and looked up. The stairwell was dark. If there had been a light in any of the rooms it would have shown round the door. She went back into the living room and shone the beam round the walls, not sure what she was looking for. The bookcase held an eclectic mix of romantic novels and thrillers by well-known authors, while the magazine rack contained a selection of women's magazines and a TV programme guide. She picked up the guide and shone her light on the date. This week's programmes. Someone had been living here, either now or very recently. She almost tripped over a rug and looked down at her feet.

The stain on the wood floor could be anything.

She pressed her hand against the dark patch. It was dry and no particular colour, just dark. It could be coffee, tea, red wine, anything. What she needed was some luminol, the stuff the police use to turn bloodstains blue. It has limited use, because it turns all manner of other things blue as well, but it would have been better than nothing.

150

She crouched down for a better look . . . and heard a tiny sound. Or thought she did. Creeping around an empty house in the pitch dark was making her jumpy, and it might well have been a mouse. That thought made her even more jumpy.

Realizing she hadn't a clue what she was looking for, and probably wouldn't recognize it if she found it, she left the living room and crept up the stairs. A flick of her torch showed the bathroom door was open, and so was the door into one of the two bedrooms. The other door was shut. Taking a breath, she turned the handle and pushed the door open, sweeping the room quickly with the light. The room was furnished with a bed, a bedside table, and a large wardrobe. The bed was neatly made, but if Jack was obsessive-compulsive it followed that his sister would be as well.

Gina eyed the wardrobe warily. It was big enough to hold all manner of things, including a person, and if this had been a television programme she would have scoffed at the idea of someone opening a wardrobe in a dark, deserted house. Never a good idea. A bit like climbing to the top of a building when you're being chased.

She crept across the room and pulled the wardrobe door open before she could change her mind.

151

A black fleece jacket hung from the rail but otherwise the cupboard was bare. She shut the wardrobe door and moved to the bedside cabinet. A quick feel around inside the drawer told her that it was empty. As she closed the drawer she heard a noise from downstairs.

Her ears twitching like a rabbit's, she turned off the light and stood still, the silence humming in her head. There it was again. Wood against wood. The sash window rising ever so slowly, creaking against its runners. Someone had managed to force the window the rest of the way up. Someone too big to get through the small gap she had created. Her first thought was the man from the nightclub. With her torch turned off it was difficult to see across the room, restricting her to the area where she stood. If she moved she would bump into something. With panic pushing her heart rate up until she could hear the blood thumping in her head, she stared at the dim shapes of the furniture. A bed, two bedside cabinets and a wardrobe. She reached out with her left hand and touched the bed, feeling her way down the side until she came to the foot. Opposite the end of the bed was the wardrobe.

She had just squeezed inside when she heard someone creeping up the stairs.

152

15

Whoever it was had a bigger torch than hers. Something akin to a searchlight swept her hiding place. She clenched her car keys in her hand, the long shaft of the ignition key protruding between her knuckles. Not a particularly formidable weapon, unless you could poke it in someone's eye, but it would have to do. A moment later the wardrobe door was wrenched open and she leapt forward. The light from the big torch completely blinded her for a moment and her makeshift knuckleduster met thin air. Before she could recoup she was picked up and thrown on the bed.

'Bloody hell, Gina! Pack it in, will you? It's me.'

She pulled herself to the side of the bed and sat up. The surge of adrenaline had racked up her heart rate and almost stopped her breathing. 'What the fuck do you think you're doing, Adam! Do you know how much you scared me?'

'Not half as much as you scared me. You came out of that wardrobe like a banshee, waving your arms around and screaming at the top of your lungs.' He grabbed her wrist and pinned her arm above her head, staring at her clenched fist in disbelief. 'Did you just try to kill me with a car key?'

'The urge is still there. What on earth are you doing here?'

He stood his torch on the bedside table, the beam pointing at the ceiling. 'You left a message, remember? I tried phoning you at home and then on your mobile, but you had it turned off.'

'Turning off my phone while I was breaking into someone's house seemed like a good idea at the time.'

He ignored her. 'I went to your flat and you weren't there. You'd taken your car so I knew you weren't out running, and I remembered mentioning the houses.'

At that moment there was a loud bang from downstairs. It sounded like a door slamming.

'I didn't leave a door open,' she whispered, the adrenaline flooding back. 'I came in through the window.'

Adam got to his feet. 'So did I.' He grabbed his torch and made for the stairs, Gina just behind him. They stumbled down the stairs together and Adam flung open the back door just in time to see someone vaulting over the gate. Gina tried to catch her breath, her

154

hands on her knees, while Adam gave chase. A few moments later she heard what sounded like a motor bike leaving in a hurry.

Adam didn't attempt to vault the gate on his way back. He pushed it open and walked up the path, obviously out of breath. 'I'm quick,' he said. 'Army training. But that guy had a head start — and youth — on his side. Also a very big bike. Sorry.'

'I was sure it was going to be the nasty guy from the club,' Gina said, 'but that looked like the DJ. Roddy McBride.'

'You sure?'

She nodded, and then shook her head. 'No. But it wasn't Mr Nasty.'

Adam took her arm and opened the gate. 'Let's get away from here. We've made enough noise to wake the dead. I hope the next-door neighbour hasn't come back.'

'Lucinda Valentine? She's probably at the hospital.'

'The Valentine woman lives next door? For God's sake, Gina! What else haven't you told me?'

She followed him through the field and out on to the road. 'Lots, I expect. You're never around to tell anything to.'

He followed her home, just as she had expected. She could have refused to let him in, but she didn't.

'There's no wine left,' she said, as she shut the door behind him. 'So, coffee or beer?'

'You had plenty of wine the other day. What on earth did you do with it?'

'Would you believe I drank it? I had one bottle left after you went, and by my reckoning that does not count as plenty. It's barely an evening's worth.' She shrugged out of her damp jacket. 'I can't be bothered to make coffee, so we're having beer.'

He took the bottle she handed him and flipped the top with his thumb. 'How did you find out the Valentine woman lives in that house?'

'I drove over there on Thursday evening and spoke to her. She doesn't know me, so I made up a story about how I was looking for someone. She must rent the house from the Beaumonts, which makes sense as she works at Willow Bank. But if Roddy's renting the other house, why would he run away? Perhaps he's squatting there illegally. He certainly made a quick getaway.'

'Get Megan to have a word with him. He'll tell her more than he'll tell you. Incidentally, I spoke to Steve Gilmore, Donna's supposed boyfriend. The police have already been to see him and ruled him out as a suspect. He said Donna slept around, so the baby could have been anyone's. Said he dropped her

156

months ago, as soon as he found out she was pregnant. I told him if the baby was his the police could prove it, and he said fine, go ahead, Donna and the baby are both dead so he can't be done for maintenance. Nice lad.'

'So you've still got nothing to write a story about.' Gina frowned when her stomach made a gurgling noise. 'What's the time?'

He looked at his watch. 'Nearly three o'clock. We'd better get you something to eat.'

Over lunch at an Indian restaurant a short drive from her flat, Gina told him about her conversation with Shelly in the park. 'How did this girl recognize you?' Adam asked curiously. 'You're not that famous.'

'She saw the television interview with Donna's mum. They mentioned me, you said.'

'No one mentioned you. Donna's mum said she recognized her daughter from the sketch, and how good it was, but she never mentioned you by name, and they didn't show a photo of you. Angie Price is not one to share the limelight with anyone.'

Gina stared at him over her plate of chicken korma. 'Angela Price doesn't know who I am, does she? Last time she saw me she thought I was your photographer.'

'Exactly.'

'Don't sound so smug. I don't know what point you're trying to make. Shelly obviously knew me. She called me Miss Cross.'

'The point I'm trying to make,' he said slowly, 'is how she knew you. Who told this Shelly person you were Gina Cross, the forensic artist who works for the police? Not many people know that.'

'You sound like Michael Caine,' she said, trying a smile, but her stomach had tied itself into a knot and she pushed her plate away.

'You know what?' He pushed his own plate out of the way. 'This is beginning to get more interesting. I take it you didn't get the girl's last name?' He smiled when Gina shook her head. 'Actually, she was quite clever. You told her more than she told you.'

'She did ask a few questions. You think I was set up, don't you? But why?'

'To stop you poking your nose in where it's not wanted. It was probably quite easy to work out who drew the police sketch. You're the only professional artist in Castlebury and everyone at the police station knows you, so anyone with half a brain could put two and two together.'

'So now you agree something strange is going on?'

He grinned at her. 'I didn't say that. I just said it was getting more interesting. There might even be a story in it somewhere. I'll poke around a bit more and let you know what I find out.'

Her phone suddenly trilled and she put her hand guiltily in her pocket to shut it off, conscious of stares of disapproval from other diners. 'Sorry, I should have turned it off.' As Adam asked for the bill, she took the phone out of her pocket and looked at the dial. 'It was Reagan. Shit, that can only be bad news. I'd better go outside and call him back.'

When Adam joined her she looked at him in dismay. 'They found another body. Another young girl in practically the same place as before. Near the cycle path. He wants me there straight away.'

Adam took her arm and guided her to where he had parked his car. 'Stop freaking out, Gina. The last dead girl wasn't Sophie.'

'How lucky can you get?'

He pulled away from the kerb as fast as he could in the late afternoon traffic. It was starting to get dark and everyone was heading for home. 'You don't have to do this, Gina. You're freelance. You don't have to look at another dead body if you don't want to.'

'Yes, I do. Reagan needs to know who this girl is, and he needs to know fast. Drop me at home and I'll pick up my car.'

He turned his head to give her a quick grin. 'No way.'

There was no need for directions. The drizzle had given way to a brilliant orange sunset and the purple and white crime scene tape looked almost pretty. A tent-like enclosure had been erected round the body, the area outside cordoned off with more tape. Gina pushed through the tent flap, closely followed by Adam. The light inside was impossibly bright and Gina had to wait for her eyes to adjust. When she eventually looked down, her breath caught in her throat. This wasn't Jack's sister, and for that she was grateful, but there had been two deaths tonight.

The kneeling pathologist looked up at Gina and sighed. 'She's carrying a four or five month foetus. Please don't tell me you can see it.'

'Not exactly, but I know it's there.' Bending closer so she could look over Avery's shoulder, she realized the girl's face looked wrong. Distorted. The eye socket was flattened, causing the eye to protrude behind the closed eyelid, and the nose was obviously broken, although the girl had died too quickly for bruising to form in that area. 'What was the cause of death?'

Sheila Avery climbed painfully to her feet.

'The victim was probably hit hard enough to cause a bleed in her head, or force a piece of bone into her brain. All I can tell you for the moment is that she got hit in the face with something and died almost instantly.' Avery moved her gloved fingers slowly over the shattered eye socket. 'It wasn't anything solid, like a rock.' She closed her eyes, frowning, while her fingers kept exploring. 'Probably a fist, but it could have been done with the back of someone's hand if they hit her hard enough. People don't realize a single blow to the face can kill.'

'Are we looking at domestic violence?' Reagan asked. He turned to speak to Gina and noticed Adam for the first time. 'What the bloody hell are you doing here, reporter man? You better not have a camera with you.'

'I drove Gina here. You interrupted our dinner date.'

'Sorry about that. You can go now.'

For a moment Adam looked as if he might argue, then he backed out of the tent without a word. Reagan watched him go then turned to Gina. 'If he writes a story, you're in trouble.'

'Do you want me to go, too?' She certainly didn't want to stay. Domestic violence? That was a load of crap. A young girl had been killed and her baby had died with her, but

161

domestic violence? She didn't think so.

Reagan waved an arm. 'Do your picture, then you can get reporter man to take you home.'

Gina took the pad and pencil he handed her. The policeman knew Adam's name but wouldn't use it. The two men didn't get on and Gina thought it was probably because they were so alike. Both bloody awkward.

Sheila Avery moved out of the way so Gina could get closer to the body. 'Don't know why Reagan called you. We already took photos.'

Photos that showed someone's daughter cruelly beaten to death, whereas her sketch would show a pretty girl, eyes open, hair freshly combed. A person, not a victim. Avery didn't trust Gina's sketches, she thought they were fantasy, nothing to do with the violence in the real world. But Gina wasn't going to apologize for her gift. She could take a piece of paper and a pencil and make people whole again. That was what made her keep coming back to look at dead bodies.

Reagan watched Gina draw for a moment and then turned to Avery. 'So we don't need to look for a murder weapon.'

The pathologist was waiting for Gina to finish her sketch so the body could be moved to the mortuary. 'No, just for someone with a sore hand. Maybe even broken.' She stared at Gina's sketch. 'Even if this one was a right little scrubber, you'll still make her look like a fairy princess.'

Gina finished drawing and handed the sketch to Reagan. 'Just so long as someone recognizes her. If you show them your horror pictures, her own mother won't recognize her.'

Avery shrugged. 'Someone's got to look at the real thing. Can't always pretty them up.'

But by then the family would be prepared. As prepared as you can ever be for sudden death. Gina hoped this young girl would be mourned. Not dismissed as lightly as Donna had been. 'Please let there be someone out there who cares,' she whispered to no one in particular, and left the tent to find Adam.

The activity had escalated with the arrival of the forensic team, and Adam was talking to the crime scene manager. Donald Parminter looked up as Gina approached.

'I see they've called in the Witch of the East,' he said with a smile.

'This is a nasty one, Don,' Gina told him. 'Another pregnant teen, this one with the baby still on board. Someone smashed her face in. Killed her instantly.'

'With a lump of rock?'

'No, it looks like it was a fist this time, but

still a violent blow to the head.'

He sighed. 'If you've finished here, Gina, get the boyfriend to take you home. This lot are behaving like a herd of elephants. If I don't get them sorted there'll be no evidence to find, it'll all have been trampled into the mud.' He looked down at the damp ground. 'They launched a new system in 2007, some sort of footwear intelligence technology with images of thirteen thousand shoe-print types, so remember what shoes you were wearing tonight.' He turned to yell at a passing uniform. 'Get some bloody booties on or go home. I don't need any more footprints.'

Adam took Gina's arm and they ducked under the tape, making their way back to his car. 'This is definitely another murder,' Gina said. 'And I think this body was moved as well. It's too much of a coincidence for two girls to finish up in the same place.'

'You think the two deaths are related?'

She looked at him in amazement. 'And you don't? Both young girls, both pregnant, both murdered, both found dead in the same place. It doesn't take a genius.'

He unlocked the car and walked round to the driver's side, waiting for her to climb in beside him. 'Castlebury is full of teens, and probably a good proportion of them are pregnant. Besides which the cycle path is

164

frequently used by students and young lovers.' He put the car into gear and drove away from the crime scene. When the silence became positively uncomfortable he laughed out loud. 'If you could see your face. I'm just playing devil's advocate. It could be a coincidence.'

She turned in her seat to look at him. 'If you knew how much I dislike you sometimes, you wouldn't do this.'

'Oh, I probably would, but I apologize for winding you up. Looking at a dead body can't be much fun. However, I still don't think these two deaths have anything to do with Jack's missing sister.'

Gina reached over and turned the radio up until James Morrison made conversation impossible. She didn't need his negative comments. She was trying to put the bits of the puzzle together. All she had to do was get them in the right order.

'Are you sulking?'

'No, I was just thinking I need a drink, but I don't have any.'

'Why am I not surprised?' He pulled away from the kerb again. 'Back to my apartment, then. I've got plenty.'

Gina loved Adam's apartment. It actually belonged to his mother who spent most of her time abroad. Situated at the very top of the building, it had amazing views over the river and surrounding countryside. Gina had painted several of her little watercolours from a seat on the balcony. The inside was sparsely furnished but not bare, with thick rugs on the polished wood floor and two cream sofas covered in red velvet cushions. Kicking off her shoes, she sank gratefully into the cushions while Adam poured wine into crystal glasses. The room was lovely, with its high ceilings and panoramic views.

As he sat down beside her, Gina yawned. The day was catching up with her. All she wanted to do was rest her head on his shoulder and go to sleep.

'Can you smell burning?' he asked conversationally.

Gina sat up in her nest of cushions and sniffed the air. 'It's not in here. It must be outside.'

Adam got to his feet. 'Christ, I hope there's not a fire in one of the apartments. This place is old, mostly timber. The metal beams hold it up, but they kept all the old wood because the building is listed.' He reached the double doors on to the balcony and threw them open. The smell was worse, rubbery and acrid, but whatever was on fire was at the front of the building and out of sight. 'Grab your coat. We'd better see what's going on.'

He shut the door of the apartment behind them and Gina felt a little flutter of fear. She remembered an old film called *Towering Inferno*. As the lift door closed behind them she also remembered you weren't supposed to use the lift if there was a fire. They stepped out into the foyer where several people were standing around looking vaguely concerned. The smell was stronger here.

'You stay inside. I have to see what's going on.'

She knew he could scent a story the same way she could scent danger. A few minutes later she followed him outside and saw him standing in front of the garages where a pall of evil-smelling smoke hung in the air.

He came towards her and led her back towards the entrance.

'It's all under control. Couple of blokes put the fire out with extinguishers, but they've called the fire brigade just in case. No one's hurt and the fire's out now, just a load of smoke left.' He took a deep breath and tried a smile. 'My car doesn't look too great, though.'

'It was your car on fire?' She looked at him in disbelief. 'But there was nothing wrong with it. What made it catch fire?'

He steered her towards the lift. 'I have no idea. It's a good job the tank was nearly empty or it could have blown up.' He pushed the button to take them up to the top floor. 'I'll report it to the police in the morning, but there's nothing I can do tonight.' His smile was better this time. 'Except get us another drink.'

She didn't know what to say to him. His little sports car was his baby. At the beginning of the year it had finished up in the river, but it had survived. Now it sounded as if this might be the end of it. She wanted to give him a hug, but the expression on his face warned her to keep her distance.

'How bad?' she asked.

He shrugged. 'Leather gone, paintwork blistered, God knows what else. I've had it restored once. I don't think I can do it again.'

She had no understanding of a man's passion for his car. She often wished her Metro would burst into flames so she could claim off the insurance and buy something new and reliable. Something with four wheels that would get her from A to B without breaking down. She knew it was no good talking about insurance claims to Adam, he would consider that as bad as selling funeral packages in a hospital.

She let him pour her another drink, but she could see his thoughts were elsewhere, and she could smell the smoke on her clothes and in her hair.

'There's no need to run me home, Adam. You may need to talk to the fire department. I'll get a taxi downstairs.'

He didn't argue. No doubt he would have a rental car organized before morning, but even a Rolls Royce would be a poor substitute for his beloved sports car. It wasn't until she was on her way down in the lift that she began to think it was all a bit too much of a coincidence. The moment Adam started asking awkward questions, his car caught fire.

16

'Someone set light to Adam's car?' Megan was very good at the wide-eyed, incredulous look. 'While you were at his apartment?'

Gina nodded. 'You'd have thought some-one had put his mother on a bonfire, the way he reacted. No one was hurt.'

'But he loves that car. It's a classic Austin Healey.'

'It's older than mine. I can't understand why it cost so much. He could have got a new one for that. Why do men like old cars?'

'And young girls? Yeah, you've got a point there.' Megan filled the kettle. 'How did it catch fire? I know it's old, but he really looks after it.'

'Don't know.' Gina found a couple of mugs and spooned in instant coffee. 'It seems strange that it was Adam's car that caught fire. There were three other cars in the garages. And we'd both been asking ques-tions, hadn't we?'

'So, you didn't stay the night and comfort him? Did you get a taxi home?'

'No, in the end I decided to walk.'

'For fuck's sake, Gina! There's a murderer out there.'

'Someone who targets pregnant teenagers. I hardly fit the bill.'

The first customer of the day took Gina's mind off Adam and his problems, and lunchtime brought an unexpected visitor. She had been about to reverse the sign on the door so they could eat their sandwiches in peace, when Grace Lowry scuttled into the studio almost furtively. For a moment Gina didn't recognize the woman and it was Megan who said, 'Mrs Lowry?'

Sophie's mother looked ill. No amount of carefully applied make-up could hide the dark lines under her eyes or the pinched look around her mouth. Gina locked the door and pulled the blind down over the glass. Deciding the woman looked as if she needed a drink, she opened the fridge door and looked inside. Perhaps it would be a good idea to keep a bottle of gin on hand, in case of emergencies.

'Please have a seat.' She waved a hand at the visitors' chair. 'Do you drink beer, or would you rather have tea or coffee?'

Grace Lowry sank into the chair and rewarded Gina with a weak smile. 'Tea, please. I'm really sorry to barge in like this, but I didn't know . . . ' She took a shaky breath. 'I had to talk to someone, and I can't go to the police. If Brian or Jack find out they'll never speak to me again.' She took a tissue out of her bag and wiped her eyes with a trembling hand. 'Sophie's not answering her phone. She didn't call me at the usual time yesterday so I tried calling her, but her phone appears to be turned off.'

Gina blinked. 'You've spoken to Sophie recently?'

Grace shook her head impatiently. 'No, I told you, not since the day before yesterday. She phones every day between five and six when Brian goes over to the church. She didn't phone yesterday and I can't call her, her phone won't answer. Something's wrong and I don't know what to do.' She took the mug of tea Megan handed her. 'Thank you. Sophie's pregnant but Brian doesn't know. He wouldn't be able to handle something like that. Sophie's going to have the baby at Willow Bank and Dr Beaumont is going to arrange for an adoption, but Brian mustn't know that either. He'll hate it that I lied to him, but I did it for the best. I kept telling them she was all right, that there was nothing to worry about. I thought telling everyone she'd taken a gap year would be fine. Students do that, don't they?' Grace covered her face with her hands. 'Why did Brian have to go and make such a fuss?'

'He was worried about her,' Gina said gently.

Grace took her hands away from her face. 'He was worried about his reputation. Losing his job with the church. That's all he ever cares about. You have to help me find her, the baby's due at the end of the month.'

Gina glanced at the calendar. Three weeks at the most. 'I think you have to tell them, Grace, and I think you should tell the police as well. Sophie could be in danger. The police will take it seriously if you tell them everything you've told me. You haven't committed a crime; you were just trying to help your daughter.'

Megan had kept quiet, but now she swung her swivel chair round angrily. 'I think it's a crime, even if Gina doesn't. Letting everyone think Sophie was missing was a horrible thing to do. Don't you care about Jack at all? Maybe your husband deserves this, but Jack doesn't. He's always looked after Sophie and tried to take care of her. He was worried sick. How could you do this to him?'

Grace was crying now, her shoulders shaking. Gina closed her eyes. As far as she was concerned, emotions weren't meant to be shared. 'Can you tell me where Sophie was staying? Was it at the Beaumonts' rental house?' Presumably Grace couldn't talk and cry at the same time, and Megan, having said her piece, had shut up. She was sitting staring at a blank computer screen, too cross to even look at Grace Lowry.

'Yes,' Grace said eventually. 'You see, that's why you can't tell anyone. Doctor Beaumont can't be involved with the police. He's a respected surgeon and he was just trying to help. He's been very kind.'

'Amber knows, though, doesn't she?' Megan said. 'She's known all along.'

Grace didn't answer, her expression a silent confession. Gina was trying to sort out fact from fiction. 'Where does Roddy fit in? He was at the rental house yesterday, but the place was empty. There were no clothes in the cupboards or drawers.'

'I don't know anyone called Roddy. A woman called Lucinda Valentine who works at the hospital was looking after Sophie. Lucinda has medical training. She was going to call me when Sophie went into labour so I could be with my daughter.'

The tears started again and Gina thought she heard Megan sigh.

'We have to talk to Amber,' Megan said.

'You can't tell Celia. Amber's mother doesn't know anything about this.' Grace was getting agitated. 'Doctor Beaumont doesn't want her to know he's helping us. She wouldn't understand.'

'We still have to talk to Amber,' Megan

repeated. 'You can't protect Sophie *and* Doctor Beaumont, not if you want to find your daughter, and Amber knows where she is, I'd bet on it.'

Gina felt her heart rate pick up. The feeling of impending doom was back with a vengeance. Sophie was out there somewhere, and someone had just murdered another pregnant girl. If this was a jigsaw puzzle, it was like having two different puzzles on the board at the same time with no way of sorting the pieces. At the moment nothing seemed to fit. 'We'll do what we can, Grace, but I really can't see any way of keeping this from your husband. And you ought to tell the police. Sophie could go into labour at any time.'

'She was safe,' Grace Lowry said. 'I made sure she was safe. She would have taken her gap year and gone back to university and no one would have been any the wiser.' Her voice shook. 'Sophie left it too late to have an abortion. I believe she thought it would all go away if she didn't talk about it. She won't tell me who the father is, but I know.'

'The schoolteacher?' Gina asked.

Grace looked at her in surprise. 'How did you know?'

'Jack told us,' Megan said. 'He doesn't keep secrets like you do.'

'Sophie told us it was over. He was moving

away, but it took a while for him to arrange a transfer to another school. You'd think he'd know better, wouldn't you? A teacher.'

'At least not to get his pupils pregnant.' Megan frowned. 'Wasn't Sophie on the pill?'

Grace shook her head. 'Her father wouldn't hear of it. So silly. I mean, it's not as if we're Catholic, birth control is fine within our church, and he knew his daughter better than anyone. She was always a rebel. Told me she had sex when she was fifteen just to see what it was like. She wanted to shock me, of course.'

Megan grinned. 'She wasn't much of a rebel if she waited until she was fifteen.'

Grace ignored Megan. 'I want to find her, but I don't want anyone to lose their job over Sophie's mistake, or my foolishness. It wasn't supposed to be like this.'

'It never is,' Gina said. She looked at Grace Lowry's red eyes. 'You'd better tell your husband you've got flu, or he'll wonder what's wrong with you.'

'Yeah, you look awful,' Megan said, without a shred of sympathy. 'We'll talk to Amber. Don't worry, she won't want to drop her father in the shit, either.'

Grace promised she'd go home and go to bed. She wanted to stay in Castlebury, and a dose of flu would be a good excuse. She said

176

she was hoping Brian would return to his parishioners and leave her behind. Jack wouldn't be in the dark about his sister much longer, Gina thought. Megan would tell him as soon as she got the chance.

As soon as Grace Lowry disappeared out of the door Gina breathed a sigh of relief. 'I hate emotional women.'

Megan gave a snort of disgust. 'We should have got the old girl drunk. Do you reckon she told us everything?'

Gina shook her head. 'Not for a moment. I don't think Doctor Beaumont is as much of a saint as Grace thinks. Why would he risk losing his job over Sophie?' She thought of her jigsaw puzzle again. 'We've still got some missing pieces.'

'Like I said, if we talk to Amber we may find out where Roddy fits in. What were you doing at the rental house?'

'Ah,' Gina said, 'that's a long story,' but she told Megan anyway.

'You tried to stab Adam with your car key? Wicked. And you saw Roddy running away? What on earth was he doing in that house? Mrs Lowry said Sophie was staying next door with Lucinda.' Megan looked thoughtful. 'Unless Amber and him go to the empty house together. She'd have a key, wouldn't she? Or she'd know how to get hold of one.

It'd be a good place for a quick shag.'

'She might still have been there for all I know,' Gina said. 'We didn't hang around, and it was so dark half a dozen people could have been hiding in that house. I kept hearing noises while I was creeping around.' She didn't mention the stain on the floor.

Someone banged on the glass door and Gina looked at the clock in horror. They had been closed for nearly two hours. She opened the door to an impatient customer who wanted to buy a tube of acrylic paint, and then moved to the back of the studio to finish a portrait. At times her brain seemed capable of working independently from her hands, and while she worked on the portrait of a student in graduation robes she let her mind wander.

Something had been odd about the empty house. No, not the house. The path leading up to the house. Some of the weeds between the paving stones would have been four or five inches high before they were crushed underfoot. She could visualize the path and the weeds and tufts of grass lying flat on the stones. She put down her paintbrush. If someone had trampled the weeds underfoot they would have been lying every which way, but they weren't.

They were all leaning toward the gate.

The rest of the day passed incredibly slowly with hardly any customers, so Gina sent Megan home and locked up early.

She slipped off her shoes as soon as she got upstairs to her flat and chose a microwave meal from the freezer completely at random. She squinted at the label. Four minutes on high, that would do, whatever it was it was going to be quick. Just as she was about to take the first mouthful, her doorbell rang.

Adam was standing at the top of the stairs holding a bottle of wine.

'I wanted to apologize for practically kicking you out last night.'

Gina held the door open. 'How's the car?'

'It'll live, but it's going to cost me.' He walked past her and put the wine on the table. 'Someone tipped petrol on the front seat and set it alight, so the insurance company won't pay out. Not yet, anyway. But I managed to get a rental car out of them.' He looked at her open packet of fish pie. 'Finish your food. Do you want a glass of wine to go with it?'

'A glass of the white would be nice.' She picked up her fork. 'You don't believe this was just wanton vandalism, do you?'

'I'd like to. But if my car was torched because I've been digging where I shouldn't, perhaps I should have listened to you.'

'In that case you owe me one.' She tossed

179

her food container in the bin. 'I need you to take some pictures for me before it gets dark.'

He screwed the cap back on the wine bottle. 'I'd better not drink any more then.'

17

Gina insisted Adam park his hire car at the top of the lane in case Lucinda was home. 'If she is, we can pretend we're just out for an evening stroll. Even if she recognizes me from last time, it won't matter. I told her I was looking for someone who lives round here.'

'You can pretend you've found me,' he said, as they started down the lane. 'If we hold hands we'll look like a couple of lovers out for an evening stroll.'

Lucinda's car wasn't in the drive so they ducked under the wire fence and into the field. When they got to the back of the empty house Adam pushed the gate open, but Gina stopped him going inside the garden.

'Look,' she said. 'See how the weeds have all been flattened in one direction? Some of them have been pulled out by the roots. Just walking on them wouldn't do that.'

He bent down for a closer look. 'You're right. Something heavy was dragged from the house to the gate. Could've been a body, but it could equally have been a mattress or a heavy bag. Anything, really. It's not against the law to drag something down a garden path.'

'Just take the photos,' Gina said. Why did he always have to be such a dickhead? 'Do you think there's a chance Sophie might still be in there?'

He looked at the house. 'No, I don't think Sophie is in there, and the stain on the floor you were talking about was made before she went missing, so put your imagination on hold. Sophie hasn't been murdered, and she wasn't hauled away in a bin bag.' He squatted down on his haunches and pointed his camera at the weeds. 'But something was dragged out of that house.'

'Should we tell the police?'

She saw him hesitate, weighing up the odds. An investigation of Willow Bank by the police could very well lose Dr Beaumont his job, and any scandal involving the Lowry family would probably lose the vicar his parish. Jack would be devastated, and Jack was his friend.

'Not yet,' he said. 'Not until we know Sophie is in real danger. You said she has another few weeks to go before the baby's due, and I'm sure she'll get in touch with someone if she goes into labour. You wouldn't want to do it on your own, would you?'

Gina shuddered. 'I wouldn't want to do it at all. Why would anyone? Have you seen the size of a baby's head?'

He gave her a look she couldn't quite fathom. 'Does that mean you don't ever want children?'

'I haven't seen anything yet to make me change my mind. Besides, it's usually a good idea to get married first. Or am I being old-fashioned?'

'Don't let what your father did to you mess up your life, Gina.' Before she could answer, he turned away to study the ground outside the back gate. 'Tyre prints. Even though its been pissing down with rain, you can still see them. Someone unhitched the wire and drove through the field.'

They followed the tracks back to the wire fence and he shook his head. 'I was wrong. They pulled up a couple of posts and drove over the wire, then they put them back in again.'

Just as they were about to leave the field a car turned into the lane. Adam pulled Gina back out of sight. 'Is that the Valentine woman?'

Gina poked her head round the corner of the house. 'Yes.' She had a sudden thought. 'Can you take a picture without using the flash?'

'The light's just about good enough. Why?'

'See if you can get a picture of Lucinda as she steps out of her car. A close-up if possible.'

He looked at Gina curiously for a moment and then eased the camera lens through the bushes. They were only a few yards away when Lucinda walked up the path to her front door. The digital camera was almost silent and Adam had a steady hand. He had time to take several pictures before Lucinda went inside the house and closed the door.

'We can't walk past her window,' Gina whispered to Adam. 'She'll see us. We'll have to go back the way we came and see if there's another way to get to the lane.'

There was, but it involved something akin to trekking through a rain forest. 'I've got twigs in my hair,' Gina said, as she climbed gratefully into the still warm car. 'And my feet are soaked.'

'That long grass holds the rain for days.' Adam picked something off his jacket and threw it out of the car window. 'That was still moving.' He started the engine and turned on the heater. 'Can we go now, or is there something else you'd like me to photograph for you?'

'No thanks, that'll do.'

By the time they got back to her flat, her socks were steaming. She had been toasting them in the warm air from the car heater. 'Come in and dry off if you want, but I need those pictures as soon as possible.'

She took off her socks and trainers and got a towel from the bathroom to dry her hair. 'Do you want a coffee?' When he nodded, she started towards the kitchen. 'Sit down while I fill the coffee machine.'

'I think I've got something moving around on my back,' he said suddenly, and before she could speak he'd pulled off his shirt and was trying to look over his shoulder. 'Can you see anything?'

Of course she could. He had the most beautiful body, tanned to a golden brown by the Thai sunshine, the scar that ran from his navel to his hipbone just visible over the top of his jeans. There was a gleam of sweat between his shoulder blades and stuck in the damp patch, its legs wriggling uselessly, was a tiny brown beetle.

Keeping her mind firmly on the insect, she plucked the creature carefully from his back and held it on the palm of her hand. 'Hardly a scorpion, but I bet it tickled.'

He laughed, shrugging back into his shirt. 'Thanks. It felt like a bloody great centipede.' His blue eyes studied her thoughtfully. 'I can understand you wanting a picture of the path, a body could have been dragged down there, but why do you want pictures of Lucinda Valentine?'

'She's had cosmetic surgery. Quite a lot of

unnecessary stuff. A boob job I can understand, and teeth are always worth doing, maybe even a nose job she didn't really need, but why would she want an artificial mole stuck on her face?'

'Some people think a mole is attractive.'

'Not this one. Did you see it? It's just a big ugly brown blob. When you see her for the first time, you can't take your eyes off it.' She suddenly realized what she had said. 'That's it, isn't it? When you look at her all you see is the mole, not what she really looks like.'

'Quite clever,' Adam said, 'but it's been done before. Like bright red hair, or a purple jacket. Ask a witness and that's all they remember. It's like a magician using distraction to take your eyes off what he's really doing. You see what he wants you to see.'

'Like that Shelly girl in the park. I thought I was getting information from her, but instead she was trying to find out what I knew.' Gina flopped down on the sofa and took a sip of her wine. 'She was very good. She must be an actress, or something.'

'Then maybe there is a way to find out who she is.' He sat down next to Gina, so close she could feel the heat from his body. 'There's only one proper stage school in Castlebury. Give me a sketch of her and I'll sit outside and see if I can spot her when she comes out.'

'I can't, Adam, you know that. I can't remember faces. That's why I needed a photo of Lucinda Valentine, and why I'll need to go with you to look for Shelly. I can't draw her, but I'll recognize her when I see her.'

He didn't argue. 'I'll find out what time the class chucks the students out. I doubt the girl really knows anything, but someone probably paid her for her little act. It would help to know who that was.' He looked at his watch. 'I'd better go. I'll call in at the studio tomorrow. I should have the photos by then.' He stopped by the door and turned to look at her. 'Get a good night's sleep.'

The next day was quiet. People rushed around on Monday to get the things done they'd forgotten to do the week before, but Tuesday was a nothing day and Gina felt restless. She gave in halfway through the morning and phoned Adam. For once he answered on the first ring. 'Do you have the photos yet?' she asked.

'Lunchtime,' he said. 'I'll drop them in to you and I'll pick up some sandwiches on the way. What do you want?'

Sandwiches sorted, Gina settled down to some serious work until Adam arrived.

He came through the door carrying containers of sandwiches, a four-pack of beer, and a large brown envelope. Megan took the beer, Gina grabbed the envelope, and Adam was left to dish out the sandwiches. He knew their favourites now so there was no arguing over who had what.

Gina tipped the photographs out on to Megan's desk. Adam had taken several long shots of the garden path and a close-up of the broken weeds. The pictures of Lucinda were not so good. The light was going and leaves from the bush obscured her face in several of them. None was the full-faced view Gina would have liked. She chose one that showed Lucinda on the point of turning towards the camera, three-quarters of her face visible.

'Why didn't you wait until she was fully turned around? It would have been a perfect shot.'

'She turned to look at the bush because she heard or saw something. Luckily she lost interest and went inside.'

Gina looked more closely at the picture. At least the mole was in full view, and she could already visualize what Lucinda would have looked like before her surgery. The woman's nose would have been several centimetres longer. Her lower jaw would have receded slightly because of the overbite, her eyebrows would be closer together, and the attention-grabbing mole would be nowhere in sight.

Not a great change, but enough.

'As I only had half her face to work with, I'll have to assume her cheekbones are symmetrical and her ears are the same both sides, but I can draw her well enough for you to check police records.'

'That's what I'm going to do, is it?'

'Yes, please.' She picked up the photo and walked to the back of the studio where she propped an A4 sketchpad on her easel and clipped the photo to the top where she could see it. Now, Lucinda Valentine, let's see what you really look like, she thought, as she started sketching in an outline of the woman's face.

'Nothing like the way she looked at the clinic,' Megan said half an hour later, watching over Gina's shoulder. 'But you haven't really changed anything much, have you?'

Adam joined them, standing beside Megan. 'I was once told there are only five faces,' he said. 'Every one is a variation of those original five. It only takes something really small to make a person different. If you add hair and eye colour, disfigurations, and blemishes like the Valentine woman's mole, the possibilities are endless.'

'And weight and height,' Megan said, joining in enthusiastically. 'If you had two Adams, but one was short and fat, he'd look

189

completely different, even with the same face. I'd look different if I had a body like Kylie Minogue,' she added wistfully.

'Or if you had a big, ugly mole, like Lucinda.' Gina glared over her shoulder. 'Will you both stop breathing down my neck? This isn't easy, you know. I've got to concentrate.' She shook her head when Megan handed out beer, she wanted to get this right, and removing cosmetic surgery was much harder than straightforward reconstruction. First she had to strip the face back to the skull, layer by layer, and then build it back up again without the extra bits. A bit like restoring a building that had been the victim of bad DIY.

Megan dealt with a couple of customer queries, and Adam actually sold a woman a £90 easel when all she had come in for was a sketchpad. Gina worked for two hours, stopping only for a cup of tea, and at the end she felt exhausted. Normally, she'd make a job like this last all day, doing a bit at a time, but she wanted to get the sketch finished so Adam could check it against the police database. Theoretically, it was a million to one chance that Lucinda would have a record, but Gina had a gut feeling, and she had learnt to trust the little nudges her intuition gave her. She sat back and stared at her drawing for a few moments and then got up and walked to the back of the studio.

'What are you doing?' Megan asked.

'Finishing touches.' Gina had picked up a watercolour palette and a little pot of water. A few moments later Lucinda had honey blonde hair, which went much better with her pale skin, and light blue eyes. 'She couldn't alter the colour of her skin, but she could change the colour of her hair and eyes with a bottle of dye and contact lenses.' She handed the sketch to Adam. 'It'll take a minute to dry, but that's the best I can do from a photo. If I had her standing in front of me I could be certain I'd got it right, now I'm not sure. Even a lack of symmetry in a face changes it. People looking in a mirror look different because they see themselves back to front.'

Adam held the sketch carefully by one corner. 'This'll do fine. Even if you had her in front of you, I doubt she'd want to stand still long enough for you to paint her portrait. I'll take it to my friend at the police station in the morning.' He unclipped the photo from the easel and looked at Megan. 'Can you hold the fort for a while? We're going to go and find us an actress.'

18

'They knock off at half four,' Adam said. 'So they should start appearing any minute.'

The drama school was in a road to one side of the castle. An old building looking a bit the worse for wear, with steps leading up to a double door and a sign proclaimed it was a School of Performing Arts for Gifted Pupils. None of the students who were now spilling out of the doors looked particularly gifted, Gina thought, but who was she to know?

Half an hour later they were about to give up the surveillance. 'She's not there,' Gina said, disappointed, but not surprised.

'Hang on.' Adam swung his long legs out of the car. 'Give me five minutes. There's always a chance.'

A chance of what? Gina watched him walk towards the school entrance and disappear inside. Just over five minutes later he was back, a big grin on his face.

'There was always a chance she might have used her real name,' he said. 'People often use their own first name, and just make up a surname. There are two girls called Shelly at the school, and one of them is off sick. I've got her address.'

Gina looked at him in amazement. 'How did you do that? Surely they're not supposed to give out the students' addresses to any old body.'

He looked offended. 'I'm not any old body, and I look trustworthy.' He ignored her humph. 'I said I was holding auditions for a London play and I'd spoken to a girl called Shelly a few days ago, but couldn't remember her last name. The woman looked in the register and gave me two names. She said one of the girls had just left through the front doors, and the other was at home sick. He waved a piece of paper. '*Voilà*! The girl's address.'

Gina shook her head. He was as devious as a benefit cheat. 'So what do we do now?'

'We pay poor, sick Shelly a visit.'

Shelly Pullman lived in one of the newer blocks of flats. The building was nearer to the centre of town than the university accommodation, a bleak block of concrete with industrial looking ironwork on the outside. Modern architecture. Gina remembered the block being built about five years ago, near the train station with its regular service to London, and full of expectations for an élite clientele of commuters, but already it had an air of despondency. It was doing its best, but not quite making it. No competition for the mill apartments.

'How are we going to play this?' she asked.

'Keep back out of sight until we find out if the girl's in and I put my foot in the door. All we want to do is find out if she's the girl who met you in the park and if she really knew Donna. She might have been telling the truth. If she wasn't, you'll come as a nasty shock.'

Shelly might have been a good actress when she had a script, but confronted with a real situation she was hopeless. The expression that crossed her face when she saw Gina was a dead giveaway. She tried to shut the door, but Adam's foot was firmly in place. She looked over her shoulder, as if expecting help from within, but no one came to rescue her. Gina moved in closer.

'Did you really know Donna Price?'

The girl shook her head, defeated. Her nose was red and her eyes bloodshot. She either had a hangover or a really bad cold. An enormous sneeze she only just got a tissue to in time suggested it might be the latter. She turned back into the flat, Gina and Adam following closely behind.

A burgundy duvet tumbled off the sofa, an empty mug and a packet of paracetamol sat on the floor, and the table was piled with

194

books and manuscripts. Otherwise the room was clean and fairly tidy. An open door led into a small kitchen.

Shelly rolled the duvet into a bundle and tossed it into a corner. The room smelt of cough medicine and vapour rub.

'It was just a job,' she said. 'I was given a script with all the names and everything and he said I could ad-lib if I had to. I just had to find out what you knew about Donna. He said you and Donna's mum were trying to make trouble for Willow Bank. Saying if Donna had got an abortion she wouldn't have died.' Shelly paused to blow her nose. 'I saw the mum on TV and didn't like the look of her, so I said OK. It was just a job,' she added defensively.

'You were very good,' Gina said with grudging respect. 'You had me fooled.'

'But not me,' Adam said. 'It wasn't just a job, Shelly, it was a con, and I think you knew that.'

The girl shrugged and flopped down on the sofa. 'I like acting, and I didn't take any money from you or anything, so I don't reckon you can do much about it. A friend of mine went to Willow Bank to have her baby. They were very good to her, took care of everything after she had the baby and gave her some money to get a flat. They don't need people like you causing trouble.'

Gina looked at Adam then back at Shelly. 'What happened to your friend's baby? Did she keep it?'

Shelly looked uncomfortable. 'No, she had it adopted. But no one forced her. She wanted to go to university, get a degree.'

'We're not trying to make trouble for the hospital,' Gina said. 'We're just trying to find out how Donna died. Someone dumped her in a ditch after she was dead and I think she deserved more than that. Who gave you the acting job, Shelly?'

'A man. He said the school had told him I was the best. Said a hundred quid for half-an-hour's work.' She looked up at them defiantly. 'It was good fun.'

Adam sat down next to her and waited until she turned to look at him. 'What did this man look like?'

Shelly frowned. 'I've no idea, I only spoke to him on the phone.'

'How about his voice? Old, young?'

'Not that young. And he had a very slight accent of some sort, but I couldn't place it.'

Adam stood up and walked to the open door. 'If you want to be an actress, Shelly, don't give people the impression you'll do anything for money. You might get the wrong sort of job. By the way,' he said, as if it was an afterthought. 'What was your friend's name? The one who had her baby at Willow Bank?' He smiled when Shelly shook her head. 'I didn't think you'd remember.'

'So something is going on at Willow Bank,' Gina said as she climbed back into the car. 'What are they trying to cover up?'

Adam put the car into gear and pulled away from the kerb, looking for somewhere to turn round. 'I'll see what I can find out about Lucinda Valentine. She must have a good reason to change her appearance so drastically, but I'd be surprised if Beaumont is involved in anything dodgy. He has a reputation as a top class consultant and I can't see him getting mixed up in anything illegal. He'd lose his licence.' He reversed into a side street and then swung the car back up the hill.

'But he must have employed the Valentine woman. She works there, and according to Megan she knows the Beaumonts personally.'

'I suppose she could be running some sort of scam on her own that Beaumont knows nothing about. Difficult though, in a small private hospital.'

Gina was silent for a moment. It was all beginning to come together in her head. Pieces of the puzzle slotting into place. 'It's all there, isn't it? Willow Bank has a fertility

197

clinic, which means a list of women desperate for a baby, and Lucinda finds girls who are desperate to have an abortion. She doesn't even have to go looking for them. Hand out a few leaflets, and they come to her.'

'Like Megan.'

'Yes, like Megan. Do you think she's in danger?'

'Not if she doesn't go back there. They'll think she's just changed her mind.'

'A doctor at Willow Bank told Megan they'll pay her to answer some questions for them, some sort of special study they're doing.'

'Saying they'll pay for information could be a way of getting Megan to go back to the hospital. If you're right, it would be best if she stays away.' He drove in silence for a few minutes. 'It would be best if you stay out of it as well.'

'Was that an order, or a suggestion?'

'Give it a rest, Gina. You know trouble follows you around like a bad smell. Let me do my job and check on Lucinda Valentine. Reagan told you to stay out of it, so why don't you do what he says for once?'

'He told me not to interfere with the Donna Price murder investigation. I'm only interested in finding Sophie.'

'No you're not. You keep telling me the two

cases are connected. If they are, this is about Donna as well as Sophie. You can't have it both ways.'

He always twisted everything she said, but she couldn't be bothered to argue. He would no doubt win. He stopped outside the studio and held her arm as she was about to get out of the car. 'Can't you do what I ask, just for once?'

'You don't ask, Adam, you tell. That's the problem.'

She walked into the studio and let the door slam shut behind her, making Megan jump.

'Don't tell me you two have been arguing again. You're worse than a couple of kids. Did you find the Shelly girl?'

Gina sighed and slipped off her shoes. Megan was right. Why did she bother to argue with Adam when she knew it wasn't going to get her anywhere? 'Yes, we found Shelly, and yes, she was pretending to be a friend of Donna's. She's a drama student.'

Megan looked puzzled. 'So what was the point of sitting next to you in the park?'

'To find out how much I know. This must have something to do with the hospital, but Adam doesn't reckon the doctor would risk his reputation, and his licence to practise medicine, for an adoption scam. He's got too much to lose.'

'You think that's what this is? An adoption scam?'

'It makes sense, doesn't it?'

'I suppose.' Megan pulled a face. 'After they did the test on my wee, the doctor took a blood sample as well. Said they need to know I'm healthy.' She looked at Gina. 'I already told them I don't want a baby, so what's the point in sticking a needle in me?'

'I think that is the point. They want a healthy mother and a healthy baby. That's the other option, Megan. Carry the baby full-term and have it adopted. A fertility hospital with adoption as a sideline makes perfect sense, doesn't it? They wait until people are in a state of despair with fertility treatments that don't work, and then bring up the idea of private adoption.'

'Some people would pay anything to have a baby,' Megan said quietly.

'Thousands of pounds.' Gina chewed her bottom lip. 'We know what those funny questions were about now, don't we? Blonde, blue-eyed parents get a blonde, blue-eyed baby. No wonder you were asked if you knew the nationality of the father. No ethnic kids for Willow Bank parents. These are real designer babies.'

'I know it's probably illegal or something,' Megan said, 'but is there anything wrong in giving an unwanted baby to a couple of people who're really desperate to have one? How is that wrong?'

'If someone's making money out of it, it is wrong. They aren't giving the babies away, Megan, they're selling them, and two girls have died. I don't want you to go back there. It's not safe.'

'It's as safe as it was before,' Megan said. 'They still think I'm just a scared no-good who dropped her knickers one time too many. They had a file on me at the clinic. I'm famous for screwing up my life.'

'Promise you'll tell me when they call you back. By then Adam will have done some more digging and we might know who Lucinda Valentine really is.'

Gina was worried Megan might go back to the hospital without telling anyone. She just hoped the hood of her jacket had hidden her face when she knocked on Lucinda's door. All the woman had to do was put two and two together.

An hour later Gina was glad to put the closed sign on the door and tell Megan to go home. It had been a hectic day, and all she wanted to do was get upstairs to her flat and take off her shoes, but as she turned the corner she realized that was not going to happen.

Amber Beaumont was sitting on the bottom step.

19

Adam pulled away from the kerb outside Gina's studio with a screech of tyres. Why, he wondered, did he let someone the size of a garden gnome wind him up? Thank God he managed to keep his cool on the outside. If she knew what she did to him on the inside she'd have a field day.

He knew why Gina was scared of relationships. He'd tried a couple himself, and they hadn't worked. He'd been fine in Thailand with no one to answer to, but get involved with someone and that's the end of life as you know it. He still hadn't worked out whether it was a price worth paying.

He debated where to go first. He wanted to interview Dr Beaumont at Willow Bank and find out what was going on. Normally, he would have walked in and asked to see the doctor without a second thought, but Grace Lowry's confession had complicated things. If Dr Beaumont was just trying to help Sophie, there was no point in antagonizing the man. It would probably be a good idea to see his police contact first and collect all the available information, before he confronted the doctor.

He found a lay-by and pulled in, taking his mobile phone out of his pocket. His friend would want to meet him somewhere anonymous. It was not a good idea for a police officer to be seen talking to a reporter. Bradford Norman's messaging service picked up and Adam left a message saying where he'd be for the next half-hour.

The hotel coffee shop was in a glass-roofed annexe where two elderly ladies were sipping glasses of white wine and chatting in hushed voices, but otherwise the place was empty. Later, the conference room would empty and the quiet would be shattered by a crowd of loud-mouthed businessmen, but at the moment the atmosphere was of serene gentility. Adam found a table in a corner overlooking a paved courtyard and ordered a pot of coffee for two. Even if Brad managed to get away, he wouldn't be able to drink any alcohol while he was on duty.

The policeman arrived five minutes later in an unmarked car, wearing jeans and a sweater. 'Luckily I was out on a job on my own. This gets more risky every time, you know. Now you regularly get articles published in the tabloids, people know your name.'

'But not my face. I'm pretty careful about that. I need my anonymity as much as you do. What are you working on?'

Adam had tossed the question into the conversation casually, but Bradford laughed. 'You know damn well what I'm working on. What we're all working on. A bloody murder, that's what.'

'Anything new?'

'Not a lot. Normally forensics will pick up a few clues, but moving the body buggered that up. She was hit on the head with a rock or a big stone of some sort, probably still at the murder site, but we have no idea where she was killed.' He sighed. 'Good old plodding police work. Someone will have seen something, but we have to find them.' He took the sketch Adam handed him and unrolled it on the table. 'Who's this?'

'We know who she says she is, but she's had a lot of work done on her face and probably changed her hair and eye colour. Gina reckons that's how she looked before she had the work done.' Adam passed over the photo he had taken outside Lucinda's house. 'That's how she looks now. Oh, and the mole isn't real, either.'

Bradford looked up in surprise, and then smiled. 'Gina Cross, your little psychic artist, she drew this?'

'Forensic artist. And she's not mine.'

The policeman laughed. 'No, you're right, I

can't imagine her belonging to any man, but she has to be something other than an ordinary forensic artist if she's right about these changes. She's made this woman look completely different. And how does she know the mole isn't real? It sure looks real in the photograph.' He poured coffee for both of them. 'And why would an attractive woman decide she needs a big ugly mole on her face?'

'Exactly,' Adam said, watching Bradford add three spoons of sugar to his coffee.

'Don't give me that shit.' Bradford stirred his coffee and then lined up the sketch and the photo side by side. 'Come to think of it, my wife could do with Gina's help, the little witch has taken ten years off this woman's age.'

'She doesn't like being called a witch.'

'I know,' Bradford grinned. 'But it's great fun. You can actually see her hackles rise.' Serious again, he said, 'Trouble is, she spooks a lot of people, me included. She looks at you like she's paring you down to the bone.' He leaned forward, squinting at the drawing. 'How would little Gina know the woman's hair was originally this colour? And the eyes, she's changed the colour of those as well.' He sat back in his chair again. 'Like I said: a witch.'

'Leave her alone, Brad,' Adam said. 'She's

just good at her job.'

The policeman raised an eyebrow. 'Now you're being over-protective. I had no intention of getting anywhere near her, she might put a spell on me.'

'Can you run both the sketch and the photo through a facial recognition system? Can a machine like that handle a sketch?'

'You talking about one of those machines you see on the telly? Stick a picture in and it goes flickerty-flick through loads of faces nineteen to the dozen, and then stops on the one that matches. Is that what you're talking about? Because, if so, we don't have one.'

'Someone must. One of the main police stations. Can't you call in a favour or two and get it done for me? It'll be worth a bob or two.'

'It's not about the money, although I can do with the stuff or I wouldn't be here talking to you. The fact is, I don't even know if a machine like that exists except on the telly. For facial recognition you need a mug shot already on record somewhere. They ran a trial up in the Midlands somewhere, with seven hundred and fifty thousand photos of known criminals, trying to identify them from video surveillance cameras, but there were loads of problems. How many crooks stare at a CCTV camera so you can get a good look at their face? Besides, nothing is likely be fully operational until 2012, so there's no way anyone could be identified from a sketch or an old photo at the present time.' He paused to take a sip of his coffee. 'Not in this country, anyway, and even in the States they couldn't get a match from a sketch. They'd need a digital image of some sort. But,' he held up his hand as Adam started to roll up the sketch, 'we do have the PCN which is the Police National Computer. We don't live in the sticks here, whatever people may think, and QUEST — that's an acronym as well, but god knows what it stands for — might be able to help. You can stick in names and physical characteristics and stuff, and it'll look for a match. Or CRIMELINK, that one matches similarities in crimes. If they've done this before they should be on a computer somewhere.'

'This woman has a North American accent, so she probably came over from the States quite recently. You got any contacts across the pond who can help?'

'Might have.' He grinned. 'You're going to owe me big time after this. You know that, don't you?'

'I already owe you big time, just for meeting me,' Adam said seriously. 'The woman's name is Lucinda Valentine — you won't forget that, will you? But if she's changed her face she's probably changed her name. And she works at the private hospital in town, Willow Bank. At the moment she's renting a house from Dr Beaumont.'

'Nice man. I met him once. Good hospital too. It's expensive, but they got a waiting list. People come over from abroad.' He swallowed the rest of his coffee and got to his feet. 'Christ, that was hot. I'll do what I can, Adam. Tell you what, give me the sketch and I'll fax it over to a mate of mine in California, get him to pass it around the different precincts and see what he can find out. If she's a con artist, someone might recognize her.'

Adam thanked his friend and poured himself another cup of coffee. Bradford would never give out classified police information, but he had a wife and three kids, and a little extra money came in handy. Adam found him invaluable. There's nothing like having a friend on the inside.

He gave Bradford time to get well away, and then drove back to his apartment and parked in the new parking space he had been allocated. He got out and slammed the door of the Ford. No one was going to set light to this car. He thought of phoning Gina, maybe suggest he take her out for a meal after she closed the studio, but she'd managed to make him look like a bully yet again. He really didn't know how to handle her, and that was a first. He admired her fierce independence, but finding a way through her defences was proving to be a problem. Perhaps she really was a witch. She'd certainly managed to put some sort of spell on him.

20

Amber didn't look as if she was going to move out of the way, so Gina stepped over her. She got to the top of the stairs and put her key in the lock before she turned round and looked down.

'If you want to talk to me, you'd better come in.' She watched Amber unwind her long frame and slowly climb the stairs. The girl was wearing ripped black jeans and a T-shirt saying I'M VERY GOOD. 'Is that just your opinion?' Gina asked, holding open the door. 'Or do you have a testimonial?'

'Fuck off,' Amber said, without any real heat. She pushed past Gina and walked into the flat. 'Bit small, isn't it?'

Gina didn't bother to answer. She kicked off her shoes and opened the fridge. She tossed a bottle of Stella to Amber and opened one for herself, handing over the bottle opener. 'So?'

'What do you know?' Amber flipped the top off her beer and made herself comfortable on the sofa.

It took Gina a moment to realize it wasn't a rhetorical question. She pulled a chair out from the table to sit on. 'Not a lot. Why?'

'Because, whatever you think you know, you've got it wrong. None of this is my dad's fault.'

That was a surprise. 'Who suggested it was?' she asked carefully. 'I think you know where Sophie is, though, and why she opted out of going to university.'

Amber finished her beer and put the bottle down hard on the glass table, making Gina wince. 'I asked you what you know.'

Gina wasn't going to let herself be bullied by some kid, but the only way she was going to get anything out of Amber was to volunteer some information herself. 'I know Sophie's pregnant and the baby is due in two or three weeks. And I know she needs all the help she can get. No one is blaming your father for trying to help her.'

Amber had perfect lips, shiny with a peach gloss that accentuated the colour of her skin, but now those perfect lips curled into a sneer. 'You think you know it all, don't you? Do you know who got her pregnant?'

'A teacher, wasn't it? That's what Grace Lowry said. Some teacher got Sophie pregnant and then took his wife and kids up North.'

Amber laughed, but it wasn't a pretty

sound. 'That's what everyone thought. You got more beer?'

Gina took another bottle out of her fridge. She resisted the temptation to have another one herself. She had a feeling she was going to need all her wits about her if it came to a verbal sparring match with Amber.

The girl popped the top of her beer and let the cap fall on the floor. She tipped the bottle and downed half the contents in one go. 'The teacher had nothing to do with Sophie getting pregnant. I found that out today. The bitch lied to all of us, including her mum. Me and my dad, we helped her all we could, found her a place to live and everything, but she never thought to mention she was shagging Roddy.'

Gina blinked. 'I thought he was your boyfriend.'

'So did I.'

Gina almost felt sorry for the girl. 'Where is she, Amber? We have to find her before she has the baby.'

Amber shook her head. 'I don't know. Lucinda was looking after her. Roddy's missing too. It's his baby, so they've probably gone off somewhere together.'

'How do you know it's his baby?'

'Because he sent me a fucking text.' Amber suddenly looked very young and not nearly so confident. 'All the time we were in Spain, staying at my Dad's place, I knew she was pregnant because she told me, but she never said it was Roddy's.' The second bottle hit the glass table, harder this time. 'She's a scheming, lying little — '

'Don't say it,' Gina said quickly. She knew what was coming and it was one four-letter word she had trouble accepting. 'Before you break my table, why don't you tell me where your father fits into all this?'

Amber's long fingers, now tipped with scarlet, played with her hair, twisting the sleek black strands into curling dreadlocks. 'Lucinda found a home for Sophie's baby. A couple who can't have kids. They're going to be really upset if Sophie doesn't give her baby to them, because it was promised, and if they make a fuss my dad's going to get into trouble.'

'Is he taking money off them? The couple who are getting the baby, are they paying him?'

'No, of course not. He wouldn't do that.' The girl's eyelids flicked, a sure sign she was lying, but Gina let it go.

'Lucinda's American, isn't she?'

'Yeah,' the girl's dark eyes widened. 'How'd you know?'

Gina smiled. One up to her. 'I have my

sources. What's her part in this?'

Amber shrugged, a slight rise of gleaming shoulders. 'She's a nurse, midwife as well, or says she is. She's been looking after Sophie.'

'Why does Sophie need looking after? I would have thought she'd have sailed through a pregnancy at her age.'

Another shrug. 'Lucinda's supposed to bring Sophie to the hospital when the baby starts coming, but now she's missing and no one knows where she is.' There was a long pause and Gina waited, trying to be patient. 'Lucinda's not been at the hospital long, and I don't like her. My dad's supposed to be in charge, but she bosses him about.'

'What exactly does she do?'

'She runs that clinic for pregnant teens. Some of them have their babies at the hospital.' There was a pause. 'Lucinda says there's a charity pays for it.'

'What about the adoptions? Your dad's been involved before, hasn't he?'

'You mean the one all the fuss was about? That was over a year ago, and no one took him to court or anything, but that's why he's so worried about what's going on now. If anyone finds out he'll be in real deep shit, but now Sophie's gone and sodded off some-where with Roddy and doesn't give a fuck that my dad could lose his job. I really hate her.'

'What was the fuss about a year ago, Amber? And what is going on now? Does it involve Lucinda's clinic?'

Amber suddenly looked wary. 'I thought you knew. You said you knew.' She stood up. 'I gotta go. I shouldn't have come here, but I thought you might know where Sophie is, and my dad needs her back at the hospital.'

'Sit down a minute, Amber, please. Two girls are dead. Both were pregnant when they died, and we know one of them went to Lucinda's clinic. Do you know anything about that? Because, if you do, you have to tell me before more girls die.'

Amber stayed on her feet. 'No. I heard about it on the telly, but I didn't know Lucinda was mixed up in it. She'll get my dad into trouble. Everything was fine until she turned up, my dad was helping people, now everything's going wrong.' A tear trickled down Amber's cheek and she brushed a hand across her face, looking in surprise at the wet smear. She headed for the door. 'Like I said, I gotta go.'

Gina didn't try and stop her. She'd spooked the girl out by asking questions. What she needed to do now was find out what Dr Beaumont had done in the past that had caused a fuss. If there had been any report of it in the media, Adam could find out. That is, if she ever spoke to him again.

A few minutes later she was sitting down to the leftover half of a pizza, hot from the microwave, and her second bottle of beer, trying to make the new pieces fit the puzzle. If Dr Beaumont was involved in anything illegal, Amber wasn't going to talk about it. The girl was fiercely protective of her father and feeling guilty for getting him involved in Sophie's troubles. But Sophie had turned out to be a real dark horse. How would Mrs Lowry feel, Gina wondered, if she found out her daughter was pregnant by a DJ who played at a club where drugs were handed out like Smarties? Was that better or worse than being pregnant by a married teacher? On consideration, it was probably worse. The teacher was out of the picture, but Gina had a feeling that Roddy might be a little bit harder to get rid of.

And if Sophie had run off with Roddy, where the hell had they gone?

She dumped her pizza plate in the sink and was about to change into her dressing gown, when the phone rang.

'Gina?' Megan said. 'I've got Jack here in a real state. He's just found out his mum lied to him. He rang her up and she broke down and told him she'd known where Sophie was all along, but now Sophie's really gone missing. She told Jack his sister's pregnant, and he was going to phone his dad, but I stopped him. Can you come round and talk some sense into him, please, before he does something stupid?'

Gina sighed. 'Hang on to him until I get there.'

Two beers in quick succession made driving a bit dodgy, so she put on her trainers and walked. Before moving into her new flat Megan had rented Jack's little Victorian house only a few streets away, but now walking back home was not going to be much fun. Perhaps Jack would give her a lift, Gina thought hopefully, as she jogged through the evening drizzle.

Megan opened the front door and headed back into the living room. Jack was sitting in Megan's only comfy chair, Blossom, the Siamese, sprawled on his lap.

'How long have you known?' he asked. He didn't sound angry, just resigned.

'Only since yesterday. Your mum was just trying to protect both her children the best way she knew how. She didn't want to worry you when there was no need. The baby was going to be adopted and Sophie was going back to university with no one the wiser. She

217

seemed to think your dad would have a heart attack if he was told the truth.'

'He's got a right to know, though. Sophie is his little girl. He'd want to know if she's in trouble.'

'What do you think he's going to do if he finds out, Jack?' Megan asked. 'He's going to go ballistic and cause trouble for everyone.' She walked over to her floor to ceiling windows and threw them open, letting in the damp air and the sounds of the street. Blossom looked up curiously, but didn't move. 'It's his fault Sophie's in this mess.'

Jack put the cat carefully on the floor. 'How do you make that out?'

'Oh, don't get on your fucking horse,' Megan said crossly. 'He told his darling daughter not to go on the pill, didn't he? Really clever, that.'

'Her teacher took advantage of her and got her pregnant. She's only a kid. I think he's the one who has a lot to answer for.'

Gina took a breath. 'It wasn't her teacher who got her pregnant.' Ignoring the silence she walked over to the table and pulled out a chair. Her bottom was getting numb from sitting on hard chairs. 'Amber came to see me. She'd only just gone when Megan phoned.'

'Whatever she told you, she's lying,' Jack

said. 'We all know it was the teacher.'

'No, you don't. That's what you all want to believe. Your dad would love to think an older man had seduced poor, innocent little Sophie, and the villain is now miles away playing happy families with his wife and children. Your mum wants it all to go back to the way it was. The baby is going to disappear, adopted by a lovely couple who will give it a marvellous home; Sophie is going back to university, and your dad will never know anything bad ever happened. But it isn't going to be like that. Not now.'

'We have to find her,' Jack said. 'I don't care who the bloody father is. All I know is that she's out there somewhere, pregnant and all alone. According to Mum, the baby's due any time now. Sophie can't handle it on her own.'

'She may not be on her own. Amber got a text from Roddy McBride, the DJ, telling her he's the baby's father, and Amber thinks Sophie may have run off with him, but she has no idea where they might have gone.'

'Roddy?' Megan said incredulously. 'Roddy McBride? I thought he was hot for Amber.'

'So did Amber. She actually cried real tears. She thought Sophie was her friend.'

'Probably her only friend. No one else likes her.' Megan shook her head in disbelief. 'I didn't know Roddy had it in him. Shagging a vicar's daughter. Wow.'

Jack picked Blossom up and settled her back on his lap. 'The thing is, we still don't know where Sophie is. She could be with this DJ chap, or she could be on her own. We should tell the police what we know.'

'That's the problem, Jack, we don't know anything. All we have is guesses, and your father won't welcome the publicity.'

'Then I have to speak to my father. Sophie is more important than his reputation.'

When the doorbell rang, Gina looked at her watch and then at Megan. 'Are you expecting anyone? It's gone ten o'clock.'

Megan looked worriedly towards the door. 'It's not your dad, is it?' she asked Jack.

Jack shook his head as the bell rang again. 'Perhaps someone should answer it and find out who it is, rather than guessing.'

21

Gina walked out into Megan's tiny hall and peered through the spy hole in the front door. Adam looked really strange in goldfish mode, his nose enormous, his head bulbous and elongated. She had thought about getting a spy glass fitted in her own door, but she had read that it was possible for someone to shoot through it and the bullet get you right in the eye. She was still thinking, as she opened the door, that if you saw the barrel of a gun when you looked through the glass, instead of someone's face, you might be a tiny bit suspicious.

He was holding two bottles of Shiraz. 'You didn't take your car so I guessed you'd be here.'

She took the bottles from him. Jack could do with a drink and Megan rarely kept any alcohol at the flat. 'You'd better come in,' she told him. 'Jack's here as well. He's spoken to his mother and got a bit spooked out.'

Megan fetched tumblers from the kitchen. 'How about we sit down with a glass of wine and share information?' She beamed at them.

'It's like, you know, the Fantastic Four together again.'

Adam poured the wine, half filling the tumblers, while Gina went over her conversation with Amber. 'Doctor Beaumont got himself into some sort of trouble at the hospital a while ago, evidently. Amber thought I knew about it but when she found out I didn't, she clammed up.'

Adam kept quiet. He didn't want to throw any more information into the pot until he had checked it out.

'I don't know anything about that,' Jack said. 'I'm sure Doctor Beaumont wouldn't get mixed up in anything dodgy. I've known him for years. He built that hospital up from scratch and now it must be worth millions. He doesn't need to make money from anything dodgy.'

Gina sighed. 'No, you're right. I'm just trying to make the pieces fit the puzzle.'

'Jumping to conclusions,' Adam said, with a disparaging shake of his head. 'You have to check your facts at least three times before you make any sort of allegation.'

Megan gave him the finger. 'You might have to, you're a journalist, but I can allegate all I want.'

Gina was about to tell Megan there was no such word, but she couldn't think what the

222

right word should be. 'Anyone got any ideas where Sophie might be?'

'Ask the DJ,' Jack said, 'if you think he's really the father.'

Adam agreed. 'One person might be able to disappear, but if they're together it will be more difficult for them.'

Gina yawned, and Adam got to his feet. 'Time to go, I think. We all have to work tomorrow.'

Adam offered to drive her home, but she shook her head. 'Jack can take me. He only lives round the corner from me.'

Adam took her arm. 'Jack walked as well. Come on, I'll run you both back up the hill.'

He dropped Jack off first, and on her own in the car with Adam Gina found herself unable to think of a thing to say. Thankfully, there was only a minute or two of silence before they reached the studio.

'Thanks Adam,' she said, reaching for the door handle.

He put his hand on her arm. 'You OK?'

She managed a smile. 'Fine. Just tired. Thanks for the lift.'

He didn't try and stop her, and she heard him drive off before she had her front door open.

She slept well, but that was probably due to the drink, rather than an untroubled mind.

She moved her head carefully as she got out of bed the next morning, just in case, but the headache she was expecting didn't materialize.

Down in the studio, she worked hard until lunchtime, catching up with a backlog of work, and then sent Megan out to get sandwiches. They sat outside in the little courtyard, making the most of some fairly warm sunshine for the time of year, trying to think where Sophie might be.

'I can try and find Roddy,' Megan said. 'When he's not at his mum's, he stays with mates. He's never bothered to rent anywhere because he travels about a lot, but if he's still in England, I can probably find him.'

'Not if he doesn't want to be found.'

Megan grinned. 'I'm working on being your assistant detective, like in that programme on telly. *The Ladies Detective Agency.*'

'That was set in Botswana. Grace Makutsi is African and I'm not a detective.'

Megan's grin got wider. 'So? Everything else fits.'

Gina laughed. 'OK. Try and find him, I don't imagine he's dangerous, not if he's lived in Castlebury all his life. But if you go to the club, don't run foul of that Crawford bloke, he is dangerous.'

224

They both looked up at the sky as a large raindrop hit the metal table. 'Bloody English weather,' Gina said. 'It was sunny a few moments ago.'

They cleared up the sandwich packets and coffee mugs and headed back inside. Someone knocked on the studio door and Gina looked at her watch. 'Ten minutes to go,' she said. 'What shall we do?'

'Oh, open up,' Megan said, throwing the sandwich packets in the bin and dropping the mugs in the sink. 'We can't afford to lose a customer.'

The rain brought people in off the street, and Gina had discovered that even if they didn't buy anything then and there, they often came back. By the end of the afternoon she realized she would have to replenish her stock of watercolours, which was more difficult in the winter. Now was the time to get outside with her sketchpad and top up the stock, but finding Sophie was dominating everything else at the moment.

She closed up half an hour early, when the last customer had gone, and sent Megan home. They had both worked hard enough for one day. Climbing the stairs to her flat she half expected to find Adam or Amber sitting on her doormat, but the entrance was free from obstructions. Wondering whether the post-mortem examination had already taken place, she picked up the phone.

'Are you alone?'

There was silence for a moment, then Mick gave a little giggle. 'Gina darling, what are you suggesting?'

'Oh, shut up, Mick.' She didn't have time for his innuendoes. 'Has the PM been done on the second girl yet?'

'The dead one?'

Was he being deliberately dense? 'How many post-mortems are done on live people, Mick? Just answer the question, will you?'

'My, my, we are in a tizzy, aren't we? The answer is yes. She hasn't been identified yet but, as there might be a serial killer on the loose, Sheila Avery was given permission.'

Gina looked at her watch. 'If you're going to be there for the next half hour, I'll pop in.' She hung up before he could say anything else, grabbed her bag, and headed out again.

She hated the way it got dark so early at this time of year. An English autumn could be beautiful, with the trees almost as colourful as those in New England, but most of the time it was too dark to see them. The rain had set in and she turned on her headlights against the gloom, heading for the hospital. When the clocks went back it would get dark even earlier.

'Sheila was right,' Mick told her when she arrived at the mortuary. 'Nasal bone straight up into the brain. The poor girl wouldn't have known what hit her.'

'I bet she did,' Gina said. 'It was a fist, I reckon, and she'd see that coming. Knew who threw the punch, as well, I expect.' She sat on the edge of Mick's desk. 'So no one has come forward to claim her? Did Avery put her photos out, as well as my sketch?'

'The sketch went out on Anglia News and the photos to Detective Reagan. You'd think someone would have missed the poor little thing by now.'

Gina sighed. 'Not if she's another Donna. Her mum only came forward to get fifteen minutes of fame on TV. She's a nasty piece of work, that woman.' She looked at Mick. 'Can you do me a favour? Can you let me know if the girl is identified?'

'Because?'

'Because Reagan told me to stay away. He won't tell me anything, and everyone at the station treats me like a new form of plague.'

'Not to get anywhere near you if they value their lives?'

'Exactly.'

'Just because it's you and I love you, I'll see what I can do.'

'How's it going with the hunt for Donna Price's killer?'

Mick shook his head and a pink curl tumbled on to his forehead. 'No idea. The last I heard they were questioning all the students who might have used the cycle path, and that's going to take forever. She was hit on the head with a rock or a big stone, but nothing special about that either, according to Sheila Avery. The killer most likely dropped it amongst a load of others exactly the same. Then it rained for a couple of days and that would've washed off any blood. A perfect murder weapon.'

'Does Reagan still think we have a serial killer on our hands?'

'You don't? Same type of killing, a blow to the head, even though Avery is sure that was a fist and not a rock. Someone who loses their temper easily and no rocks about the second time.'

'But why pregnant girls? There's no sense to it.'

Mick pushed the curl back into place with a flick of a chubby finger. 'They were both teenagers who got themselves into trouble. Could be someone with a religious axe to grind.'

Gina thought of Sophie's dad. She couldn't quite see the vicar brandishing a bloody great rock, but it was a thought.

She thanked Mick and left, sitting in her car while she mulled over what to do next. She could catch up with Megan who was probably off to the clubs, but that wouldn't help the still-hovering headache. And there was something niggling at the back of her mind. She remembered reading somewhere that the best place to hide something is in a place that has already been searched. Her mind made up, she started the engine and headed for the country lanes again.

If it hadn't been for the lights of the bungalows, the lane would have been scarily dark. Lucinda's driveway was empty and there was no gleam of light through the Venetian blinds on the front window, so hopefully the woman was still at the hospital. The layout of Lucinda's house appeared to be the same as next door, with the kitchen at the front and the living room at the back. There was always a chance that Sophie was living there, but there seemed no reason for Lucinda to lie.

So what about next door? The empty house with the bloodstain on the floor.

Gina left her car at the bottom of the lane and walked past the two cottages. As she slipped under the wire into the field, she looked back over her shoulder and saw a black car pull up in front of one of the bungalows. She stood still for a moment. The headlights went off, but as far as she could see no one got out. Strange. She waited a few moments longer and then shrugged. What someone did in their own car was none of her business.

Her eyes were becoming accustomed to the dark, but her feet kept going down potholes, and when there was a sudden noise behind her she spun round, startled. Something ran past her, only a few inches from her feet, and she stifled a scream. She really didn't like fields very much at all, particularly in the dark. She stood still for a few minutes until she had overcome the desire to run back to her car.

At the back of the house she lifted the gate as she opened it to stop it catching on the paving slabs and making a noise. The house looked darker than ever, the garden even more overgrown, but she thought she could see a tiny glint of light through the downstairs window behind the bush. She moved closer, testing each paving slab before she stepped on it in case one of them rocked and tripped her up. The sky was overcast with a hint of rain in the air, and the garden smelt of wet wood and fungus. Small noises coming from the field behind the house made her pull her hood up over her head. Whether it was rats or only baby rabbits, she didn't want to listen to them.

Lucinda's house was as dark at the back as it was at the front, but there was definitely a glow of light coming from the window of the empty house. Trying desperately not to rustle bushes or trip on stones, she moved to the back door. Now what? No way was she going to try and jemmy a window again. It was going to have to be the bold approach. Before she could change her mind, she knocked on the door.

The light in the window went out but nothing else happened.

This wasn't working. Even though Lucinda didn't appear to be home next door, Gina was wary of shouting. She pressed her mouth against the crack in the door and called out as loudly as she dare. 'Sophie? Are you in there? It's Gina, Jack's friend. Please open the door.'

The door opened so suddenly she stepped back in shock and almost fell. There was a shape in the gloom, much too tall to be Sophie, and then a hand grabbed her arm and pulled her inside.

22

'What are you doing here?' Roddy McBride hissed, as he closed the door behind Gina. 'The woman next door will be home any minute.'

'Lucinda Valentine. I know. Is Sophie here?'

Roddy walked into the living room and turned on a low wattage table lamp. 'How did you find me?'

'I didn't know you were going to be here. I'm looking for Sophie. The baby's due in a few days. Where is she, Roddy?'

He shook his head. 'I don't know. I really don't know. Lucinda doesn't know either, or says she doesn't. Sophie was staying here, waiting for the baby to come. Amber's dad had arranged an adoption, but we decided to keep it.' Just for a second a little smile played round his mouth. 'It's mine. Did you know that?'

Gina nodded impatiently. 'Yes, I know that. What happened, Roddy? Start at the beginning and tell me exactly what happened.'

He was quiet for a moment. 'D'you want a beer. Got a couple in the fridge. Sophie won't drink now. Before, it didn't matter, the baby was going to belong to someone else.' When Gina shook her head, he went into the kitchen and came back with a can of beer. 'I knew it was mine, right from the start, but we both had things we wanted to do. Sophie wanted to get a degree and I wanted to do gigs all over the world. No time for a baby, but she'd left it a bit late to do anything about it. She told her mum, and Mrs Lowry asked Dr Beaumont if Sophie could have the baby at his hospital. Quiet like, with nobody knowing, not even Sophie's dad. Doctor Beaumont offered to arrange an adoption, and it seemed like a good idea. Sophie went away with Amber for the summer so her dad wouldn't see her getting bigger, and told her tutors she was taking a gap year. She knew her dad wouldn't check, he left that kind of thing to her mum, and her brother was away in Thailand. Sophie lived in her brother's house for a while.'

'But then?'

'By the time Sophie got back from Spain the baby was moving around. It was like, you know, a real person. She got me to feel it and it was, like, in there rolling around and kicking.' He pressed his lips together. 'So we decided to keep it.'

'Give up the gigs and university?'

'Sophie thought her mum would look after the baby some of the time and she could get a degree doing evening classes. She was going to tell her dad, she reckoned he'd come around in the end, but her mum said not to.' He finished his beer and took a breath. 'Couple of days ago she was going to tell Lucinda she'd decided to keep the baby.' His Adam's apple bobbed. 'When I got back here she'd gone, so had all her clothes and things. Now I don't know where to look for her.'

'Do you think she might have left of her own accord, Roddy?' Gina said gently. 'Maybe she thought about keeping the baby and got scared. Perhaps she changed her mind again. Went to stay with a friend.'

'She told all her mates she was going back to Spain to work for a year. None of them knows she's still in this country, or that she's pregnant.' He put his hand in his pocket and held out a gold earring with a small blue stone. 'Besides, she wouldn't go without this. They were a present from her mum and dad. She lost the other one.'

'It's not lost; her brother has it.' Gina thought for a moment. 'Is the whole of Willow Bank in on this adoption scam?' He was quiet for so long Gina thought he wasn't going to answer. 'I've changed my mind about the beer,' she said.

He brought two more cans from the kitchen. 'Might as well sit down. I don't know all of it, but I'll tell you what I do know if you want.'

Gina sank into a reasonably comfortable chair and pulled the tag on the can. She glanced at the label. It was difficult to see in the gloom, but the brand was one she hadn't heard of. A supermarket special. Her stomach rumbled audibly. 'Got anything to eat?' she asked.

He shook his head. 'Beer is all. Doctor Beaumont made a mistake a while back trying to help some woman who couldn't have a baby. She said he promised her a baby to take home, and when she didn't get the baby she tried to sue him. Doctor Beaumont's lawyer made out the woman was nuts. She'd had loads of fertility treatment costing thousands of pounds, and the lawyer said all the stress had sent her daft.'

'How do you know all this?'

'Amber told me. She was really worried for her dad at the time. Then some people in America found out what he'd done and threatened him. Lucinda Valentine told him she'd find girls who didn't want to keep their babies and all Dr Beaumont had to do was deliver them and not record the birth. Amber thinks he's doing it to help people.'

'But he gets a cut of the profits?'

Roddy shrugged.

'How many people knew all this?'

'Not many. Doctor Beaumont, Lucinda Valentine, Amber, Sophie and me.' He thought for a moment. 'The gynaecologist's a daft old git who thinks they're doing a drug trial. Oh, and Crawford, the guy you met at the club. I never worked out what he does. I know he has a gun.'

'I thought he was a bouncer at your club.'

'He was keeping an eye on me and Amber. Amber knew her dad was going to arrange for Sophie's baby to be adopted, but when she found out the baby was going to some rich woman whose IVF had failed, she asked her dad what the fuck was going on and he told her.'

'And then Sophie decided to keep the baby.'

Roddy swallowed. 'They won't let her do that, will they?'

Gina gnawed her bottom lip. God, what a mess. 'Sophie must be at Willow Bank. That's the only place she can be.'

'You think they've kidnapped her?'

'Not necessarily. She might have gone into labour early, or gone to the hospital of her own accord.' Gina set her empty beer can on the floor and sat staring at it. 'But I don't believe Doctor Beaumont is as innocent as he pretends to be. I can't believe he'd start selling babies just because someone threatened him. This isn't a one off. I think he'd already got a nice little sideline going and Lucinda and her husband decided to cash in on it.'

'If they've got Sophie they'll take the baby away and we'll never get it back.' He downed the rest of his beer and tossed the can in a waste bin. 'If Sophie was OK she'd have texted me.'

'I'll try and talk to Reagan again, off the record.' She wasn't interfering in his case, she told herself. This was about Sophie. 'Who put Lucinda's leaflet under my door?'

Roddy looked sheepish. 'I did. Amber told me you'd been round to her house asking questions. Sophie was freaked out about them taking the baby away from us and I knew you worked for the police. Lucinda was on the other end of that phone number, and I wanted the police to stop her handing our baby over to some poxy stranger.'

'Even if Doctor Beaumont got struck off?'

He lifted his shoulders. 'I don't really care.'

Gina looked at her watch and stood up. 'I have to go.' She felt the beer as soon as she got on her feet. Only three halves, but too much on an empty stomach. She had read somewhere that alcohol affected the system in relation to body mass, and she didn't have a lot of that. 'I think I'd better call a taxi. Adam can run me back tomorrow to pick up my car.' She looked at Roddy. 'It'll be all right, won't it, parked outside the bungalows?'

'Yeah. People'll think you're visiting someone. It won't get broken into round here. Can't have a taxi pull up outside, though. The Valentine woman might be back any minute.' He turned the light out. 'I'm going to kip down here in case Sophie turns up, but you can have a taxi meet you at the pub. I'll walk you there and pick up another pack of beer.'

Gina used her mobile to call a taxi and then slipped out of the back door with Roddy. The hike through the bushes wasn't as bad this time. He found a path through the undergrowth that left her legs scratch free. The walk to the pub took another ten minutes and the taxi arrived a few minutes later. As she climbed into the cab, she watched Roddy walk dejectedly into the bar.

★　★　★

The man in the black car sat staring at the dark house. What was she doing in there? He'd followed her round the back and seen her knock on the door. He'd only had a brief glimpse of the man who hauled her inside the house, but it had been enough. Crawford knew Roddy McBride only too well. So why was the little forensic artist visiting McBride in an empty house? The big man reached under the dash for a pack of cigarettes and took one out, lighting it with the onboard lighter. An hour later he looked at his watch and grinned to himself. Well, well, well, who'd have thought it? It didn't look as if she was coming out again. He lit another cigarette and settled down for a long wait. Her little red Metro was still parked at the end of the road, and he had a good view of it. His brief was to watch and wait, and that's exactly what he intended to do.

She couldn't go anywhere without him knowing about it.

23

The steps to Gina's flat were empty. She had half hoped she would find Adam sitting there, the proverbial bad penny, but no such luck. As she had noticed before, he was never around when she needed him. She let herself into her flat, checking the answer phone and her mobile again in case she'd missed a call. She got a pack of macaroni cheese out of the freezer, trying to decide what to do next. Eating was a priority, she needed something in her stomach to soak up the beer, but then she would have to decide whether or not to phone Adam.

When the doorbell rang, it made her jump.

This time, Adam didn't attempt to come in. 'I'm sorry,' he said. 'I shouldn't try to tell you what to do.'

Gina held the door open. 'I'm glad you said try.' At least he had apologized, although he should know by now that she didn't respond well to being ordered around. She let him follow her inside. 'I was going to call you after I'd eaten. If I'd sat on my backside like you wanted me to, I wouldn't have found Roddy. He was at the empty house, but Sophie's not with him. He doesn't know where she is.'

Adam glanced at the unopened macaroni carton. 'You haven't eaten yet?' When she shook her head, he smiled. 'Right then, I've come to take you out. We can talk over dinner.'

She yawned, looking at her watch. It was almost nine o'clock. 'Thanks Adam, but it's late, and I don't think I've got the energy to go out.'

'Takeaway?'

'Not pizza. I can't face another pizza.' She looked longingly at her macaroni cheese. 'I've got another one of those in the freezer.'

'Salad?'

'Yes, I think so. There should be a bag in the fridge drawer.'

While she put mats and cutlery on the table, he found a bag of salad and fresh tomatoes. Ciabatta rolls, bottled olives tipped into a dish, and a rather strong virgin oil Gina had bought on a whim, gave the meal a rustic, Italian feel.

'I've got red wine in the car,' Adam said. 'I didn't bring it up with me in case you thought I was trying to seduce you.'

'Red wine always works,' she said with a smile. 'I've got balsamic vinegar to go with the oil, and we can have the salad with the macaroni. Do you want extra cheese on top?'

While he ran back down the stairs to his car, she microwaved the macaroni, added more cheese, and put it under the grill to brown. The rolls only took a moment to warm through and then she sliced them for dipping. 'I don't cook,' she told him when he came back upstairs. 'This is as near as I get.'

He sat across the table from her. 'I saw Jack today. His father still hasn't got a clue what's going on. He's gone back to look after his parish. Jack's mum is still here in Castlebury, staying at Jack's house. She's spoken to Lucinda Valentine and the woman swears she doesn't know where Sophie is.'

Gina held a dripping piece of ciabatta in one hand and a forkful of macaroni in the other. She wondered how food that had been thrown together could taste so good. When her mouth was empty, she took a sip of wine. 'I think Lucinda knows exactly where Sophie is. I think Sophie's at the hospital. That's the only place she can be.' She told Adam about her conversation with Roddy. 'I think Sophie was moved to the hospital as soon as they found out she wanted to keep the baby, and then Lucinda told Mrs Lowry her daughter had gone missing. They need that baby, Adam. It's probably already been paid for.'

He finished his food and pushed his plate away. 'If Sophie is at Willow Bank, she's in the best place. If the baby is that important, they'll look after the mother. They won't want another incident like Donna.'

Gina picked up the plates and loaded them into the dishwasher. 'Who killed Donna?' she said, as she came back into the room. 'And how about the other girl? The one who died with her baby still on board? What if she decided to keep *her* baby and someone got angry and bashed her face in? Do you really think Sophie's in the best place?'

Adam poured the last of the wine into her glass and Gina tried to remember how much she had drunk already. Reluctantly, she handed her glass back to him. 'You drink it. I'm sure I've had enough, and I need to talk this through with you while I'm sober. The sixty-four dollar question: shall I go and see Reagan, or will that make things worse?'

'It may not make things worse, but what good will it do? You have no evidence that points a finger at the hospital or the Valentine woman. Reagan can hardly send a task force to raid the hospital and rescue Sophie on your say-so, so what's he going to do? If he speaks to Valentine or Beaumont they'll deny everything and make you look a right idiot.'

She took the glass out of his hand, took a sip, and handed it back. 'I'm just worried about Sophie.'

'First babies are rarely early, so I've been told, which means we still have a couple of weeks before we need to panic.' He put down his glass and leant across the table to take her hands. 'Donna probably had an argument with an old boyfriend, or she confronted the father of her baby and he panicked. There's no evidence the second girl had anything to do with Donna or the hospital. Sophie is safe, I'm sure of it.'

Gina shook her head. She didn't need evidence. She could see the lines that tied the three girls together, Sophie, Donna, and the unidentified body. Also, and this was something that really frightened her, a tenuous, almost invisible thread joining Megan to the other three.

She took her hands back reluctantly. 'I know you're trying to make me feel better, but something is wrong, Adam, and I'm scared for that baby. Once it's sold, it's lost for good, Sophie and Roddy will never see it again.' She stood up and pushed her chair back under the table. 'Have you heard from your friend yet? He was going to show my sketch of Lucinda around, wasn't he?'

Adam flipped open his phone. 'I'd completely forgotten about that, but no time like the present.'

He watched the radiating waves on the dial

of his phone for a moment and then cancelled the call. 'Not answering, and I can't leave a message. Bradford's not supposed to have any contact with journalists. He'll check out his missed calls and get back to me.'

She yawned again. 'I forgot to ask. Can you do me a favour and run me back to pick up my car tomorrow some time? I had a couple of beers to keep Roddy talking and then realized I'd had too much alcohol to drive back here. I left my car parked outside one of the bungalows.'

'Sure, no problem. I'll come by at lunchtime if I can, if not, early evening.' He started for the door. 'Gina, I'm sorry I can't make this all go away, and I don't want to seem as if I'm bossing you about, but I'm sure it will all sort itself out without you. You scare me when you go diving off on your own and I don't know where you are.'

'I don't like having to be accountable to anyone, Adam. I don't want you to worry about me. I'm not your responsibility. I'm not your wife.'

She had no idea why she said that, and when he looked at her it was her turn to be scared.

'Is that all it would take? If I was married to you I could boss you about?'

'That wasn't what I meant,' she said

uneasily. No eyes should be that blue, particularly not a man's. 'I thought you were leaving.'

'I was, but this is interesting. So you have considered getting married one day.'

She moved away from him. 'Not really. Have you?'

'Once or twice, but it didn't work out. I'm waiting for the perfect woman.' He caught her round the waist and pulled her against him. 'And if that ever happens, I'll make damned sure my wife does what she's told.' He bent his head and kissed her lightly on the mouth, then held her at arm's length. 'But all that's irrelevant as far as you're concerned, isn't it Gina? You're the girl who doesn't want to get involved with anyone.' He put a finger on her lips to stop her speaking. 'I think you're just scared.'

She was. Absolutely terrified. Marriage, sharing a house, babies. Probably a dog or a cat, or something equally smelly and hairy. And finding someone in bed with you when you woke up in the morning. Every morning. No, it just couldn't be done. But — and this was a little but that sneaked in when she wasn't looking — was it really better to spend your life alone?

Adam waved a hand in front of her face. 'You are tired, aren't you? I thought you'd gone to sleep standing up. Go to bed, Gina. I'll see you tomorrow.' He grinned. 'And I promise not to propose.'

After he'd gone, she walked to the window and opened it, watching the tail lights of his car disappear up the hill. Being married to someone as bossy and opinionated as Adam would be a nightmare. She wasn't surprised he hadn't found his perfect woman.

As she got ready for bed, she wondered why she'd included babies in the things she didn't want to do. Soon, she wouldn't have an option. It would be too late. Her thirtieth birthday loomed on the horizon and her biological clock would start to grind to a halt. Not that it mattered, of course. The last thing she wanted was a baby. She wondered if she would have felt differently if her parents had been alive. If she had a mother desperate for a grandchild, or a father eager to bounce another baby girl on his shoulders, would it really make a difference? Or did she really lack the maternal gene altogether?

The next day Adam arrived just after they had closed the shop for lunch.

'Bring your sandwich with you,' he told her. 'I'll drop you at your car, but I can't be too long because I've got an appointment with Bradford Norman.' Once she was safely buckled in, he swung the car out on to the road and headed out of town. 'Brad got back to me. He thinks he may have a hit on your sketch. There was a similar case of babies being sold to order in a couple of the southern states a few years ago. Maybe a wider area, according to the records, but the couple involved moved too fast for the police to catch up with them. Then it all went quiet and the case was put on hold. He has got some photos to show me that may tie it all together.'

'It reminds me a bit of the film *Gone in Sixty Seconds*,' Gina said. 'Where they had to steal a particular make of car in a race against time. This is the same, isn't it? The hospital has to deliver a blonde, blue-eyed baby to a client within a specific time frame.' She turned to look at Adam. 'Do you think they want Megan as a back-up in case something else goes wrong?'

'Possibly. Like I said, keep her away from Willow Bank.'

'They only want her back to get the results of her blood test. She won't be in any danger. I doubt everyone at the hospital is involved in the adoption scam.'

He didn't answer for a minute or two and she could see frown lines creasing his forehead. 'You didn't tell me they did a blood test on Megan as well. I know she took the urine sample from a pregnant friend, but the blood must have been her own.'

'Of course it was,' Gina said. Adam's tone of voice was worrying her. 'Does it matter? The nurse told Megan they just wanted to make sure she was healthy; no drugs in her system or anything like that. They wouldn't be able to tell the blood and urine were from two different people, would they?'

'Maybe not, but they would be able to tell the person who gave the blood wasn't pregnant. If the urine sample gave a positive reading and the blood didn't, they couldn't both be from the same person.'

Gina swallowed. 'So they know Megan is trying to con them.'

He pulled into the lane and parked behind her car. 'They do now.' He waited while she got out and then rolled down his window. 'I've got to go. I don't want to keep Brad waiting. Just don't let Megan anywhere near Willow Bank.'

She watched him drive away before she unlocked her car and got in. She drove to the end of the lane to turn round, glancing at Lucinda's house. The woman's car wasn't in the driveway and there was no sign of life in either house. She wondered if Roddy was still in the empty house, hoping Sophie might come back. Just as she was about to drive away, something banged the back of her car. Puzzled, she put her foot on the brake and looked in the rear-view mirror.

Crawford's face was staring at her from behind the car.

For a moment her mind went blank. She couldn't remember what gear made the car go forward and she was afraid to put her foot on the accelerator in case she ran him over. Why this bothered her, she had no idea. Before she had time to sort herself out, he opened the passenger door and slid in beside her.

'Don't try and go anywhere.'

She reached for the door handle, but he draped an arm casually over her shoulder and the excruciating pain that shot into her head completely incapacitated her. The scream that bubbled up inside her died before it could be heard, and all she could manage was a feeble moan. Most of her body appeared to be paralysed and she remembered Adam telling her there was a pressure point in her neck that could kill her. Now was not the time to cause trouble.

'You don't need to speak,' Crawford told her conversationally. 'All you need to do is listen.' He took his arm away and she felt a tingling sensation, but she still couldn't move. 'If you want your friend's sister back safe and sound, you need to stay away from the hospital. Running to the police won't help. Beaumont has friends there. Whatever you tell the police, they won't believe you.' He leaned towards her, invading her space. 'So back off, little lady. Don't start a fight you can't win. Make any more trouble and there might be another body in the ditch.' When she tried to speak he laughed. 'It'll take about half an hour to wear off, then you can drive home and get on with your life. No one need get hurt here. It's up to you.'

He got out of her car and slammed the door. She watched him walk up the road, get in the black car with the tinted windows, and drive away.

She managed to get her car moving after fifteen minutes. She did think of knocking on the door of one of the bungalows and phoning Reagan, but she could imagine his reaction. He'd probably have her committed to the nearest mental institution.

Driving proved quite difficult with dead feet and tingling hands, but she wanted to get home, and waiting any longer to recover the use of her limbs was not an option. She managed to get almost to the main road before disaster struck.

Her right foot was still numb, and halfway round a corner she pressed too hard on the accelerator and drove straight into a ditch. The whole thing happened quite slowly, but her foot wouldn't move fast enough from the accelerator to the brake. Not waiting until she was fully functional had proved to be really stupid.

She sat quite still for a moment, before undoing her seat belt and getting out of the car. Apart from a peculiar trembling in her extremities, most parts of her body appeared to be working again. Her car had a slight dent in the front where it had hit a tree root, but otherwise everything seemed to be intact. Whether she could drive it out of the ditch or not was another matter.

Five minutes later she knew she couldn't. Moving the car backwards and forwards just drove it deeper into the mud. She tried her mobile phone, reasonably sure she wouldn't get a signal, and she was right. So, forcing her legs to behave themselves, she started walking. She had no sense of direction but always took markers when she was driving, and a particularly strange looking tree told her she wasn't far from the pub.

'You're back.' The woman behind the bar continued polishing glasses. 'Drink?'

'Yes, please.' Gina didn't often drink spirits, but she asked for a neat brandy.

'Early,' the woman said.

252

Gina had to think about that one. Early for brandy? Early to be in a pub? Or just early in the day?

'Yes,' she agreed, covering all the options. 'My car went into a ditch just round the corner. Shook me up a bit. I need to phone someone to get me out and I couldn't get a signal on my mobile.'

The woman handed Gina what looked like a double brandy. She didn't offer soda. Coming out from behind the bar she opened a door into a back room. 'You lot. Out here. Now.'

The first person to appear was an older man with a ruddy face. Gina thought he looked a bit like Inspector Reagan. He was followed by two other men, both younger, both dressed in jeans and waxed jackets with heavy boots on their feet.

'Another one in a ditch,' the woman said. 'Go see if you can help.'

'Finish your drink,' one of the younger men said to Gina. 'Happens all the time round here. No room to pass. Shakes you up a bit, though.'

She nodded, finishing her drink in one go and shuddering as the fiery liquid hit the back of her throat. It was easier to agree. 'Thanks, I'll show you.'

The men stood on the grass verge looking

at her car, and then all three of them climbed into the ditch and put her car back on the road with one concerted shove. Gina thanked them profusely and blew a kiss out of the window as she drove off. She didn't like the country with its creepy-crawlies and dark little lanes, but the local people were lovely.

24

Adam met Bradford Norman at a different location, this time in a small wine bar hidden in the back alleys of the town. Brad was already sitting at a table, two glasses of beer in front of him. He waited until Adam was seated, pushed a glass towards him, and then handed him a fat envelope.

'Not much doubt in my mind,' he said, 'but a hand-drawn sketch won't count as evidence. You've got file notes in there as well, and a couple of photos, the one you took of Lucinda Valentine and one from the LAPD.'

Adam tipped the photos out of the envelope, careful not to put them down anywhere. The table was damp with beer and splattered with unidentifiable smears. He peered at the first photo and then reached into his pocket and took out his reading glasses, balancing them on the bridge of his nose. The light was so dim he could have done with a torch, but the likeness to Gina's sketch was immediate. A fair-haired Lucinda Valentine looked back at him. There was no sign of a mole.

'That's a chap called Crawford,' he said,

pointing to a man standing next to the younger version of Lucinda.

Brad leant across the table to look at the photo. 'Her husband.'

Adam raised an eyebrow. 'That's something we didn't know.'

'You've got a copy of everything, which is not a lot. As I said, they moved too fast for the LAPD to keep up with them.'

'Well, it looks like they're working over here now. I'll have to speak to Reagan, but whatever is going on at Willow Bank involves Dr Beaumont and, indirectly, Jack's dad. His daughter is pregnant and missing, and we think these two,' he pointed to the photo, 'are organizing illegal adoptions.' He thought for a moment. 'Do you know anything about the second girl who got killed? The one who had her face smashed in?'

'Natalie Mitchell. Her dad was arrested yesterday. Found out his darling daughter was pregnant and lost it, evidently. Punched her in the face in a fit of temper and killed her. Once we pulled him in he couldn't wait to confess. All a terrible accident, he said. Just meant to teach her a lesson.'

'So her death has nothing to do with Donna Price, even though they were both hit in the head and the bodies found in the same place?'

Bradford grinned. 'Yes and no. Daddy was so filled with remorse, he confessed on Facebook. That's how we found him. Someone on the Facebook website put two and two together and tipped us off. But — and this is the funny part — someone also emailed the girl's father and suggested he dump the body of his daughter in the same ditch as Donna Price. Make it look like a serial killer and throw the police off the scent. They were assuming all policemen are stupid.'

'And they're not?' Adam said in mock surprise.

He bought Brad another beer and thanked him for the information. He needed to get back to somewhere with some light, and a table clean enough to spread out the documents he had been given.

* * *

Gina tried to phone Adam as soon as she got back to the studio but, unsurprisingly, his phone was switched off. She left a message for him to call her.

'You've only just left him,' Megan said. 'What do you need to phone him about?'

'I just wanted to thank him. He had to leave in a rush because he had an

257

appointment with someone.' She'd gone upstairs to her flat to change her muddy boots before she went into the studio. She was feeling fine now, and there was no need to worry Megan unnecessarily.

Adam rang back half an hour later. 'What's up?' Short and sweet as usual.

'Did you get anything from your police contact? Anything useful?'

'Could be. I'm sorting out the stuff Brad gave me now. I'll come round this evening. Do you want me to bring food?'

'Indian,' she said. 'And onion bhagees and all the other bits. Oh, and red wine.'

'Right. I'll make a shopping list,' he said. 'See you later.'

Gina was beginning to feel a tightness over her rib cage. She had gone off the road in a car once before, and knew the damage a seat belt can do. This was mild by comparison, and she got through the rest of the day with just a couple of paracetamol tablets. Even so, she was glad to lock up and climb the stairs to her flat.

The luxury of a warm bath soothed her nerve endings and eased the rest of her aches and pains. She had been going too slowly to do much damage, but the odd bruise was beginning to make itself felt. By the time Adam arrived, she was feeling back to normal.

She could smell the food before she opened the door and was salivating by the time she let him in. He dumped the bags on her kitchen counter and looked at her curiously. 'You sounded funny on the phone. What's up?'

'Please can we eat first? I'm starving, and I hope you brought wine because I don't have any.'

'As per your order, ma'am. A bottle of South African Cabernet Sauvignon. I see you've set the table, so I'll get the glasses.' He poured the wine and then stood blocking the kitchen door. 'But you don't get to eat until you tell me what you rang me about. I'm sure it wasn't just to order dinner.'

'After you left me . . . ' Why was it so difficult to talk about it? 'Crawford suddenly appeared and got into the car with me. He warned me to stay away from the hospital or Sophie would get hurt. Maybe finish up like Donna.' She took a breath. 'You know that business with the nerves in the neck? The place where if you press hard enough you can kill someone? Well, he used it on me. My hands and feet were a bit numb for a while, that's why I drove my car into a ditch, but three nice farmer men from the pub pushed me out, and I'm fine, so can we eat now, please?'

He closed his eyes for a moment, and then

moved out of her way. 'Are you hurt?'

She grinned at him. 'You sounded really concerned there for a minute.'

'Christ, Gina, why do these things always happen to you? You're not safe to be let out on your own.'

'Gee, thanks,' she said. 'Sympathy was just what I needed.' She had heated plates and tipped out the food, still hot, and smelling even more wonderful close up. 'Let's eat, and then I'll tell you all about it.'

In between mouthfuls of red wine and curry, she told him about her encounter with Crawford.

'Crawford is Lucinda Valentine's husband,' Adam said. 'He's in the photo Brad got faxed over from America. I think we have something tangible now to show Reagan.'

'Should we do that? I don't care about the doctor, but Mr Lowry's parishioners won't be happy with their vicar's daughter running off with a DJ and getting pregnant. Particularly when he preaches abstinence before marriage. He'll lose his job, Adam.'

'I don't think we can leave things the way they are. What they're doing at Willow Bank is illegal at the very least.'

'Will telling the police what we know help Sophie, or make it even more dangerous for her?'

He shook his head. 'I don't know.'

She picked up the plates and took them into the kitchen before sitting back down at the table. 'Show me the photo.'

He handed her the print. Lucinda and Crawford, standing on a street corner somewhere, caught by a surveillance camera. In the background a man was waiting to cross the road.

'The third person in the photo, the man in the background . . . '

'What about him?'

'He looks like my father.'

Adam stared at her. 'Your father?'

She shook her head. 'No, it's not my father, it just looks like him, like he'd look now. But it's not him.'

'I can find him for you,' Adam said quietly. 'If he's still alive, I can find him for you, Gina. That's my job.'

'I don't want you to find him. I want him dead. Because if he's dead, he has an excuse for not trying to find me.'

There had to be a reason her father hadn't come looking for her. Her mother had died when the plane crashed into the sea, but Gina had discovered her father wasn't on the plane, and no amount of searching had thrown up any clues as to where he might be. All she knew was that she had been left with her grandmother when she was four years

261

old, and had never seen either of her parents again.

Adam picked up the photo and stared at it. 'You're quite sure it's not him?'

'Quite sure.' She took a breath and stared at the photo. She had to let her father go. Forget the images that popped into her head when she was least expecting it. Forget the days, only half remembered, of picnics and beaches and rides on ponies. Forget the house where they'd lived. A house near the sea, with a big kitchen and a little pink bedroom. She could see the house quite plainly in her mind and she could remember the picture of fairies on her bedroom wall, the blanket with the satin edge she liked to stroke, and the sound of her mother's laughter downstairs; but now she wasn't even sure the house existed, and she had learned not to trust her memories.

'Crawford got that scar quite recently,' she told Adam. 'Less than two years ago, so the photo must have been taken before then.'

Adam was staring at her again. 'How do you know that? How could you possibly know that?'

'The same way I know that man is not my father. And please don't look at me as if I'm a freak, Adam. I get enough of that from everyone else.'

He tipped the papers from the envelope on to the table. 'There might be something in with this lot. Something that will help. Like where they were when the photo was taken.'

She picked up a sheet of paper. 'This is dated three years ago, but I bet Crawford and Lucinda didn't sit around doing nothing for a couple of years. They've been doing the same thing somewhere else, but didn't get caught. Or almost *did* get caught. That's when they moved on, isn't it?'

Adam was already reading the first of two pages that had been stapled together. 'They were registered as Mr and Mrs Crawford in America, so he used his real name but she didn't. The idiot used his passport to open a bank account, that's how the Los Angeles police got on to him. Mind you, they may not be married. No one bothered to check once they disappeared.' He turned over a page. 'Same thing happened out there, by the looks of it. Someone didn't get a baby they'd paid for and complained to the police. The Crawfords weren't using a hospital in Los Angeles, just advertising locally for pregnant girls and then collecting the babies and selling them after they were born, but the MO was more or less the same. Willow Bank must have been a real bonus. A nice medical facility with a maternity unit and a built in supply of clients.'

'Did they come to England when they read about Willow Bank, or do you reckon they were already here?'

'I'll find out what they were doing for those missing years. Like I told you once before, people leave a paper trail of some sort however careful they are. Crawford nearly got caught because he opened a bank account. They will have made other mistakes. The LAPD weren't that bothered because nobody died. Or at least, not as far as they know. We were lucky to get a copy of the file. The more information we can get, the better.'

He stacked the papers together and then held out his hand for the photo. He glanced at it briefly before dropping it in the envelope with the papers. 'If you don't let me track him down, Gina, you'll never know why he didn't come and get you.'

She sighed. 'Please don't fight with me, Adam. My ribs hurt, I'm tired, and we only have a few days to find Sophie or go to the police. We can't leave it any longer, can we? She might be alone somewhere with no one to help her.'

'Are you sure her mother wasn't lying again?'

'What would be the point? Mrs Lowry

came to me. I didn't ask for the information. She was quite happy when she thought Sophie was being looked after by Lucinda. She wanted the baby gone and everything back to normal. Now she's scared that's not going to happen, and she's worried sick about her daughter. I think she's blaming herself.'

'So she should,' Adam said dismissively. 'I'll phone the hospital and see if I can get an interview with Dr Beaumont. It's no good turning up without an appointment, he'll smell a rat, but in a face to face with him I can probably find out whether he's farming babies for money, or whether he's doing it because he's being blackmailed. By the way, I checked the hospital records and got another bit of information. The doctor is mortgaged up to his eyeballs. He actually owns the hospital. He's not just a figurehead.'

'So it's not only his job he's worried about?'

'No. If he can't keep up the mortgage payments, he'll lose the hospital. It's just possible he found the Crawfords. Not the other way around.'

Gina closed her eyes. 'Go home Adam. I need to sleep.'

He smiled at her. 'It's been a long day for you. I'll stay if you want. Settle for a cuddle.'

'Since when have you been able to settle for a cuddle?'

He looked hurt. 'I remember one time.'

'Yeah.' She held the door open for him. 'The time I was unconscious.'

25

Megan unlocked the door into the studio and saw the message light flashing. She looked at her watch. Not quite 8.30. Someone was eager. She slung her bag on the floor and settled in her swivel chair. She liked unlocking the studio first thing in the morning and having the place all to herself. Four years ago she wouldn't have believed it was possible to actually enjoy working.

She had left home to get away from her mother, an alcoholic with a police record for soliciting, and moved in with an on/off boyfriend who was a registered drug addict living in a one-bedroom flat provided by the council. He persuaded Megan to help with the rent and then spent the money on drugs. When she took the job with Gina he was under threat of eviction and she was bordering on desperate.

The message on the answer phone was from the hospital, brief and to the point. They wanted her back as soon as possible to discuss the results of her blood test. What was there to discuss, she wondered? Unless the hospital had discovered something nasty in her blood. A terminal illness, or something.

Before she frightened herself to death, she turned on the computer and checked the appointments for the day. The first one was scheduled for ten o'clock and she wanted to go to the hospital as soon as possible. If there was something wrong, she needed to know, not sit about all morning thinking she might have leukaemia. She decided to hop on a bus and go to Willow Bank right away. With a bit of luck, she'd be back well within the hour. She knew she ought to wait for Gina to come down from her flat, but then she'd have to argue the point and that would waste time. Gina was bound to try and stop her going, or want to go with her, and Megan didn't want anyone with her. Not if it was bad news.

In the end she decided to leave a note.

The bus was full of school kids, but she didn't mind standing for the short journey. Her mobile rang, but she glanced at the dial and turned it off. She got off the bus and walked the few yards to the hospital entrance. Not for the first time, she wished she had been going through these doors when she was expecting Rosie. Not that she thought the outcome would have been any different, and the treatment she had received at the general hospital was second to none, but swanning around in a fluffy white dressing gown at

Willow Bank seemed a much better option.

She pushed open the double doors and got a big smile from the girl behind the reception desk. Everyone here was happy happy happy. The waiting area was huge. A curved counter took up most of one long wall, a large plasma screen was showing breakfast television with the sound turned down, and cream leather sofas and chairs were artistically grouped round small tables stacked with magazines. *The Lady* and *Homes and Gardens* seemed to dominate. Megan couldn't see one copy of *Chat* or *Take a Break*.

'How may I help you?'

Megan walked up to the counter. 'I have to see someone about my test results. I had a message to call in.'

The girl consulted her computer screen. 'You're red-flagged. That means Ms Valentine wants to see you personally. If you'll take a seat for a moment, I'll page her.'

Megan walked across the enormous expanse of polished floor to a leather chair. She sat down and picked up a magazine. Red-flagged? What did that mean? Perhaps she really did have something wrong with her — or they'd found out she'd lied to them. That thought was more frightening than having a terminal illness. All she could do was sit tight and wait. No one was going to try to murder her in a posh private hospital. Someone might try and save her.

Feeling restless, she took a wander round the reception area before sitting down again. She was glancing through a magazine full of designer furniture when Doctor Beaumont appeared from a doorway and started talking to the receptionist.

Megan cursed herself for not sitting nearer to the desk where she might have been able to hear what was being said. When the doctor started across the room towards her she nearly dropped her magazine. Had they found a fatal illness that had been lurking undetected for years? Doctor Beaumont stopped in front of her and smiled, while she desperately tried to read his dark eyes. She could feel her heart racing, banging against her ribs, and fleetingly thought that if she had a heart attack at least she was in the best place.

'Megan, isn't it?'

She nodded, not trusting herself to speak.

'We're particularly busy this morning, so I'm going to send you home and schedule another appointment.'

Megan got to her feet. Now she knew there was nothing seriously wrong with her, she found her voice again. 'No problem,' she said. All she wanted to do was get out.

But she was never going to make it to the door. Lucinda Valentine appeared from nowhere and blocked her path.

'We're ready for you, Megan.'

The doctor looked as if he was about to say something, but then he patted Megan on the shoulder and smiled. 'They must have found you a slot.'

She followed Lucinda along a carpeted corridor to another waiting area. If Lucinda left her to wait she'd do a runner, she decided, but Lucinda didn't stop. The woman opened a door and waited for Megan to go ahead of her. It wasn't until the door closed and another door slid across the inside that Megan realized they were in a lift.

'The examination rooms are on the next floor,' Lucinda said.

'But I'm only here for my results. There's nothing wrong with me.' Megan was beginning to wish she'd left when she had the chance.

The lift door slid back and Lucinda led the way onto another corridor. Halfway along she stopped and opened a door into a small room with a desk, a couple of chairs, and a high bed that looked like a padded table. A metal cupboard stood against the wall and a glass fronted wall unit held boxes of drugs and an array of surgical instruments.

Lucinda stood by the door and waved to a chair in front of the desk. 'We need paid volunteers for research purposes and you said you might be interested. If you sit down, I'll get someone to talk to you.'

Megan walked into the room but remained standing. So that's what this was all about. 'I've changed my mind,' she said. 'I don't think I should take part in a drugs test if I'm pregnant.'

Lucinda smiled. And then shot out a foot and kicked the door shut.

'But you're not pregnant, Megan, are you? You're playing some sort of game.' The American accent was more noticeable now. 'I said, sit down.'

She didn't raise her voice, but Megan sat, feeling a small prickle of fear. 'I don't know what you mean.'

Lucinda walked round to the other side of the desk and put her hands on the top, leaning across until her face was only inches from Megan's. 'I think you know exactly what I mean. Your urine says you're pregnant, but your blood says different. There were traces of class A drugs in the urine, but the blood was clean. I would ask you for an explanation, but there isn't one, is there? You're not pregnant and never have been.'

She put up her hand when Megan went to

speak. 'Oh, I'm so sorry, I forgot. Yes, you were pregnant, weren't you? You had a baby girl. Blonde, with big blue eyes, just like mommy.' She took a pink file out of the drawer and slapped it on the desk. 'But your sick, screwed-up, drug-addicted boyfriend beat you up, didn't he? And poor little baby Rosie was born dead.'

She pushed herself away from the desk. 'Do you still blame him, Megan? Do you try and forgive yourself by blaming him, even though it was your fault? You let him get you pregnant, didn't you? That was your fault. And you could have left him any time — no one was stopping you — but you didn't. That was your fault, too.' She shook her head sadly. 'You can't always go blaming other people, Megan. In the end it was your fault your baby died, and now you have to do something positive.'

Megan swallowed, trying to clear her throat, but her voice was still barely more than a whisper. 'What do you mean?'

Lucinda folded her arms across her chest and studied Megan thoughtfully. 'Feeling sorry is good. But you'll have to do a lot more than that before you feel right about yourself, and we can help you.' When Megan didn't answer, she smiled her cat and mouse smile again. 'You don't want any more children, do you? You told me that at the clinic, and that's a good idea considering your past history. But it could happen accidentally, couldn't it? The same as last time. Some addict you meet at one of those clubs and there you are, pregnant again. And we all know you don't want that.'

This time the smile was different. Megan could see something predatory lurking behind the dark contact lenses. Excitement, and something else. Something that made the woman's breath quicken. Anticipation.

'We have a team of surgeons here, all very good at their job, and one of them excels in gynaecology.' Lucinda leant forward again, her face so close Megan could smell the mint on her breath. 'He'll do a hysterectomy free of charge, Megan. Isn't that just great?'

Megan shot back in her seat, almost tipping the chair over. 'No! You can't do that. I might want another baby one day.'

'Oh, my. You do keep changing your mind, don't you?' Lucinda tipped her head on one side, as if she was thinking. 'But if you promise to behave yourself, we might be able to cancel the operation. We need you to tell us everything you know, and everything your little psychic friend knows, about this hospital and what we do here, and then we need you to stop interfering and leave us alone.' She stood up and opened the door. 'Have a think about it.'

'I still don't know what you're talking about,' Megan said bravely. Lucinda was a bully and Megan was used to bullies. They were like terrorists. You never gave in to them. 'When I came here the first time, the doctor told me I was pregnant.'

'He made a big mistake then, didn't he?' Lucinda didn't even turn round. 'And so did you.'

Megan watched Lucinda Valentine walk out and shut the door behind her. This was a hospital. No one could stop her leaving. Lucinda was just trying to frighten her. She tried the door handle, a simple lever, but the door wouldn't budge. The bloody woman had locked her in. She looked round the room. Nothing much of interest. No computer she could hack into, and no files marked secret. Just three drawers in the desk, the glass-fronted cabinet, and the metal cupboard standing against the wall. The top drawer of the desk was full of felt tip pens, paper clips, and other odds and ends. Nothing that looked remotely helpful. The other two drawers wouldn't open. The tall metal cupboard held boxes of antiseptic wipes and paper sheets to go on the examination table. Megan opened the door of the cabinet and stared at the row of instruments. Lucinda would be back any moment with more threats of bodily mutilation, and she didn't know how far the woman was prepared to go to get the information she wanted. Megan knew if it came down to having her stomach cut open and her organs removed, she'd tell Lucinda anything she wanted to know. A scalpel would be useful, but she wasn't sure if she would be able to use it. She'd seen a knife fight once, and made a vow that she would never ever cut anybody.

As if on cue, the door opened and Lucinda walked back into the room, smiling when she saw Megan standing in front of the open cabinet.

'Ready to talk?'

Megan shook her head. 'You can't keep me here. I can scream real loud when I want to.'

'I only want to talk to you, Megan.'

Lucinda was close now, and Megan wondered if it was worth grabbing a knife and hoping she had the guts to use it, or whether to just open her mouth and start screaming.

'I can't tell you anything because I don't know anything. I thought I was pregnant, that's all, and if I'm not, then fine.'

The woman walked up to Megan and shut the cabinet door. 'If you decide to do something, don't spend time thinking about it, just do it.'

She smiled, and Megan felt a sharp stab of pain, over almost before it registered. There was a syringe in Lucinda's hand and Megan rubbed the top of her arm, frowning in disbelief. 'What have you done?'

Lucinda guided her across to the bed. 'You'd better lie down, Megan, before you fall down. You might hit your head on something.'

Megan felt the edge of the bed hit the back of her knees. She sat unwillingly, her limbs not responding to the messages from her brain. She'd felt like this before, when she'd taken a dodgy pill at one of the clubs. 'I feel bad,' she mumbled, trying to get the words past an unresponsive tongue.

'I know you do, honey,' Lucinda said soothingly. She pushed Megan back on to the bed and lifted her legs, arranging them neatly side by side. 'Just lie back and relax, the doctor will be in to see you soon, and when you wake up it will all be over.'

26

Gina was surprised to find the studio locked. It was almost nine o'clock and Megan usually preceded her by at least half an hour. She let herself in and saw the note propped on Megan's desk. So Megan had already been in and gone again. Puzzled, Gina picked up the note and then dropped it back on the desk. Her hand was shaking as she called Megan's number. The call cancelled out. She tried Adam next, and for once he answered straight away.

'Megan's gone to Willow Bank.'

'Bugger! I thought I told you — '

'Don't even start,' she said. 'The little idiot left before I got here. Says she won't be more than an hour.'

'Might be true. If they send the bloods outside for checking, it's possible no one's put two and two together.'

'Do you really believe that?'

'No.'

'So what do we do?' She could feel her agitation building, her heart starting to race. 'Shall I call Reagan?'

'Might be an idea.' He was silent for what

seemed like an age. 'Look, I'll be over in ten minutes, traffic willing. Wait until I get there and we'll go and see Reagan together.'

'He doesn't like you.'

'Too bad.'

He hung up and Gina put the phone back in its stand. Should she wait for Adam? What she wanted to do was rush round to Willow Bank and drag Megan out of the hospital, but they'd deny everything and then what was she going to do? Come to think of it, what was Reagan going to do? She picked up the phone and dialled 1571 but there were no new messages and no saved messages, so Megan had deleted the call. She tried 1471 but caller identity had been withheld.

Gina ran a hand through her hair, swinging round at the sound of the bell over the door. A couple of teens wandered in casually and headed towards the shelves at the back. Gina stared at them as if they had just descended from an alien spacecraft.

'Do you want something?'

'Brushes,' the girl said. She turned to the boy beside her. 'What size do we want?'

'Can you be quick?' Gina said. 'I'll have to close the shop in a minute.'

'But you've only just opened.'

'And now I'm going to close again. If you

hurry up, I'll serve you. If not you'll have to leave.'

The boy grabbed a couple of paintbrushes from the display, muttering under his breath. He handed them to Gina. 'Thanks for being so fucking helpful.'

She took his money and rang up the sale, handing him his change without a word. As soon as they left she put the closed sign on the door and read Megan's note again.

Had a call from Willow Bank to collect my results. Left at half past eight. Should be back in an hour.

She had been going to warn Megan to stay away from the hospital, but now it was too late. She looked at her watch: 9.15, Megan would be at the hospital by now. She tried calling the girl on her mobile again and got told the party she had called was unavailable. Christ! Why hadn't she come down early for once? She looked at her watch again. Where was Adam? Even in traffic he should be here by now. If he didn't get here soon, she'd leave anyway. Go to the hospital and find out what had happened to Megan. Speak to Dr Beamont. Jump up and down and shout Megan's name, if necessary. Anything except stand here and wait. She tried Megan's mobile yet again. Still nothing.

The bell rang again as Adam pushed open the door.

'Where the hell have you been?'

'I've been exactly ten minutes, like I promised. Nearly hit a bus and missed a couple of pedestrians by inches if you want a blow-by-blow account.'

'Reagan won't be able to do anything, we don't have enough to give him.'

'He might be prepared to listen, but I can't give him the police notes because he'll find out who I got them from, and the photo has an index number on the back, so I can't give him that either.'

Gina looked at Adam in despair. 'Is it worth going to see Reagan at all, or should we just go straight to the hospital?'

'And do what? For all we know we may be worrying unnecessarily. Have you tried Megan on her mobile?'

'Of course I have. Turned off, smashed, flushed down the loo. I don't know. All I know is, I can't speak to her.'

It was Adam's turn to look at his watch. 'Do you want to give her a bit longer before we do anything?'

'No. If she was OK she'd be back by now.'

'If I go with you to the police station, I'm going to put Reagan's back up, aren't I? Then he won't tell either of us anything.' Adam thought for a minute. 'You go and see Reagan and I'll go to Willow Bank. I'll ask for an interview with Beaumont and take it from there.' He smiled at her. 'I'll be very diplomatic and I promise not to cause a major incident. The Crawfords must be about ready to run again, but I think it all depends on this last baby.'

'Sophie's baby. It's already promised, and if they've got her at the hospital they may try and get her to deliver early.'

'Couldn't that be dangerous?'

'They'll take the risk. Sell the baby and go.' She looked at Adam. 'Don't try and scare them. If they get desperate, you don't know what they might do.'

'Yes, I do know. They're con men, preying on desperate people.'

'They're killers, Adam. Donna died, and Sophie could be next, particularly if they try and get her baby out too soon.'

Unexpectedly he put his arms round her and pulled her against him. She rested her head gratefully on his chest, listening to his heartbeat. 'I'm scared for them, Adam. Sophie and Megan. And I don't know what to do.'

'We'll sort it, love. I promise you.' Gently, he pushed her away and held her at arm's length. 'Go and see Reagan. Convince him to do something.'

She let him out and locked the door behind him, and then sat down at Megan's computer to cancel her client's morning appointment. She had no idea what she was going to say to Reagan, or what excuse she could make for poking her nose into one of his cases yet again. Left alone, it would resolve itself. The Crawfords would leave Castlebury and Donna's murder would never be solved. Dr Beaumont would still have his hospital and, with luck, the Lowrys would get their daughter back. If Mrs Lowry had her way, the vicar would never know his daughter had been pregnant, and Sophie could go back to university and finish her education.

Except that wasn't going to happen, because Sophie had decided to keep her baby. Now her life was in danger. So was Megan's, probably.

★   ★   ★

Reagan agreed to give Gina fifteen minutes, and by talking very fast she managed to include most of what she wanted to say.

'I wasn't trying to butt in on your case, I was just trying to find Sophie.'

'Good God, Gina, you've talked daft

before, but never like this. Are you telling me you think Doctor Beaumont is selling babies on the side?'

She felt shattered. She had thought he would at least consider that what she was saying might be true. 'Doctor Beaumont isn't doing this by himself. It's the Crawfords, Lucinda Valentine and her husband. They did the same thing in America.'

'And you know all this because?'

'Because Adam checked it out on the Internet, and then got a friend in the LAPD to fax him a photo of the Crawfords. They pulled the same thing in Los Angeles, but they never got caught.' She pulled the photo out of her bag and put it in front of him. 'That's a photo of Lucinda Valentine and her husband.'

'I've met the Valentine woman. She has straight black hair and a bloody great mole on her face.' He tossed the photo back to Gina. 'This is nothing like her.'

'The mole isn't real, and anyone can dye their hair.'

Reagan stood up. 'This is ridiculous, Gina. We found Donna Price's baby on a landfill site, if you remember. No one sold it. Someone hit the poor girl on the head with a rock. Probably someone she knows. And the other girl was killed by her father. Do you realize how ridiculous this all sounds?'

He shook his head, standing up and heading for the door. 'I have to go. I told you fifteen minutes and your time is up. Go back to your studio, paint some pretty pictures, and get all this nonsense out of your head. Doctor Beaumont is a good man, doing a decent job. Honestly, Gina,' he added soberly, 'if looking at dead bodies is messing with your head, stop doing it.'

'Just check it out,' she told him. 'Look on the Internet. Check with the LAPD. Ask about the Crawfords. They were operating in LA a couple of years ago. And then imagine a blonde Lucinda Valentine without a mole.' She tossed her sketch on his desk. 'This is what she looks like now.'

He held the door for her. 'Leave it be, Gina. I don't have time for this.'

She left the police station totally defeated. She wondered if she should call Adam and see if he was having better luck at the hospital, but in the end she headed back to the studio. There didn't seem to be anything else she could do.

She was sitting in Megan's seat, swinging backwards and forwards, waiting for Adam to come back from the hospital, when Crawford walked in.

Before she had time to get out of the chair

he pulled the blind down over the glass panel and locked the door to the street.

'Stay right where you are.'

She might have argued, but the large black gun in his hand stopped everything. Breath, movement, even thought. Gina had never seen a gun in someone's hand before, not in real life, and the sight was completely unreal. She had a mad moment when she wanted to laugh out loud. Farmers kept guns to shoot rabbits, and a policeman might carry one sometimes, but no one waved a real gun in your face, not in Castlebury. And Crawford, with his bald scalp and heavy build, looked like a caricature of Ross Kemp. None of this could be real. Not possibly.

'This is silly,' she said. 'What are you going to do with that?'

Without taking his eyes off her he reached into his pocket and attached something to the gun. Gina had seen enough TV dramas to recognize a silencer. Now the gun was even bigger than before. It seemed to dominate the room.

Crawford pointed the gun at a framed portrait of a woman with a little boy on her lap and shot her through the middle of the forehead.

'Been a while, but I haven't forgotten how.' Still holding the gun pointing in her direction, Crawford produced a roll of bright red insulating tape and taped both her wrists to the arms of Megan's swivel chair. When she tried to stand, the tape cut into her skin, making her catch her breath. 'I should keep still if I were you, or you'll cut off your circulation. Probably make your hands drop off.' He studied her thoughtfully. 'You going to keep quiet, or do you want me to tape up your mouth as well?'

She had just been thinking of screaming. The road outside wasn't usually busy until the evening rush hour, but someone would be passing by. She looked at the sticky tape and thought about having it over her mouth.

'I'll be quiet,' she said. 'What do you want?'

'We want you to keep out of our hair until we leave, and this is just a taste of what we can do.' He picked up a small watercolour and dropped it on the floor, smashing the frame with his foot. 'Your boyfriend got his car back on the road yet?'

'Please don't,' Gina said, as he swept the remaining pictures from the shelf, stepping on each one, his weight enough to smash them beyond any hope of repair. She thought of the time she had spent, sitting on the bank of the river, painting those little pictures, and how quickly they were being destroyed. What had once taken hours to create was now just a mess of paper and glass on the floor of her studio.

The tubes of paint came next. Opened, they brought out what must have been a latent artistic talent in Crawford, and he used them to redecorate her studio. Humming to himself as he squeezed yellow ochre onto the walls and used a squiggle of magenta to create a new design on her visitors' chair. Megan got a dollop of carmine in each of her desk drawers, where clients' records were kept in meticulous order, and he used the last of the cobalt blue to highlight Gina's hair.

'Why?' she asked, the paint mixing with the tears on her cheeks, but he didn't answer. He was too busy snapping her paintbrushes in two. Somehow the desecration of her studio was far worse than the burglary of her flat earlier in the year. He was destroying months, sometimes years of work in a matter of seconds, and that hurt more than anything. When he put a boot against her new shelving, sending it crashing to the ground, she could keep quiet no longer.

'Stop it! That's enough!'

Fuelled by anger and frustration, she pushed off from the desk and used her feet to propel herself across the room on the chair, the wheels skating on the polished wood floor. She was on him before he could move, lifting both her feet to catch him square in the crotch. Clutching himself with one hand, he slapped her so hard across the face with his free hand the chair skittered back across the room and smashed into the wall.

'Bitch!' He grabbed her by the hair and slapped her again, then wound the tape round and round her head, sealing her mouth shut. 'Go crawling to the police again and I'll burn this place down.'

For one awful moment she thought he was angry enough to tape her nose as well, but he stopped just short of suffocating her, satisfied with winding the tape so tight it cut into her cheeks and crushed her lips against her teeth. She sat limp in the chair and watched him leave, all her energy drained.

27

Adam drove slowly through the hospital gates and parked in one of the free parking spaces. He thought of the times he had visited the general hospital following up on a story. It had sometimes taken him half an hour to find a parking space and, by the time he came out the parking meter had cost him a small fortune. Willow Bank was in a different league. In the spacious, free, half-empty car-park, his little Ford looked like a poor relation.

He had sent Gina to the police station to give her something constructive to do and keep her out of danger. He knew Reagan wouldn't believe her story. The Crawfords were clever. They made a few hundred thousand and moved on, wherever girls wanted to get rid of babies and wealthy women were prepared to pay for them. Supply and demand. The building blocks of a good business.

But you should never try and sell what you don't have, and that is where it had all gone wrong. Donna's baby had been stillborn, leaving the Crawfords with nothing to sell.

They had back-up in the form of Sophie, but Sophie had changed her mind, and by now the client would be getting restless. Leave it much longer and the client would pull out, all the hard work and organization for nothing.

Adam pushed open the doors and walked inside. He had never visited Willow Bank before, and now he wondered why. The people who walked through these doors would have enough stories to fill a book. He walked up to the reception desk and returned the girl's smile.

'Adam Shaw. RMP. I need to speak to Doctor Beaumont. I won't keep him more than a few moments.'

'RMP?'

'Army. Royal Military Police. Just a couple of questions, that's all.'

'Can you tell me what it's about?'

'Just tell him it's about Donna Price.'

He had to do something to get the doctor to talk to him. He watched the girl swing her chair round so she had her back to him and use a phone on a desk behind her. He couldn't hear what she was saying, so he leant on the counter trying to appear casual, but he could still only catch the odd word. He stood up as the girl turned round and gave her his best smile. She smiled back and he wondered if they did teeth-whitening at the hospital as well as everything else.

'Doctor Beaumont will see you in a few minutes. If you take a seat I'll give you a call when he's free.'

He walked over to a leather armchair, but didn't sit down. Megan should have left a long time ago. How long does it take to give someone their test results? He looked at his watch and then walked back to the counter. The girl looked up with another brilliant smile and he realized she thought he was hitting on her. For a moment he considered chatting her up, but she looked so hopeful it would have been cruel.

'I think a friend of mine had an appointment today. Megan Pritchard. Can you tell me if she's still here?'

The girl looked crestfallen. She glanced at her screen. 'I think so. She's still on the board. She hasn't been deleted yet.'

Adam found the choice of words a little unfortunate, but he smiled his best smile again. 'I thought I might be able to give her a lift home. How long will she be?'

'I don't really know, Mr Shaw. It depends how long her treatment takes.'

Something tightened in his gut. 'Treatment? I thought Megan was just here to pick up her test results?'

'I'm not supposed to discuss the patients,

but I'll leave a message for her. Just come over to the counter before you leave.' The girl hadn't quite given up, she smiled seductively. 'My name's Cheryl.'

'Thank you, Cheryl,' Adam said. 'You've been very helpful.'

The girl's smile disappeared, and Adam looked over his shoulder to find Doctor Beaumont standing behind him.

'Good afternoon, Mr Shaw. I can give you a few minutes. We'll talk in my office.'

Without waiting to see if Adam was following him, Beaumont pushed open double doors into a corridor. Adam caught the doors before they closed in his face. The good doctor was obviously not pleased by his visit. A few doors down the corridor branched to the right and ended with a single door. A brass plaque stated that the occupant was a Dr Lucas Beaumont. The list of medical abbreviations meant absolutely nothing to Adam, and he was pretty sure they would mean nothing to a prospective client. They could all be made up and no one would be any the wiser.

The doctor pushed open the door and ushered Adam inside, seating himself in a black leather chair behind a large, highly polished walnut desk. He waved Adam to a seat on the other side of the desk.

'I hope your reason for being here is to interview me about fertility treatment, Mr Shaw. If that is the case, I can give you a few minutes of my time.'

'Why else would I be here?'

The doctor's face remained blank. 'I have absolutely no idea.'

So that was the way it was going to be played. Adam hated games.

'Megan Pritchard,' he said. 'Still here, evidently, when all she wanted was her test results. Sophie Lowry, pregnant and now missing. Donna Price dead, her baby stillborn.' He waited, but the doctor said nothing, his face inscrutable. 'I think you know who killed Donna Price, Doctor Beaumont.'

'I have no idea what you're talking about, Mr Shaw. As far as I know, no one called Donna Price has ever been inside this hospital. I know Sophie Lowry is missing because her mother told me so. I have known the Lowrys for a number of years. Her mother didn't tell me the girl was pregnant. If I had known, I might have been able to help.'

'But you did help, didn't you, Doctor? Grace Lowry told me how you kindly offered to arrange an adoption for Sophie. And it wouldn't be the first time, would it? I dug up a newspaper article about another time you helped someone. The woman was quite annoyed when she didn't get her promised baby, wasn't she?'

'I suggest you leave, Mr Shaw. We have nothing else to talk about.'

Adam sat back in his chair and stretched out his legs. 'I'm not leaving. Not until I get the whole story. I know most of it already.'

'If you carry on with this witch hunt I'll lose my hospital.'

'No you won't. Not if you're innocent.'

'Yes, I will,' the doctor said quietly. 'Once they start digging. The case that nearly went to court, you know about that? Well, it wasn't the first. When the hospital opened I had a much bigger mortgage than I could afford and the hospital wasn't making a profit. Not to begin with. I needed staff and I didn't have the money to pay them. I told myself I was helping people. I don't agree with abortion, so I was saving babies too.' He gave a dry laugh. 'All completely altruistic. The fact that I made a bit of money on the side was just a bonus for being such a good person.'

'How many?' Adam asked.

'Four that actually came off. The difference then was that if a girl changed her mind, it didn't matter. The women weren't ordering babies in advance. I just arranged a private adoption if I heard of a baby that wasn't

295

wanted. One woman paid me fifty thousand pounds. Said it was cheap. She'd spent eight months in a private psychiatric hospital after the IVF didn't take, so she told everyone she'd been pregnant all that time.' Dr Beaumont looked Adam straight in the eye. 'He's three now, their son. A lovely, happy little boy. And his real mother was able to finish her degree.'

'You can try and justify it all you like, but I think Crawford or his wife murdered Donna Price. Her baby was born dead and she ceased to be of any use to them. The same thing could happen to Sophie. Where is she?'

The doctor sighed. 'She's here at the hospital. All I can do is make sure she's delivered safely.'

'Even though she wants to keep the baby?'

'Who told you that?' The doctor sounded genuinely surprised. 'I spoke to Sophie's mother a couple of days ago, and you have your facts wrong, Mr Shaw. Sophie wants the baby adopted.'

It was Adam's turn to sigh. Mrs Lowry was being economical with the truth again, and there wasn't time to explain. 'Do you know where Megan is? I need to get her out of here.'

'Lucinda wanted to talk to Megan. The girl's only a few weeks into her pregnancy.

She's in no danger. She's probably left by now.'

'No, she hasn't. Her name is still on your board. And Megan isn't pregnant. She lied, and Lucinda Valentine knows. She won't let Megan just walk out of here.'

'That's ridiculous. This isn't a prison.' He picked up his phone and pushed a button. 'Can you tell me if Miss Megan Pritchard is still here?' He listened for a couple of seconds and then put the phone down. 'She left a few minutes ago, safe and sound. If you hurry you might catch her.'

Adam didn't bother to thank the doctor. He followed the corridor to the reception area but hesitated before he rushed out into the street. He walked up to the counter and stopped the receptionist just as she was about to answer the phone.

'Just a minute, before you deal with that can you tell me if Megan Pritchard has actually left?'

The girl smiled at him, her porcelain crowns gleaming. 'Yes, she has. I gave your message to Miss Valentine and she said Miss Pritchard had already got transport arranged and didn't need a lift, but to thank you all the same.'

'Did you see Megan leave?'

'I'm sorry,' the girl looked anxiously at the

still ringing phone. 'I have to answer this.'

She turned her back on Adam and he stood undecided. Did he go racing after Megan when he had no guarantee she had really left, or did he go back and challenge Dr Beaumont again? In the end he decided there was no point in wasting more time until he had checked to see whether Megan really was on her way home, so he made his way to the car-park and climbed into his car.

There was no sign of Megan at the bus stop, so he drove slowly, following the route she would take if she walked back to the studio. He checked her flat on the way to make sure she hadn't gone straight home, but no one answered the bell and he could hear Blossom making her pissed-off-Siamese noise inside. She didn't like being left alone for too long.

When he eventually arrived back at the studio, the closed sign was still on the door. Gina had been at the police station a lot longer than he expected. Thinking she might have gone upstairs to her flat, he parked out the front and walked round the corner to check. Seeing her car parked at the bottom of the stairs he went up and rang her doorbell.

Nothing.

She should have given him a key. He tried the bell again and then knocked on the wood with his knuckles. Still nothing. Deciding she must be in the shower, or vacuuming for some obscure reason and couldn't hear him, he decided to sit in his car and read the paper for twenty minutes, then try the bell again. No use sitting on her steps, he'd tried that once before and she hadn't been pleased.

He made his way back to the car and was about to get in when he noticed something odd. The blind covering the back of Gina's window display was caught up on something. When he got closer, he saw it was part of a picture frame. A broken picture frame. The two portraits displayed in the front of the window were intact, so where had the piece of polished wood come from?

Puzzled, he tried the door to the studio, and it opened at his touch, not even latched.

As he pushed the door further open it caught on something but he gave it a shove, fear knotting his belly. Someone had pulled down the blinds at the back of the room, so the inside was dim, but he could see enough. The floor was littered with debris; paper, brushes, and tubes of paint lay amongst broken frames and shards of glass, Gina's pretty little watercolours shredded to bits.

He turned at a sound, and saw her as she tried to move towards him, the broken glass on the floor stopping her progress. Her hair and face were covered in paint, a red line slicing her features in half like a gaping wound. For a moment he thought the red mark was a knife cut, and a moan escaped his lips, until he saw the gash in her face was red insulating tape. He looked round for something to cut her free, remembering a box of etching tools with knives like scalpels. They had been put on a high shelf out of the reach of children, but now they could be anywhere.

Gina made a noise again, nodding with her head, and he saw a pair of scissors lying on the floor. He grabbed them and started on the tape round her mouth. The stuff was stuck to her face and hair, and he found the best way to get it off was to make a lot of little cuts and gently remove the tape a piece at a time. Eventually the only bits left were the ones across her mouth. He hesitated, knowing he was going to take skin off with the tape, but Gina wiggled her fingers trying to get her hands loose, and he realized she wanted to do the painful bit herself.

After he cut her hands free, she eased the tape from around her mouth, moving her jaw to get the circulation going again.

'Saves having a face wax,' she said, tossing the last bit of sticky tape on to the floor, and then she burst into tears.

She cried so rarely in front of him, he had

no idea what to do. A few moments ago he had felt like crying himself while he tried to extricate her from the tape cutting into her skin, and now he did the only thing possible: took her into his arms and let her rest her bruised and paint-splattered face against his nice clean shirt.

'They're not going to kill Sophie,' he said a few minutes later, as she eased herself out of his arms. 'Dr Beaumont will take care of her. So I think now is the time to give up.'

'Taking her baby away will kill her anyway,' Gina said. She pushed herself away from him and pulled a tissue from the pocket of her jeans. 'So now is the time to fight.'

28

Megan regained consciousness slowly. What had she taken, she wondered, to give her this feeling of euphoria? Whatever it was, she wanted more. She kept her eyes closed, hoping to hang on to the delightful sensation of floating on air while wrapped in a feather duvet, but she could feel it ebbing away. Sighing, she tried to turn over, and found she couldn't. Not paralysis, the sort you get from an overdose of ketamine, but restriction, as if something was holding her down.

She opened one eye — and saw her feet.

Not possible. She was lying flat on her back, so what were her feet doing up there where she could see them? She tried to move her arms and couldn't. Couldn't sit up, either. Even so, the panic came slowly, no doubt due to the drugs she must have taken. Or been given. That thought stirred up memories of Lucinda Valentine sticking a needle in her arm — and then the panic hit hard and fast.

She was lying on a bed, her wrists secured either side with Velcro, and by lifting her head she could see a strap across her stomach. Her legs — and here the panic quickly turned to terror — her legs were spread wide apart and anchored to poles on either side of the bed.

She was also stark naked.

She must have screamed because Lucinda appeared almost immediately, slipping into the room and shutting the door behind her.

'If you make a noise again I'll gag you.'

'What have you done to me?'

The overwhelming need to cover herself caused Megan to convulse on the bed, almost tying herself in a knot. Having a baby had done away with most of her inhibitions, but she had never experienced this sort of exposure before. Any remnants of dignity had been stripped away with her clothes, leaving her completely helpless. Involuntarily, her eyes went to the glass cabinet, where the steel instruments were laid out in their neat little rows. Lucinda followed her gaze, and smiled.

'What have we done to you? Nothing yet. But think what we could do.' She moved to the foot of the bed, causing Megan to squirm again even though she knew it was futile. 'My husband has paid your friend, Gina Cross, a little visit, so I don't think she'll be troubling us any more, but you have to realize how serious this is, Megan. There's a great deal of money at stake.' She unlocked the door of the glass cabinet and picked up a scalpel. 'It's no fun being helpless, is it? Anything could happen.'

Megan felt the scream bubbling up in her throat, but she didn't know what Lucinda would do with the scalpel if she made a noise, so the sound that came out of her mouth was a small squeak that would have shamed even a mouse. She tried to press her knees together, but that wasn't going to happen, so she closed her eyes and clenched every muscle she could think of. She was determined not to wet herself. She could only take so much humiliation.

She heard Lucinda laugh, and then a click as the door closed. When she opened her eyes again she was alone in the room.

She spent ten minutes trying to get out of the straps, twisting her fingers at strange angles as she tried to release the Velcro, but only a contortionist could have reached the fastenings. She lost the feeling in her hands, and when she turned her head she saw one of the straps was slick with blood where she had rubbed the skin raw. Time to work out another strategy. Maybe she could rock the bed nearer the instrument tray and cut herself free, anything to keep her mind off what Lucinda might do when she came back.

When the door opened again she was prepared for almost anything — anything except the sight of Amber Beaumont staring at her in horror.

Megan's knees made another involuntary attempt to come together, and Amber swung round so she was facing away from the bed. 'Fucking hell, Megan,' she said to the wall. 'What have they done to you?'

'Tied me to a bed without any clothes on. Just get me out of these straps, will you?'

'I can't. I'll have to look at you. Wait a minute . . .' Amber pulled her v-neck sweater over her head and turned round just long enough to toss it over Megan's lower half. Then she undid the straps as quickly as she could and turned away again.

Megan pulled the draw-sheet off the bed and wrapped it around herself like a toga. 'You can look now, I'm more or less decent.'

Amber turned round slowly. 'Did Lucinda hurt you?'

'No, just scared me shitless, and she'll be back any minute. Do you know where Sophie is?'

'You've got to get out of here.' Amber grabbed her sweater and squirmed her way back into it. She inched the door open just enough to see outside and then closed it again. 'Do you know where your clothes are?'

Megan pulled open the cupboard door with one hand, holding the sheet tightly

305

round her with the other. The most logical place is usually the right one. Her clothes were in a bundle on top of one of the boxes.

'Turn your back again,' she told Amber, pulling on her knickers and bra and then her jeans. Her jersey top was inside out, and her hands had developed a bad case of pins and needles. Amber took it from her and turned it the right way round.

'We have to hurry, Megan.'

Megan found her trainers at the bottom of the cupboard and put them on. 'I won't go without Sophie.' She couldn't run away now, not after all she'd been through. 'I know she's here somewhere.'

Amber was beginning to look scared. 'My dad doesn't know I'm here. I came to see Sophie because I felt bad about getting angry with her, but then I heard Lucinda say she had the girl from the studio locked up in one of the examination rooms and I thought she meant Gina Cross.' She shot a glance at the door. 'We have to go, Megan.'

Megan sat on the bed to tie her laces and considered the options. It might be better to get out as fast as she could and get some help, but Sophie was in Lucinda's care and Megan had seen what Lucinda could do. 'Can you take me to Sophie without us getting caught?'

'Please let's go, Megan. You'll get me into trouble.'

Megan shook her head stubbornly. 'If you won't help me, I'll find Sophie myself.'

Muttering under her breath, Amber opened the door again. 'Sophie's upstairs. The only cameras are in reception and outside the main wards, but the staff use the lift down the hall all the time, so we'll have to use the emergency stairs.' She looked worriedly at Megan. 'We have to go past the lift to get there. Can you run?'

As they scooted past the lift to get to the stairwell, Megan suddenly had an insane desire to giggle. Just for a moment it had felt like a game, a half-remembered happy time in a school playground, but a glance at her skinned wrists brought her back to reality. The drug was still playing with her head.

'The lift is for people on trolleys or in wheelchairs,' Amber told her. 'We'll have to go up the stairs and hope we don't meet anyone coming down.' She looked at Megan and frowned. 'Your arm is still bleeding. Hide your hands in your sleeves. It doesn't matter if you look ill, this is a hospital, but try not to look as if you're coming down off something.'

'I am coming down off something,' Megan said. 'Whatever Lucinda gave me. Great while it lasted, but now I feel like shit.' She pulled her sleeves down over her wrists. 'Is Sophie in a room on her own?'

'She's got a whole suite of her own. Flat screen TV, her own bathroom, the lot.'

They negotiated the stairs safely and Amber led the way out on to a thickly carpeted corridor with a couple of doors on each side. She stopped outside one of the doors and took a key out of her pocket. 'I knew they'd got Sophie locked in, so I pinched the key. I was going to give it to her so she could leave if she wanted to.'

She unlocked the door and the first thing Megan saw was a pale, very pregnant girl sitting in an armchair watching a television screen. She was wearing one of the hospital's fluffy white dressing gowns, her fair hair tied back off her face, and Megan thought she looked exactly like a female version of her brother.

Sophie smiled at Amber. 'Thought you'd given up on me. Sorry about Roddy.'

'Roddy's an arsehole. You're more than welcome to him.' Amber waved a hand at Megan. 'This is Megan. I found her with her feet tied to poles, completely starkers.'

Megan ignored the puzzled look on Sophie's face, she hadn't got time to explain. 'We need to get you out of here. What are our chances of getting away without anyone seeing us? There must be a back door.'

'There is,' Amber said, 'but we'll have to get her downstairs first, and if Lucinda catches us she'll kill us.'

'I can still walk,' Sophie said, 'even if I am in labour.' She smiled at the shocked expressions on their faces. 'Well, I think I am, but I've never done it before, so I'm not sure.'

'That's it, then,' Megan said. 'We have to get you out right now.'

Amber looked unconvinced. 'We can't move her if she's about to drop. She's better off in here where my dad can take care of her. What if she has the baby on the stairs or something?'

'Stop talking about me as if I'm not here,' Sophie heaved herself up out of her chair. 'Being pregnant hasn't made me completely stupid. Megan's right, I've got to get out of here or they'll take the baby away from me. Lucinda said they won't even let me hold her first, just give her to someone else. It's kinder, she said.'

'How do you know it's a girl?' Amber asked.

'Because they scanned me. If it had been a boy they would have let me go. They wanted a girl.'

'Both of you stop talking and think of a way out.' Megan felt in the pocket of her jeans and then held out her hand to Amber. 'Lucinda took my phone. Do you still have yours?' She took the phone Amber handed her and pushed buttons. 'Adam? What are you doing there? Never mind. We've found Sophie. Meet us at the back of Willow Bank as soon as you can, but don't let anyone see you.' She pushed the 'end' button before he had time to ask any questions.

'We'll put her in a wheelchair and take her down in the lift,' Amber said. 'If we go right down to the basement and then walk up the stairs to the ground floor, we might make it. There's a delivery bay and a door out into the street.'

Sophie hung on to the back of the chair. 'I told you to stop talking about me as if I'm a retard. This is a bit like a bad period pain. I expect it has to get a lot worse before I have the baby.'

'Don't worry,' Megan said. 'It will.'

They found a folded wheelchair in a cupboard and managed to untangle it between them. Sophie was tucked in with a blanket over her legs, and Megan rolled up the rest of the spare blankets and sheets and put them in the bed to look like a body.

'It'll only fool anyone for a couple of minutes,' she said, 'but we might need every minute we can get.'

They wheeled Sophie out of the room and made it to the lift without meeting any staff. Breathing a sigh of relief Megan pushed Sophie's chair inside while Amber pressed the button for the basement.

Then their luck ran out.

The lift stopped at the next floor down, and when the doors opened they were faced with a young man in a green coat with a comatose patient on a trolley. Just as Megan was about to have a heart attack, he grinned at Amber.

'I think I have priority, here, Amber. My patient is lying down.'

'Two minutes, Pete,' Amber said. 'My dad asked me to take Mrs Stevens downstairs. It's a bit of an emergency. I'll send the lift back up as soon as we get out.'

He shrugged. 'Anything for the boss's daughter. Just be quick then, or I'll be in trouble.' His eyes were on Amber's cleavage and he barely glanced at Megan or Sophie.

'Mrs Stevens?' Sophie queried, as the lift doors closed again.

'It was the first name I could think of. Did you want me to introduce you as Sophie Lowry, the vicar's daughter?'

As they arrived at the basement and scrambled out of the lift, a big black lady pushing a cart piled high with towels came running towards them. 'Hold it!' The woman pushed her cart inside the lift to stop the doors closing and scowled at Amber. 'What are you doing down here with a patient in a wheelchair?'

'Pushed the wrong button,' Amber said apologetically. 'Not to worry, you go on up. Peter is waiting with a patient up on the second floor and he's in a hurry. We can wait a few minutes more.'

The woman followed her cart into the lift. 'Thanks, Amber dear. I'll send the lift right back down.'

Megan didn't only feel dizzy now, she felt sick as well. 'Where are the stairs?' she asked Amber. She needed some fresh air.

Sophie got out of the wheelchair and Amber pushed it into a corner without bothering to fold it up. They both helped Sophie up the stairs and Amber went ahead to check the way was clear. There weren't any windows in this part of the hospital and the light was dim. Megan could see a door on the other side of a small loading area, a metal door with a pull bar on the inside. She prayed it wasn't locked.

'No one will be here unless there's a delivery. You have to call from outside and tell them who you are, and then someone comes down from upstairs.'

They walked either side of Sophie so they could help support her, but they had only taken a few steps when she stopped with a little moan. 'Hang on, I've got another pain coming,'

Megan looked longingly at the door. 'It's only a little bit further.'

Sophie dug her fingers into Megan's arm. 'I know,' she said through gritted teeth, 'but at the moment I can't move, not even a little bit, so it's no good trying to make me. And I need a pee.'

'Well, you'll have to hold it. I had to, and I've been in here for hours.'

Just as they were about to start off again, someone banged on the door from the outside and all three girls stopped where they were, too shocked to move.

'It might be Adam,' Megan whispered.

'And it might not.' Amber crossed the last few feet to the door and put her hand on the bar. 'Do I open it or not?'

Sophie clutched Megan's arm again. 'Please do something,' she said, 'otherwise I'm going to have this baby right here.'

Another bout of banging spurred Amber into action. She released the bar and pulled the door inwards a few inches. When it flew open the rest of the way, nearly hitting her in the face, she gave a little squeal of fright and jumped back, grabbing Megan's free arm. The sudden wash of light made it impossible to see anything clearly, but Megan hoped they were facing a friend. If not, they were in serious trouble.

29

Adam locked the studio door before helping Gina upstairs to her flat. She hated having to lean on him, she was getting paint all over him, but her legs felt decidedly wobbly and she was grateful for the strong arm round her waist.

'I need to wash this paint off me,' she said, pleased to see her flat hadn't been turned over as well. 'See if you can find something to drink. I won't be long.'

'Do you want any help?' He smiled ruefully at her quizzical look. 'I have only the best of intentions. Christ, Gina, you frightened me there for a minute.'

Feeling stupidly pleased that he had been worried about her, she left him to forage for alcohol and stripped off in her bedroom. Apart from some nasty welts where the tape had bitten into her skin, she seemed relatively unharmed, which was more than she could say for her studio. The pain of seeing her work smashed to pieces in front of her was almost physical. So much time and effort; so much pride when the new shelving was finished and her pictures displayed, and so much fun stocking up with artists' materials. All gone in minutes.

She turned on the shower and tried to relax in the stream of warm water. It took time to get the paint out of her hair, and she was struggling with a tangle of wet curls when Adam appeared on the other side of the glass. She hadn't the energy to be angry with him. She watched him strip off his clothes and made room when he stepped inside the shower cubicle with her.

'I said you'd need help.'

She let him smooth conditioner into her hair and gently tease out the tangles with his fingers. He took a sponge and examined her body for any smears of paint she might have missed.

When he saw the expression on her face he looked down at himself and laughed. 'I'm sorry. That seems to happen whenever I get near you.' He opened the cubicle door and reached for a towel. 'Don't worry, I'll go and find you a drink.'

She blocked his way as he was about to leave the cubicle. 'It seems a shame to waste it.'

'You're hurt, Gina, and your studio's been trashed. I should imagine sex is the last thing you want to think about.'

'The last thing I want to think about is

being hurt and my studio being trashed. If you think you can take my mind off that for a while, I'd be very grateful.'

He dropped the towel. 'How grateful?'

A few minutes later they moved to Gina's big double bed, letting the duvet soak up the water from their bodies. He was so scared of hurting her, he was almost too gentle, but she found that incredibly sexy. He let her take the lead and she made him wait, teasing him until he was begging for mercy. When she eventually collapsed on top of him all she wanted to do was sleep, but she forced herself off the bed.

'Reagan didn't believe me, and we've still got to get Megan out of that hospital.' She took fresh underwear out of a drawer. 'I'm scared what they might do to her if they find out she's been lying.'

'They already know she's been lying. The blood test will have confirmed that.'

Once they were both dressed, he followed her into the living room and poured her a glass of wine. 'I think I can get Beaumont to help me. He was convinced Lucinda wasn't going to keep Megan there. Lucinda just wanted to talk to her, he said.'

'Yeah. Pigs and flying comes to mind.' She took a sip of her drink. 'Thanks, I feel better now.'

He grinned at her. 'Sex always works for me, too.'

She could hear her mobile ringing but couldn't remember what she'd done with it. Adam found it on the bedroom floor. He said 'hello' and then his face tightened. He listened for a second and then took the phone away from his ear and stared at the screen.

'Damn! Damn and bloody blast, she's hung up on me.' He looked at Gina. 'That was Megan. They've found Sophie and they want me to meet them at the back of Willow Bank.'

'When?'

'Right now.' He pulled his car keys out of his pocket and headed for the door. 'You stay here. I'll find out what's going on and ring you as soon as I know anything.'

She laughed at him. 'You are joking? What if Mr Crawford decides the studio wasn't enough and my flat needs a going over as well? Do you really want me to stay here and wait for him?'

Adam closed his eyes. 'Get a jacket. But you'll bloody well stay in the car if I say so.'

He drove with steely concentration. Fast, but within the limit. Gina knew he couldn't take the risk of being stopped before he got to the hospital. He slowed as he reached the gates.

'Megan said to keep out of sight, but that's going to be easier said than done.' He stared at the open expanse of drive in frustration. 'There must be a back entrance for deliveries.' He took the first turning left and then left again, stopping outside a pair of metal gates that barred the way to the back of the hospital.

'How do we get in?' Gina asked.

'Don't know yet.' He got out of the car and gave one of the gates a shove, turning to grin at her as the gate swung slowly open. He pulled it closed again and got back in the car. 'I'll park up the street a bit and come back on foot. Try and bluff it out if I get caught.'

Gina followed him as he made his way back to the hospital gates. He looked over his shoulder and scowled at her but didn't say anything. She noticed a security camera mounted above a door leading into the hospital and pointed to it. He nodded. There was nothing they could do about the camera. They just had to hope that Megan knew what she was doing.

They stood just outside the gates, pretending to chat, but after five minutes Gina could stand it no longer. 'That's a CCTV camera. It probably only gets checked once a week, and if we keep our heads down it will be impossible to recognize us. Let's make a run for the back door.'

They pushed open the gate and slipped inside. Adam pulled the gate shut behind them and they sprinted across the yard, not stopping until they reached the door.

'Is it locked?'

Adam pushed but nothing happened. There was no lock on the door, just a plate with a button and a speaker grill. 'We can hardly announce ourselves. Shaw and Cross, come to rescue Miss Pritchard.'

'Bang on it,' Gina said. 'If the girls are inside, they'll hear us.'

'So will anyone else who happens to be inside.'

'So what do we do? Stand out here and wait for something to happen?'

Adam thumped on the door with his fist, stepping back when he heard a metallic noise from inside. The door started to inch open and he pulled Gina to one side, kicking the door in the rest of the way.

The three girls made a little tableau, blinking in the sudden light.

'You made me wet myself,' Sophie muttered, pulling her robe more tightly round her bulging stomach. 'I told you I needed a pee.'

Megan pulled herself together first. 'Thanks for coming,' she said. 'Have you got your car outside?'

'Adam's parked just up the road. Can you walk, Sophie?'

She nodded. 'But can we hurry, please?'

Her face screwed up with pain, and Adam frowned at her. 'Are you in labour?'

'Has been for some time,' Megan said. 'Come on, Sophie, let's get out of here. We'll carry you if we have to.'

Adam hurried them outside and pulled the door shut behind them. 'Make your way to the street and I'll fetch the car and pick you up.'

They had almost reached the double gates when a van pulled up outside and the driver got out. He walked to the gates and pushed them both open, staring at the quartet curiously. Gina felt her heart thump. Much more of this and she was going to wet herself as well.

'Our friend's in labour,' Amber said. 'We're taking her for a walk to hurry things up.' She treated the van driver to one of her glittering smiles. 'My father owns this place. If you just drive in and push the buzzer beside the door, someone will come and help you.'

'Thanks love.' He gave Sophie an encouraging smile. 'My wife's had three. It won't be as bad as you think.'

'Thanks for that,' Sophie said, as he climbed back into his van. 'It's already worse than I thought.' Saying a thank you prayer that Adam hadn't still got his sports car, Gina helped heave Sophie into the rental car. She climbed into the front beside Adam while Megan and Amber squeezed in the back on either side of Sophie.

Adam started the car and pulled out into the road. 'We have to get away from here, but where to? Do you want to go straight to the general hospital, Sophie?'

'No, please don't take me there. They'll notify Willow Bank and Lucinda will come and get me.'

'She's right,' Amber said. 'Sophie is registered at Willow Bank. They won't keep her at the general, they'll ship her back to Willow Bank by ambulance — unless we leave it until the very last minute and say it's an emergency.'

'I won't know, will I?' Sophie gave a little groan. 'It feels like the very last minute right now. And don't suggest I go to Jack's house. My mum's there and she'll send me straight back to Willow Bank as well. She doesn't want me to keep this baby.'

'Take us to my dad's house,' Amber said suddenly. 'My stepmother was a nurse, and she can send for my dad if there's a problem. Sophie will be safe there.'

'Just so I know.' Adam swung the car round

322

and headed back in the opposite direction just as the van was pulling out of the hospital gates. The driver gave them a wave.

Sophie gave another moan and Gina turned round in her seat. 'You're not going to have it yet, are you?'

'She can't,' Megan said. 'There's not room.'

Gina tried to relax, telling herself the worst was over. Sophie was safely out of the hospital and no one had sent a posse after them. Not yet, anyway. Taking her to Amber's house was probably a good idea. It was the last place either of the Crawfords would think of looking.

'Did Lucinda know you were in labour?'

'No, because I didn't, either.' Sophie groaned again. 'I do now, though.'

Gina looked sideways at Adam 'She's getting a pain about every five minutes. Is that good or bad?'

'How the hell would I know? Stop fussing. We're nearly there.'

'Can you phone Roddy, please, Amber?' Sophie asked. 'He wants to be there when the baby comes.' She looked sideways at her friend. 'I'm sure you know his number.'

Just as Amber finished talking to Roddy, Adam turned into the Beaumonts' drive. Amber was out of the car as soon as it stopped, almost crashing into her stepmother as she opened the front door. Celia looked surprised to see her stepdaughter getting out of a strange car.

'We've got Sophie with us,' Amber said. 'She's having her baby and we need some help.'

Celia Beaumont started back indoors. 'I'll call my husband.'

'No,' Megan said quickly. 'We've already called him. He doesn't want Sophie to go to the hospital. He told us to bring her here.'

'Because he isn't putting the adoption through the usual channels,' Amber added, 'and if anyone at the hospital finds out, he might get into trouble. He can't be disturbed at the moment, but he'll be here as soon as he can get away.'

'Can I sit down, please?' Sophie pleaded. 'I really need to get off my feet right now.'

By the time they got inside the house, Celia had covered one of the sofas with a folded sheet and Sophie sank down gratefully. Gina looked round the immaculate, all white room. With a bit of luck they could get Sophie to deliver her baby on the white fur rug. That would mess things up a bit.

'I'll get us all some tea,' Celia said. 'Then I'll try phoning my husband again.'

'Celia has no idea what's going on at the

hospital,' Amber said as Celia left the room. 'All she knows is that Dad's trying to arrange an adoption for Sophie's baby.' She walked over to Sophie and lifted her feet on to the sofa. 'That'll be more comfortable. What he's doing isn't wrong, is it?' she asked Gina. 'He shouldn't lose his hospital because he helped someone.'

Gina decided Amber must run around with her hands over her ears singing la la la. She was saved from having to answer by the doorbell. After a quick peek through the spy hole, Amber opened the door to Roddy.

He rushed into the room and dropped to his knees beside Sophie. 'We have to get you to the hospital.'

She looked at him in astonishment. 'I've only just escaped from there. Why would I want to go back?'

He looked around the room a little wildly. 'You can't have the baby here.'

'She's going to have to,' Adam said. 'If Celia won't deliver it, I will, and if the bloody woman insists on phoning her husband, we'll lock her in a cupboard.'

Gina bent down and released the telephone cable from its socket. She tucked the wire behind the curtain. 'That might be a tad easier. Where's she keep her mobile phone, Amber?'

'In her handbag, but she always forgets to put it on charge.' She looked worriedly at Gina. 'She'll ask to borrow mine.'

Celia came back into the room carrying a tray of tea and biscuits. 'A cup of tea will make everyone feel better.' Sophie chose that moment to grunt like a pig and Celia looked at her in concern. 'Perhaps we should get you upstairs.' She reached for the phone on the windowsill. 'I'll call the doctor.'

'I'll call reception first,' Amber said. 'Find out where he is. You don't want to disturb him if he is operating on someone.' She took her phone out of her pocket and moved away from Celia, looking down at the phone as if she was trying to get the best signal. She punched in a number and waited. 'Hi, Cheryl, is Dad around?' She waited a bit longer. 'Right. Well, can you ask him to phone home as soon as he's free. It's kind of urgent. He's in theatre,' she told Celia. 'An unexpected C-section.'

Roddy poured Sophie a cup of tea and held it while she sipped. 'You can't have this baby on your own.'

'She's not on her own,' Megan said. 'But I think the baby will arrive when it's ready whether anyone's here or not. They do that.'

Sophie grunted again and Adam stood up.

'Are we going to deliver this baby or not?' he asked Celia.

Celia sighed. 'I did a brief training course on midwifery, but then decided I didn't like it. Too much responsibility when there's two lives at stake. But I can cope if nothing goes wrong.'

'I helped deliver a couple of babies in Iraq. Bare earth and no antiseptic. One of them lived.'

'Thanks,' Sophie muttered from the sofa. 'Perhaps I would be better off doing this on my own.' But the grunt she gave, coupled with something that bordered on a scream, had Roddy backing away in alarm.

'If you're going to panic, get out of the room,' Adam told him. 'That goes for all of you. You'd be better off on your feet, Sophie. We can't deliver you on the sofa. Put your arms round Roddy's neck and let him support you. Gravity will help.'

Gina watched in quiet admiration as Adam took the lead. Celia worked well beside him, she hadn't forgotten how to be a good nurse. Roddy pulled himself together and held Sophie while she grunted and moaned alternately. 'I'm not doing this anymore,' she told him once. 'I'm too tired. You can take over for a bit.'

But she got on with it, and twenty minutes

later Adam put a baby girl in her arms. 'She's yours to keep, if you're sure that's what you want.'

Roddy stared at his baby daughter in wonder. 'We used to talk to her before she was born, Sophie and me, and tell her how much we loved her. We never thought we'd really get to keep her.' He grabbed Adam's hand. 'Thank you so much.'

Celia removed the sheets she had thrown down to protect the floor and went to wash her hands. Adam followed.

The baby gave a healthy wail and Sophie started feeding her. 'If you don't like it, don't look,' she told everyone.

'More tea?' Megan asked, when everyone was back in the room, but Amber shook her head.

'I know where Dad keeps his champagne.' She opened a cupboard in a black oak wall unit, took out a bottle of Dom Perignon, and tossed it to Adam.

He caught the heavy bottle and looked at the label. 'This will do nicely.'

Celia looked worriedly at her watch. 'I don't know what's keeping my husband.'

'Complications with the operation, maybe,' Adam suggested easily. 'We did fine without him.'

They sat drinking the doctor's champagne

and the new baby was passed around the room. Gina saw Megan's lip quiver as she held the baby girl in her arms, and took her own turn nervously. She found the baby wasn't as difficult to hold as she had expected. The little thing sort of nestled against her, all soft and floppy, which was quite nice really.

'We're going to call her Hope,' Roddy said. 'Because that's what she is. Everything's going to be great from now on.'

'I'll call Jack,' Adam said, 'and let him know he's an uncle.'

Later that day Gina realized that it had been silly for them all to congregate in one room, and even sillier to be cooing over the baby when someone should have been watching the door. But she didn't know that at the time.

30

'Hi, everyone,' Lucinda said brightly. The shocked silence seemed to please her. She pushed the door wide open and moved into the room. 'You English never lock your back door in the daytime, do you? You should be more careful. Anyone could walk in.'

Celia was standing nearest to the door when Crawford appeared. He grabbed her from behind, his arm tight round her neck, his gun at her head. 'Anyone move and I'll shoot her.'

Lucinda laughed. 'Like a scene from a bad movie, isn't it? Don't be so melodramatic, honey.' She looked at Sophie. 'All we want is the baby. She's bought and paid for.'

Gina looked at Adam, but he didn't move from his place at the back of the room. 'Sophie won't give you the baby, Lucinda,' he said. 'The police are on their way here to the doctor's house right now, and you can't shoot all of us at once, so what are you going to do?'

He was talking loudly, almost shouting, and Gina wondered if he was deliberately trying to antagonize Lucinda. He took his hand out of his pocket, and she remembered he had started to call Jack on his mobile phone.

'Shooting one of you at a time will work just as well,' Lucinda said sweetly. 'And if the police were coming they'd have been here by now. Besides, you weren't waiting for the police, you were having a party.' She looked at Sophie who was holding Hope so tightly Gina thought the baby might suffocate. 'We'll just take the baby and be on our way. No one need get hurt.'

'We won't let you take the baby,' Adam said. 'And you know you can't kill us all.' He took a step towards Crawford. 'So give me the gun and get out of here before the police arrive. Run, like you did in LA.'

Gina saw Roddy start to move as well, but Crawford turned the gun towards the floor and shot Adam in the foot. A second later the gun was back at Celia's head.

'I don't need to kill anyone,' Crawford said. He looked at Adam. 'Tell them how much that hurts.'

Adam was sitting on the floor trying to get his shoe off and Gina remembered reading how many nerves there were in a human foot. Nearly 8,000. Yes, it must hurt, and his clenched jaw looked as if he was really pissed off.

Everyone had gone very still. The baby started to whimper and Sophie frantically shushed her. Roddy sat silently beside Sophie, clutching her hand, and Gina thought how young they looked. A couple of kids with far too much responsibility, and yet giving up their baby had become unthinkable, even when faced with a gun.

'Can I help him?' she asked. 'Before he bleeds to death.' Adam had taken off his shoe and a red stain was spreading over his sock. 'You can bleed to death from a shot in the foot. I read about it.'

Lucinda tossed Adam a couple of cushions. 'Keep it up high,' she said. 'Then you won't make a mess of the floor.'

Crawford pushed Celia hard against the wall. 'You sit on the floor as well,' he told her, 'and the rest of you sit where I can see you. I don't want anyone standing.'

He waved the gun around the room in an arc, waiting for them to sit. Gina sat on the floor and wriggled back until she was next to Adam. Amber looked as if she might say something, but then sat down on the sofa beside Megan.

Lucinda smiled. 'That's better.'

Gina gently peeled off Adam's sock. The bullet had taken a chunk out of the side of his foot, and the deep groove was bleeding profusely. 'This needs a dressing,' she told Lucinda, but the woman just stared back at her.

'Hard luck. He needs to learn to keep quiet.'

Gina took a tissue out of the pocket of her jeans and pressed it against the wound. She couldn't remember if she had actually used the tissue, but it was probably cleaner than Adam's sock.

There was silence for a moment, and then Megan suddenly stood up and planted herself in front of Sophie. 'I won't let you take Sophie's baby.' She looked at Crawford defiantly. 'You said you don't need to kill anyone. Well, you're going to have to kill me if you want this baby.'

'Shit,' Adam said softly. Using Gina as leverage he pulled himself upright. 'Megan, sit down. You're not helping the situation.'

Megan shook her head and Gina could see tears in her eyes. 'They're not taking the baby.'

Adam muttered a curse under his breath and just for a moment Gina thought he was going to try and protect Megan, but he took one painful step forward and wrapped his arms around her, pulling her against him. 'I've been shot once tonight and it bloody hurts. Sit down and behave yourself.' He held her while she struggled, trying to stop her stamping on his injured foot. Gina thought he whispered something in Megan's ear. She could have been mistaken, but Megan stopped struggling and slumped down on the sofa again.

'Thank you, Mr Shaw,' Lucinda said. She bent down to take the baby and Sophie started screaming. The sound was a high-pitched keening that started off as 'no, no, no, no, no,' but then degenerated into something almost inhuman.

Gina watched in horror as Lucinda slapped Sophie hard across the face. Before anyone could stop him, Roddy stood up and punched Lucinda on the nose. The woman looked at Roddy in disbelief and backed away, blood streaming down her face. Crawford fired a shot into the wall just above Roddy's head, and Megan wriggled out of Adam's grasp and threw both cushions at Crawford who shot at them automatically, filling the room with flying feathers.

'Are you OK?' Crawford shouted to his wife, waving the gun around as he tried to cover everyone.

Gina ducked as the weapon came her way. She was waiting for Crawford to shoot someone out of sheer frustration.

Lucinda wiped the blood from her face

with the back of her hand and plucked a feather from her eyelashes. She grabbed the baby from Sophie, who started screaming again, and then shouted to Crawford. 'The car's just outside. Give me time to get in and start the engine, then shoot one of them. That'll keep them quiet for a bit.'

If Adam had a plan, Gina thought, now was the time to put it into action, but he was standing quite still staring at Crawford — making sure he would be the one to get shot, she realized.

Celia had double locked the front door when she let them in, and now Lucinda was fumbling with the locks, finding it difficult to get the front door open while she was holding a screaming baby. When she eventually opened the door, a siren started up, and for a moment Gina thought it was a burglar alarm. As Crawford turned towards the noise, Adam stepped over Gina and knocked the gun out of Crawford's hand. Not to be outdone, Roddy picked up a table lamp and broke the crystal base over Crawford's head. The man dropped to the floor amidst the shattered glass and didn't get up again.

Gina pushed past the recumbent Crawford to get to Lucinda before she got away with the baby, but there was no need. Lucinda was standing transfixed in the doorway, blinded by the barrage of car headlights outside.

As Reagan appeared in silhouette, walking between the lights of the parked police cars, Lucinda turned back into the house, but there was nowhere to run. Gina took the baby and handed her to Sophie, while Reagan and another officer pulled Crawford to his feet. A young police officer strapped Lucinda's hands behind her back.

Everyone had piled out into the hallway and Megan put her arm round Gina. 'Looks like the Fantastic Four did it again.'

Afterwards

The blessing of the marriage vows was a small, family affair. Only the first few pews were occupied. Gina took her seat beside Adam and looked around. She could see the doctor and his wife. Amber was sitting beside them with a big smile on her face. She had obviously decided she could do a lot better than Roddy McBride.

Grace Lowry was sitting at the front with the baby cradled in her arms, while Brian Lowry stood by the altar, waiting for his daughter to appear.

Sophie had lost weight, but it suited her. She held her brother's arm tightly as she walked down the aisle towards Roddy. Her dress was a slim sheath of cream lace and she held a small posy of winter pansies. Roddy couldn't stop smiling. He looked as if he had just won the jackpot. A wife and baby daughter all in one go.

They were already officially married, a register office event in Castlebury that Gina decided had been a lot more fun than this sombre church affair. The party afterwards, at Jack's house, had gone on long into the night, with practically the whole staff of Willow Bank and all Sophie and Amber's friends. Gina and Adam had excused themselves early, feeling exceedingly old.

Immediately after the blessing, baby Hope was christened at the old stone font in her father's church, and Gina hoped Brian Lowry had finally made peace with his God. Sophie might have been wilful and thoughtless, but she had been forced to deal with the consequences on her own because Brian Lowry couldn't face the fact that his daughter wasn't one hundred per cent perfect.

'How did you make Reagan believe we had a problem?' Gina asked Jack. 'He wouldn't listen to me.' They were sitting in the village pub having a beer before they made the journey back home. Adam was driving, so he was drinking cola.

'But he did listen to you. He checked out the information you gave him about the Crawfords and got in touch with the Los Angeles police. When the Crawfords arrived at Beaumont's house, Adam pressed the speed dial on his phone and dropped it back in his pocket, hoping I'd pick up. I heard him mention Lucinda's name and Beaumont's house, and when he said something about not shooting you all at once, I thought it was time to phone the police.'

'They'd already started investigating Willow Bank,' Adam said. 'The gynaecologist was pissed off at being left out of the loop. He found out how much money was changing hands and wanted in, but the Crawfords told him to get lost, so when the police came asking questions, he was the first to talk. The LAPD have asked that Lucinda and her husband be shipped home for sentencing, but Doctor Beaumont will have to face charges here. If Beaumont gets a prison sentence Celia's going to run the hospital herself. But with a good lawyer, he might get away with it.'

Jack was staying over with his parents for a week or two to help Roddy and Sophie find a house in Norwich. The vicar and his wife had put up the deposit, and once everyone was settled Sophie would go back to university and Roddy would carry on with his music.

Adam stood up and pulled Gina to her feet. 'We'd better get going. We've got a long drive home.'

Gina fell asleep as they left Norwich and didn't wake up until Adam pulled up outside the studio. 'Come on, my love,' he said, running a finger lightly down her cheek. 'We're home.'

She opened one eye. 'I'm not your love, Adam.'

He smiled at her. 'You could be, if you

weren't so scared.'

She came fully awake and unbuckled her seat belt. 'Not a hope. I don't do what I'm told.' She gave a little shriek as he grabbed her before she could reach for the door handle. It is quite difficult, she discovered, to snog in a Fiesta, but a little easier than carrying out the same exercise in a sports car. When he let her go, she had a crick in her neck and a dangerously high heart rate. 'What was that all about?'

He reached across to open her door. 'I think we should give that commitment thing a try. See how it works out.'

She gave him a suspicious look as she got out of the car. 'Remember, I don't do what I'm told.'

He put his arm round her shoulders as they walked up the stairs to her flat. 'I know. That's what makes it so much fun.'

We do hope that you have enjoyed reading this large print book.

Did you know that all of our titles are available for purchase?

We publish a wide range of high quality large print books including:
Romances, Mysteries, Classics
General Fiction
Non Fiction and Westerns

Special interest titles available in large print are:
The Little Oxford Dictionary
Music Book
Song Book
Hymn Book
Service Book

Also available from us courtesy of Oxford University Press:
Young Readers' Dictionary
(large print edition)
Young Readers' Thesaurus
(large print edition)

For further information or a free brochure, please contact us at:
Ulverscroft Large Print Books Ltd.,
The Green, Bradgate Road, Anstey,
Leicester, LE7 7FU, England.
Tel: (00 44) 0116 236 4325
Fax: (00 44) 0116 234 0205

Other titles published by
The House of Ulverscroft:

MURDER IN MIND

J. A. O'Brien

As acting DI, Andy Lukeson had not
expected to head up a high-profile murder
investigation, but there he is, thrust
forward into the limelight, investigating
the murder of a woman whose death may
be linked to a string of murders long
unsolved. As he struggles to find the killer,
Lukeson's fears of the case going cold
haunt his every waking moment. Can he
get to the heart of the matter before it's
too late?

STONE COLD

Peter Taylor

Former gypsy prize-fighter, Henry Torrance, is about to be released from prison where he's been serving time for killing fellow bare-knuckle fighter Bull Jackson. Now, he's resolved to get his life on track and settle down with his girlfriend Mary. However, the criminal Jackson family is insistent that Henry should fight their latest protege and Henry's brother and father accept the challenge on his behalf. As the day of the big fight draws closer, Henry's determination not to return to his old ways is countered by the mounting pressure on him. Can he ever escape his dark past?

LOVE TO DEATH

Patti Battison

What happens when love goes bad — and it becomes an obsession . . . ? Ageing rocker Johnny Lee Rogers is performing a series of charity concerts in Larchborough. His biggest fan, librarian Lizzie Thornton, has won tickets to see his final show. She's convinced that Fate is bringing them together . . . and Lizzie's always wanted a December wedding. As the town basks in the hottest temperatures for decades, it will be no Summer of Love for DCI Paul Wells and his team. Lizzie, a group of travellers and a missing girl seem to have conspired to bring a time of torment, intrigue and murder.

M